THE BLOOD

we crave

HOLLOW BOYS BOOK FOUR
PART TWO

The Blood we Crave Part 2
Monty Jay
Copyright © 2023 by Monty Jay

Cover Art by Opulent Designs
Editing by Sandra with One Love Editing
Formatting by AJ Wolf Graphics

To the morally grey and the villains we love within it.

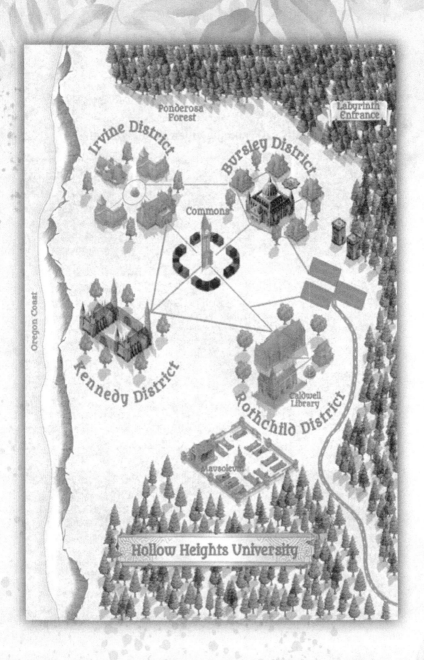

This is a **dark romance**. It deals with sensitive subject matter, sexual assault, serial murder, graphic violence, gore, issues of religion, self harm, psychopathy and others. If you have a problem with any of these topics or those similar, please do not continue.

PLAYLIST

Hostage-- Billie Elilish
Moonrise—Anne Buckle
Under Your Skin—Aesthetic Perfection
A wild river to take you home—Black Hill, Silent Island
Salt and The Sea—Gregory Alan Isakov
From Persephone—Kiki Rockwell
Silhouette—Aquilo
To Be Alone—Hozier
It Will Come Back—Hozier
A Girl Like You—Edwyn Collins

For the entire playlist:
https://open.spotify.com/playlist/7gG0JEeKAXiThJYe7rnHAG?si=
b903239341764180&pt=88c6e8884552ad090f1f28b114ed8017

"I have crossed oceans of time to find you."

—

Bram Stroker "Dracula"

TABLE OF CONTENTS

PROLOGUE

unknown

I did all of this for her.
So that we could be together.
And yet, she mourns him.

I killed so many for her, will continue to kill them, and instead of seeking comfort in my arms, she mourns.

Soon, she will see how ungrateful she has been. Soon, Stephen will own this town, and the darkened sons of Ponderosa Springs will be the end of a baleful reign. So very soon, sweet Lyra will be mine and only mine, as it should have always been. Soon, she will see why I had to do this.

Why it's only her that can love a man like me.

There will be no stopping us. Stopping me. The untouchable Hollow Boys will reap not only what they have sowed but the fruits of their legacy. Their thrones, built from treacherous demands and crowns forged from bones, are crumbling.

They are weak. Breakable. Love has exposed their humanity.

Here lies the thin line between gods and monsters. They will all see—Lyra will see—that those boys they mark with divinity are simply a false claim.

There is no divine right and no god to protect them.

They bleed, and when they do, they will flow red.

ONE
an oath to the dead

lyra

The cemetery has always been a place of refuge for me. Solemn, forgotten ground that makes the world feel less desolate, only because it's a reminder of how many souls still exist in the ether. It allows for a macabre sort of perspective no other living place can handle.

Today, the tombstones do not soothe me.

Today, they are a reminder of all that was lost. All the lives that met their conclusion. Cemeteries are a place of peace. Funerals are a bitter nudge towards a future without someone you love.

"It's so terribly sad," a woman next to me sobs into a tissue. "No one deserves to die like that."

"I never thought I'd live to see the last of the Piersons," her husband mutters, a thought I'm sure he didn't mean to say out loud. Or maybe he did. Maybe he's better than the rest, and instead of playing nice, he was tired of hiding his disdain.

This lady cries again, the wet sound making my ears burn. I whip my head from the fresh hole in the ground, where a black coffin remains motionless, and openly glare at the middle-aged woman, completely uncaring if she or her husband notice.

My grief is a tangible feeling, one that mingles with the current rage thrumming in my veins. The snow melts as it touches my skin, seeping into the fabric of my floor-length lace dress. How dare she sit here and cry for a family she openly talked shit about for years?

How dare they have a right to be here.

All these citizens with their fraudulent condolences, making this more of a social event than a goddamn mourning ceremony, only showing up to catch up on all the hot gossip.

Look at me! Look at me! they all say, showing up in their finest silks and pearls, armed with counterfeit tears and bullshit apologies.

"You didn't even know—" I start, my tone laced with untamed venom, but I'm stopped by a large hand resting on my shoulder, tugging me backwards into their space.

I cut my eyes upward, staring into Alistair's dark eyes as he gives me what I assume is a look of disapproval. A silent warning and a reassuring squeeze of his fingers.

"They aren't worth it," he mutters lowly. "Don't let them win by making it about them. It's what they want. This town will only eat you if you let them take the first bite."

I try to jerk my arm from his hold, but he just holds tighter. "You're not my keeper. I'm capable of handling myself."

It could rip me apart for all I care. As long as I take my chunk of flesh before they finish me off.

This town turned the entire Pierson family into a ghost story—a haunted tale, a fucking plague—and made sure everyone who would listen knew how evil they all were.

Now they stand here in mourning? They show up and disrespect the dead?

"I'm well aware of what you're capable of."

"Then I think you should let go of me," I say through gritted teeth. I don't want to hurt Alistair, but I also don't want him to coddle me either.

"I know you're hurting, and you want to make everyone else hurt too," he breathes. "I know what that feels like, Lyra. But you can't right now."

My molars grind against one another. "That's supposed to make it better? I'm just supposed to stand here and what? Do nothing? That's all we have been doing, and look how that turned out for us, Alistair."

Caldwell's eyebrows twitch, his mouth twisting slightly, and I can see the pain in his eyes. If I was thinking rationally, I'd be aware that what happened wasn't his fault. I would have maybe hugged him and supported him because he'd lost pieces of himself too.

But I was empty. I am empty.

This hollow, dark space that allows no light or air. So I compensate by shoving anger into that bottomless pit inside of me just to feel anything other than this constant ache.

The ache of losing him is brutal.

I don't miss him, the way you miss a pair of shoes that you grew out of, a memory of a glowing summer, or even a pet you'd lost. I do not miss him.

He is missing *from* me.

A vital organ torn from my gut. A severed limb.

Thatcher's memory was what I clung to every single second when I was passed around from different foster homes and orphanages. I held on to the boy who made me feel less alone on a night when everything had been taken from me. When I had absolutely nothing, I had him for that short, brief time. He was it. That was all I had—how could no one understand that?

I held on to him through school, the little pieces I'd gathered watching him all these years. Tightened my grip on the person who made me feel human. Seen. Safe.

My heart and soul were never mine. They had always been his, and now they belong to no one. They are lost, forgotten, alone.

I tethered myself to him, and now he's just...gone.

He is gone, and his memory isn't enough.

Yet, it feels like all I have left.

"You're always allowed to do something, Lyra. I just don't need you stabbing someone in the eye at a public funeral. That's the last thing you need right now."

Words I don't mean but can't keep down spurt from my mouth before I have a chance to stop them.

"Stop acting like you fucking care about me." I look at him, meeting his dark eyes. "I'm Briar's friend. You're only doing this for her benefit, and frankly, I don't need you protecting me. Remember what happened last time you told me I'd be safe? I almost died."

This time, I do remove my arm from his grasp, probably because he let me, but I'm free from his control either way. I've never spoken to him like this. I've never spoken to anyone this way before.

But I don't regret it. Not when all this bitterness has consumed every ounce of kindness that once lived inside of me.

"Fine." He scoffs, shoving his hands in his jacket. "Then how about this. If you do anything fucking stupid at this funeral and put Briar at risk, I will show you just how little I care about what happens to you."

I'd been waiting for him to bite, knowing I could only poke at Alistair Caldwell so long before he snapped back.

The sting of his words doesn't land as hard as I expected they would. The numbness is the likely cause, or maybe it's because I knew from the start that was our relationship.

"Fine," I agree.

The snow begins to fall in a heavy flurry, and I watch as guests pile into their cars, seeking warmth. The show has come to an end, leaving only a few people lingering in the Pierson family cemetery.

"Incoming." Alistair tosses his head to our right, and I follow the direction carefully, seeing the federal agents who'd approached us in Tillie's Diner weeks ago. Moving in sync with one another, they approach us.

"Hope they aren't trying to blend in."

"They want us to know they're here. It's an intimidation tactic, making sure we know they're watching us."

Odette Marshall shoves her hands in her pockets, offering a welcoming smile as she steps in front of me. The man she'd introduced as Gerrick brushes her shoulder, nodding at Alistair in silent acknowledgment.

"We wanted to stop by and offer our condolences for your loss," she says, so casually, dripping with fake sincerity, and I've had just about enough phony emotional displays to last a lifetime.

I'm not in the mood to play nice, especially with them.

Neither Alistair nor I say anything in response to her opening statement. We just stare blankly, waiting for her to get to whatever point she has.

"Listen," she levels. "All we want to do is help. I know you may not see that right now, but we just want those responsible for these crimes to pay for them."

"You should take your help elsewhere," I snip. Maybe it's the bite of the cold or the sting of loss, but I feel like an exposed nerve. Every whisper of air across me sends an agonized bolt of pain through my body.

"Is that your way of telling me you know more information than you're giving and want me to stop poking around?"

"No," I say. "If that's what I meant, I would've said it."

Odette smirks, rolling her lips together as she nods.

"If your plan is to interrogate us at a funeral, it's not only shit taste, but our lawyer won't appreciate it either." Alistair curls his hand around my upper arm. "We told you everything we know."

Which is true.

When the two of them showed up at the home on Pierson Point and found us already there, they were quick to request our presence at the station house.

I'd been unfeeling to the entire experience, practically silent, barely aware that Rook Van Doren's father had forked up the bill for my lawyer, who did most of the talking for me. A pleasant gentleman who made it very clear if either of the detectives or anyone else with a badge tried to speak to us without him around, they'd regret it.

"I somehow doubt that." Gerrick speaks for the first time. "Your loyalty will be your downfall, and the killer doesn't even deserve it. Thatcher—"

"Don't say his fucking name," I snap, taking a step in their general direction with no fear of repercussions. What do I have left to lose? "You don't get to say that name."

My hands curl into tight fists, my fingers bunching up the material at the sides of my dress. I feel Alistair's hand squeeze my arm, not from anger or Gerrick's comment, but to hold me back from doing something I might regret.

Like strangling this prick with my bare hands. But in no universe do I find myself having remorse for this jarhead.

"Watch yourself, little girl."

I step a little closer, pointing one accusatory finger, unafraid of his stature and blank expression. "It seems you have your priorities a little skewed if you're treating him more like a suspect instead of a missing person."

Those words echo inside me, bouncing off the walls of my vacant chest. That might be what hurts the most—not knowing if he's dead or alive. If this copycat killer has him as leverage for the Halo or has already tossed his body into the ocean as fish food.

I don't know where he is.

I can't find him. None of us can.

"Until I find his body, Thatcher Pierson is our number one suspect in the murder of those girls and May Pierson. I'd get used to it now so it won't be so difficult adding money to his books when I throw his ass in prison."

"Just how dumb are you?" I counter. "Find the easiest target and pin him with murder? Get some evidence other than your ego, dickhead."

My stomach twists, my hands flexing at my sides. The vivid image of gutting Gerrick Knight with the pin in my hair becomes more appealing by the second. The metallic taste rushing to my mouth is hard to swallow, and I know my self-control isn't wound as tightly as Thatcher's.

That was the whole point of him teaching me. How to control it so that I didn't do what I desperately wanted to do right now.

These useless cops are hunting Thatcher down for a crime he didn't commit instead of searching for him. They don't understand that he would never kill May, that none of those girls dying is his fault.

They expect me to believe they're here to help when all they've done is crucify those around me with no evidence?

"I respect you wanting to protect your friend. He's lucky to have a girl like you." Odette steps in, her tone nothing short of condescending. "But if I find out you know where he is or what his next move is, I will charge you all with harboring a fugitive. You can be loyal in a cell."

"All good over here?" Rook's hand appears on Alistair's shoulder, a forced smile on his pale face.

The tension is so thick it almost chokes me, a heavy smog weighing on my lungs.

I feel my friends step next to me. Briar's hand slips into mine and gives it a squeeze, but I can't bring myself to return the favor. Not when I feel like this. Jaded. So vacant that I can't make myself be there for anyone, not even myself.

Both she and Sage are trying too hard, desperately trying to help me, but I'm too far gone. Too secluded in the darkness to even see their hands reaching for me. I've turned into that dark spot inside of myself, allowing it to take me over.

"Perfect," Alistair says through clenched teeth. "We were just leaving."

Both detectives look at us lined up in a row, eyeing each of us with careful glances. It feels like the start of another battle in this never-ending war. A line drawn in the white snow in front of us, painting a clear picture of what side we all stand on.

I'm sure Odette and Gerrick feel that where they stand is on the right side of the law. That they are doing good by being here.

But if you're not on our side, no matter the reason, then you're against us.

They are the enemy by default.

"It will only be you who is hurt in the end," Odette says to each of us but is quick to make eye contact with me with her goodbye. "Ask yourself, would he return this favor of silence? Would he put his freedom at risk for you?"

We turn, walking away and giving our final goodbyes to the woman about to be covered in dirt. Sweet May. Possibly the only innocent person involved in this web we've found ourselves trapped in. She didn't deserve this, to die like that.

Cut up. Dissected. Robbed of her heart.

She'd done nothing but show each of these broken men a mother's love, guiding and protecting them since they were young. I know their guilt is heavy; we all feel responsible for her death and Thatcher's disappearance.

Rook squats down, pulling a coin from his pocket and flipping it. It rings in the air as it hits the wooden coffin. "We will make them pay for this, May. I promise you."

A tear slips down my cheek, and I bite back a choked sob.

"We swear on the River Styx." Alistair's voice sounds like he's choked on gravel, and I watch his gold coin tumble into the hole, landing with a thud.

"River Styx?" Sage asks curiously, blue eyes veiled with tears and pale skin tinted pink.

"Homer wrote that the gods swear by the water of the Styx. It's their most binding oath," I answer, chewing the inside of my cheek and allowing the silence to overtake us all. "It's an unbreakable promise."

TWO
to become a killer

lyra

I turn the key on the music box once again, twisting until the tension is pulled tight before releasing it and filling my room with the sound once more. The twinkling melody echoes around the four walls, and it hadn't taken me long to figure out the song's title.

"Once Upon a Dream" was a song my mother used to hum while she was working around the house or in the kitchen, trying to cook, and sometimes she'd sing while she got me ready for bed. It's a tune I'd remember anywhere, and I wasn't sure if it was fate or some kind of destiny that I found this little trinket in the Library Tower.

Either way, it brings me a strange sense of comfort, and for that, I am thankful.

My phone vibrates on the bed next to me, and I don't have to look at the screen to know it's Briar calling.

Again.

I continue to let it ring as I stare up at the ceiling, my fingers tracing the golden swirls along the base of the box until the sound runs out. Sitting the whimsical object on the bed, I scoop up my phone and quickly send a text to my worried friend.

B:

> Happy New Year, we miss you.

How could it have possibly been a month already? How is it the start of the new year without him here?

Me:

> Happy New Year. Miss you guys too.
> Just don't want to talk tonight.

B:

> Lyra…

B:

> We haven't seen you since the funeral. Why won't you let us be there for you?

I type half the message, then think better of it. I don't want to tell my best friend over a text that I don't want her over here so that she can sit and tell me it's going to be okay. That things will get better.

Not when she was so hell-bent on me staying away from Thatcher in the first place. I'm not saying I wouldn't have done the same thing in her position, but she only had surface-level information when it came to my situation.

Which, admittedly, is my fault, but he made me promise. What happened between us was to stay quiet. I would take protective Briar over Thatcher seeing me as disloyal.

Me:

> Just want to be alone is all, B.

B:

> We could come over and help you clean? I know there are at least ten empty water bottles on your bedside dresser. We don't even have to talk. Alistair is worried too.

I let myself stare into the void for another moment longer before wincing as I looked over at my nightstand, which does, in fact, have way too many plastic containers littering it.

I can't even feel embarrassed as I look at the state of my room. The hanging and potted plants scattered around in desperate need of water, dust coating the shelves that hold different taxidermy items, trash on the floor, clothes thrown about.

The only thing I've had the energy to do is feed Alvi. His two-story terrarium is the cleanest thing in my home. I'm better at taking care of my white king snake than myself.

Forcing myself to sit up, I kick a pair of dirty jeans across the room as I walk quietly to my closet, admiring what used to be my safe haven of a room, now turned into a tornado of depression.

It's the last space in the cabin I had remodeled. I'd curated every inch, taking my time to thrift every golden picture frame that showcases different bug species. I bought several different animal skulls, which are neatly placed on my floor-to-ceiling bookshelves. I selected furniture, plants, and even my black velvet headboard with the hopes of creating a space that felt like mine. My own little forgotten corner of the world.

An entire year I'd spent designing and restoring my home, only to let it dwindle into a nest of self-loathing. I can't even bring myself to be sad about it.

Not when everything feels so bleak.

I don't want to see anyone or do anything. Why would I when I'm constantly alternating between quiet depression and unbridled anger? My pain is a warpath, hostile interactions and a constant need to make everyone around me feel this loss.

Opening the door to my closet, I quickly tug the black sweater from the hanger, pressing the soft material to my nose and inhaling the faint remains of his cologne.

Tears sting my eyes, and I rub my fist in front of my chest to relieve the burning sensation that has started. I want so desperately to believe he's alive, that he's okay and somehow will find his way back.

Yet, it's been a month since May's murder, and we can't find a trail to follow. I have no answers, just a pathetic hope that he's out there somewhere, still breathing.

I'm not sure how long I stand in here—far too long to be considered healthy for my current mental state. But once I find the motivation to go downstairs and rummage through my cabinets for a tea bag, I'm soon disappointed when I find the tin empty.

I would laugh, but the humor in the situation dies when I realize I'll have to go into town to buy more. For a moment, I think of asking Briar if she could bring me some, and she would, but then she'd ask to stay.

Weasel her way inside with her soft smile, Sage in tow, with a stash of Rook's weed that she steals, and we'd spend the night on a pile of blankets in front of my TV. All of us pretending to be normal college students while the world outside my door falls to shit.

It would be fun, and I almost work up enough energy to commit, but it disappears quickly. Mentally, I won't be able to handle the pity in their eyes or be very good company because it feels impossible to hide my worry.

I'm constantly thinking about how long it will be before I see him again. Another month? Years? Never? That seems like a reality too hard to bear, and I want to put off the acceptance of his death, but every day, it gets harder to have hope.

Grabbing my frumpy plaid coat, I slip my feet into a pair of yellow rain boots that are sitting by the door. I catch a quick glimpse of myself in the mirror by the front door, wincing at the dark circles beneath my eyes.

I'm sure somewhere in the world, the gothic lace gown I wore to the funeral paired with this jacket and these boots is high fashion. Here, it's unlikely someone would pay attention to me long enough to notice.

I'm not sure why I put it on this morning, maybe to remember. To grieve or feel the pain of loss. I've always been a sucker for sinking into my self-pity.

The high lace collar that wraps around my neck scratches against my skin as the heat from my car blasts against my face. Quietly, I drive through the flurry of snow, watching the sun drift away, allowing darkness to soak the pines.

I'm pleased to see the parking lot barren, save for a few cars. I just wish the fluorescent bulbs inside the store weren't so fucking bright. Feeling like a vampire as the light burns my skin and eyes, I try to shield myself from the harsh glow.

Normally, I'd spend hours inside the store, wandering down aisles and discovering new foods to fixate on or sweets I had yet to try. Now, all I want is to get back home, curl into my blankets, and sleep for the next half century. Maybe when I woke up, this would all be over. The Halo would be destroyed, the copycat killer behind bars, and my friends would be happy. At the very least, we all would find some peace.

I'm chewing my bottom lip, trying to decide which flavor of tea I want for the next week. *Lady Grey, Chai, Lemon Delight, Ginger Black, English Breakfast, Pomegran—*

Heavy boots thud against the tiled floor, wet stomps from the snow outside. I can't explain how I know, but I feel the moment the person turns into the aisle. The hairs along my neck stand up in warning, my heart beating just a bit faster.

The sound of a cart moving echoes in my ears, and I silently turn my head. What I find is a surprise.

Clothed in a starched button-down and slacks, whistling with every step forward, is a man who has haunted my sleep.

Player One.

The man who'd tied me to a chair, beaten me until I was bruised, and attempted to drown me strolls down the aisle with lax confidence. Unaware of my presence, he looks like an average guy just getting off work, stopping by the store to grab whatever item his wife texted him to pick up. Or maybe his husband. Either way, there is a golden band wrapped around his finger, meaning he belongs to someone.

Even someone as vile as him belongs to another person, and he may not be the sole reason, but he is part of why I do not share that quality.

Why the person that belongs to *me* is no longer here.

He must sense my gaze because he looks around until we make eye contact. Recognition flares, and it's obvious he knows who I am. Hunger pools in my stomach, a familiar itch starting along my fingertips.

I feel like my blood might set on fire as the electric hum of opportunity races through me. Wrath strikes through my veins with violent speed, and I look at Player One not as my attacker but as something far better.

An outlet.

All of this miserable rage and guilt finally has a place to go, given the perfect chance to quench my thirst for revenge, even if it's for a moment. I tighten my hands into fists, turning my knuckles white.

It was all their fault—*his* fault. They are the reason Thatcher is missing from me. For all I know, this man could be the person who killed him. Knowing that he is already a dog for Stephen Sinclair means I wouldn't doubt his involvement.

What I'd done to his partner, Michael, the other man who'd laid his hands on my body and tried to end my life, was only a preview of what I wanted to put Player One through.

I warned them what I would become if they took him from me. Now there is no need to fear the reaper. They should fear the woman who loves him.

Giving a soft smile, I hide any recognition and turn back to the tea selections while he stares at the back of my head. I let him look at me, calculate his plan on how to get rid of me.

The fear I'd once harbored for the craving that lives inside of me is no longer there. I've embraced what Henry Pierson turned me into, and I'm ready to let it off the chain.

Except this time, I don't need a reason to hurt Player One. I don't need an excuse or something to ease my future guilt. I no longer care if he'd done something wrong or deserves death.

I'm going to kill him for only one reason.

Because I want to.

Nothing but the overwhelming desire to feel his blood between my fingers.

Plucking a random tea from the shelf, I turn on my heel, making my rain boots squeak. I walk out of the aisle and towards the checkout, knowing he is behind me almost every step.

He looms like a shadow as I pay, taking the bag from the rack.

"Have a good night."

"I will," I reply to the teenage cashier.

With a steady walk, I settle into the eerie calm that falls upon my shoulders. I stroll to the doors and head into the snow once again. Sliding my hand into the pocket of my jacket, I run my fingers along the smooth metal that's tucked away. It's one of the more expensive items I'd stolen from Thatcher but possibly one of my favorites. I'd taken it from him our sophomore year of high school after taking a week to figure out his locker combination. I also stole a pack of gum from him that day.

I rub my thumb along the switchblade, coaxing the memory of him. All the things Thatcher had taught me—being precise, having a plan, being in control—seem to flutter to the back of my mind as I walk to my car. My only plan is that I'll be breaking one of his most important rules.

Do not kill out of emotion.

Tonight, I am killing out of purely that.

Taking a life not to better society or help but to aid the ache inside of me. A way to pour all of my frustration and pain into something else. I want to kill so that I might feel a little better.

Player One is my mouse, caught in a tricky, unsuspecting maze. Last time, he'd been in control, and I'm sure he still feels that way as I walk to my car, parked in the dimly lit lot.

The streetlamp flickers, threatening to go out. My fingers hit the unlock button, the sound echoing. My heart is pumping at a steady rhythm, as if even my body has accepted what I am.

I'd detached my emotions, removed them from the equation, and the killer inside of me has taken over in order to guarantee my survival. My fingers hum with excitement as I pull open the back door, tossing the bag of tea on the floorboards behind the driver's seat.

I count to three in my mind. That's all it takes before he shoves me with the full force of his body, quick to push me into the back seat of my car, pressing a thick hand on my back.

Adrenaline courses through my system, my mouth staying closed as he lays himself on top of me. I struggle, kicking my feet and turning so that I'm facing him. The weight of his body presses me into the leather. Curling my fingers around the weapon in my pocket, I stare up at him with patient eyes, silent, waiting for him to do anything that isn't predictable.

"Remember me?" His voice is veiled in darkness. I feel his grip tighten around me, and I'm sure he feels consumed with power. I bet he feels like he's in control, a strong, unstoppable man.

And I'm just his prey. A loose end that needs to be tied up.

I blink, tilting my head a bit to avoid the smell of his rank breath. "You should have killed me when you had the chance."

Confusion knits his brows together, and I take that as my opening. I press the button along the side of the knife, feeling the blade break from its hold, and before he can do more than blink, I slide the edge across the front of his throat.

Skin meets metal, and I feel it melt along the sharp edge, peeling apart and opening a waterfall of red liquid. It seeps from the gash, covering the front of my body. It soaks through my dress, paints my neck, and its warmth makes my body hum.

Power drowns me, pours over me like liquid gold and stains my fingers and mouth. It swallows me, and all I want is more, greedy for how it tastes on my tongue. Power curls along my veins and takes over. I feel it thrumming in my bones, aching.

All the keys inside of me click and slide into place, as if my mind and body have finally merged into agreeance. It's in this moment, as I drown in a man's blood, that I accept myself for all the horrible things I'd once feared.

Death and decay. Lover of the macabre. A killer.

All the blood seems to send me to a different place. Lyra is safely tucked away in the closet of my mind while something else entirely takes over.

My mouth pulls into a smile as his eyes widen. Terrified hands grapple to stop the bleeding, and I watch him panic. A fly caught in a web, struggling for life, unknowingly walking himself straight into the hands of death.

It fuels my pride, my ego, watching him break apart, knowing his entire life is at the hands of my misery. I'm the last thing he gets to see before he dwindles into nothing. My face will haunt his spirit in every life. The girl he couldn't kill, the girl who'd eaten his control and spat it out at his feet.

He was due to pay, and the price had been his life.

I stay quiet, seeing the light dim in his eyes. Color drains from his face, and he chokes, gurgling some form of a plea. Blood continues to leak, a spout with no end. A bath of vengeance. A crimson meal for the depraved rage inside of me.

It dawns on me that he will be the first of many, the dominion at the front of the line, and I will not stop until all those guilty pay for what they did. What they took from me.

I inhale the deep metallic scent, feeling his body go lax against mine. The dreaded realization that there is a dead body on top of mine starts to settle in. I wait for the guilt to follow.

But it never comes.

There is only a profound relief and my adrenaline slamming into my bloodstream.

The knife falls to the floorboards, and I now have to figure out a way to get rid of his body, knowing I can't leave him in the parking lot of a grocery store. With more struggle than I'd like to admit, I press my hands into his chest and move our bodies so that I'm able to slip out of the back seat.

Once I'm standing, staring at the mess I've made for myself, I almost want the panic to set in. Some sort of emotion other than dull numbness, but nothing ever hits me.

Maybe because of all the things Thatcher had taught me, or maybe because I have nothing left to lose. What's my freedom if he's not a part of it?

The majority of Player One's body is sagging against my leather seats, but his feet dangle off the edge, reminding me of the witch from *The Wizard of Oz* when the house fell on her.

I glance around the empty parking lot before grabbing his booted feet and shoving him further into the car, tucking his knees at the chest so that his large frame fits.

When I slide into the front seat, I look at my painted hands. The blood is still sticky and clings to the steering wheel. I make a mental note to bleach the inside of this tomorrow.

I move on autopilot, starting the engine, making my way back home, all the while being keenly aware of the dead body crammed inside the back. Maybe tomorrow, when the adrenaline has faded and reality sets in, I'll feel guilty. I'll feel scared or panicked.

Until that happens, I'll use this new sense of calm to get rid of the body.

The snow has turned to rain, splashing against my windshield as I pull into my driveway. The tangy smell of death is knocked out of me as I push the door open, inhaling a deep breath of cold air.

The icy rain pours down as thunder rumbles in the sky.

My plan hadn't run further than getting him here. Now comes the issue of what I'm going to do with the body. Burn it? No, it's too wet outside. Acid? Don't have any.

I could, however, bury him. My backyard is already torn up from renovations and my pathetic attempts at trying to start a garden. If anyone asks questions, it would be easy to play off disturbed ground as home maintenance.

It's the only option I have, and there's no one else with a better idea.

One thing they never mention about killing someone is how heavy the body is after death. It's a truth I'm learning the hard way as I pull this man by the feet around the outside of my home.

My lungs burn and feet ache as I stumble backwards. The cold air makes it nearly impossible to breathe. It feels like hours of tugging, but thankfully, my backyard comes into view.

Dragging him just a few more feet until he lies near the middle, I drop his feet and place my hands on my knees. I'm doing this all wrong, I know I am. Frustration eats at me, and all I want is for him to be here.

Thatcher would know what to do. He would have shown me.

He should fucking be here. Why isn't he here?

A sob breaks from my mouth, and I feel my chest tighten unbearably. All those emotions that went hiding away when the knife was in my hand come flowing right back in.

I miss him.

They could have taken anything from me, anything at all, but

24

not him.

Lightning strikes across the sky, the clouds crying with me as thunder rattles the trees surrounding my home. Tears blend with the rain, and exhaustion hits me hard.

The snap of a branch brings my attention upward. I lift my watery eyes, expecting a tree to come tumbling down due to the storm, but they're all intact.

He stands there.

A dark figure just across from me, dressed in black, hands tucked inside of his pockets, and the rain forcing his hair in front of his pale face. The cold air has nothing on the look in his eyes.

Drips of water slip from his mouth, sliding across his angular jaw.

My mind tells me it's a ghost. A coping skill my PTSD caused in order to deal with his loss. But my heart, my addictive heart, she beats for the first time since he went missing.

It's you! It's you! You came back, you came back!

The blood rushes to my ears, thrumming as my heart pounds violently against my chest. The world seems to spin a little slower, and I feel my throat constrict around the sound of his name.

Neither of us moves.

We only stand there staring at one another.

He is devastating. A quiet, morbid god amongst humans.

I almost let my mind win. I almost believe he's a ghost.

Until—

"Hello, darling phantom."

THREE
night of the living dead

Thatcher

I've never been particularly fond of Lyra's clothing choices.
Tonight, that is not the case.
She is a vision in black.

That color might've been created just for her.

Grim's lovely bride with a dead body at her feet as her wedding gift. The temptress of light. My one and only mistake, the girl who'd cheated death.

A mother of ravens in lace fabric that wraps so delicately around her body, framing every single inch. My lips quirk a bit, seeing the streaks of crimson on exposed skin, staining the material.

She would wear an expensive dress just to let blood and the elements ruin it. But she's never cared for what wraps the package, only what lies beneath. The high collar bleeds with the wet, inky curls of her hair, making it impossible to tell where one ends and the other begins.

"Did you wear that pretty little dress for me, Lyra?"

My first words to her since I'd left, and they drip distaste, even though my eyes note the opposite. Rain pours across her porcelain face, the trembles of her bottom lip caught by the moonlight.

My return is a relief for her, and it severely hinders me.

"Wore it for your grandmother's funeral," she whispers, her voice an echo of the pain she has lived through recently. "It was my mother's."

I tighten my jaw, the muscle in my cheek jumping.

Quiet wrath brews in my chest.

I've never been one for funerals or mourning the dead. But a piece of me would have liked to see May at peace. To maybe remove my final image of her.

My whole life, I'd always thought of her as someone strong, willful, unmoving in my turmoil. Yet she couldn't have been more different on her last day. My days as a child made me immune to all the blood. The hacked body parts and exposed bone.

I'd seen women dehumanized, brutally strung up like cows to slaughter, and was made to clean up the aftermath. In my spare time, my favorite hobby was skinning other serial killers.

There wasn't anything that shocked me in the department of murder.

But it hadn't been shock that rippled through me when I saw May on the floor of the kitchen. Something slippery moved across my skin—it felt like a thunderstorm inside my own body.

I'd like to think watching her be buried would have provided me an umbrella of sorts.

"Where have you been?"

It's a valid question, one I hadn't planned on answering until Stephen was arrested for his ties to Halo, but my hunting had been rudely interrupted by her recklessness.

I don't give her a reply; I just continue to move forward. My legs close the gap until the only thing separating the two of us is the dead body of a man that should've suffered far more.

Death always seems to be that thin line cutting between Lyra and me. Always there, lingering in our space, existing between the two of us like air. Where we go, it follows.

My fingers reach out, seeking the lace fabric at her collar. When I make contact, I rub the wet material with my thumb. Her body goes soft, lax, tilting towards my touch.

The weight lifts from her shoulders, and that solid wall of iron protecting her from the world crumbles with every swipe of my finger. This only makes my job of hurting her easier. She's so very easy to break like this, pliable beneath my hands.

I lift my pointer finger, caressing the side of her neck in comforting strokes. The softness of her skin makes the hair on the back of my neck stand up, reacting without my mind's consent.

Those jade eyes practically glow, illuminated from whatever light still lingers inside, and she's staring up at me like I'm her hero.

Her angel.

"Divine," I breathe.

I've never meant anything more. Never been more honest.

"Thatch—"

"So much so, it almost makes up for the mess you made tonight," I tell her calmly. "Almost."

Her eyebrows furrow, and I press my finger against the pulse in her throat, catching the steady rhythm.

"Tell me, was it blissful ignorance, or were you looking to get caught?"

She stills, licking her upper lip, possibly sensing in the air that I'm about to remind her of who I am. That I have never been an angel, to her or anyone else.

I'd let myself get distracted, lost in her mess, temporarily blurring my image in the mirror. I was created to hurt things, to never know peace, and had forgotten for a brief moment that I was to kill any and all emotion.

There is no place for it inside of me. No home for it to live.

I'm empty, driven by ego and the control that comes from ending someone's life. That is who I am. That is the person who she has to deal with, to understand I am not her death-crossed lover. I'm the root of all evil, the seed of immorality.

"How dull are you to kill someone in a public parking lot?" I place my hand beneath her chin, tilting it up so she's looking me in the eyes. "I told you never to kill using emotion as fuel. Yet, here we are, Lyra."

A few of her tears mingle with the rain falling.

"He was there," she mumbles. "He was there shopping, and you weren't. You were gone, and I thought—"

"You thought?"

"You were dead. I thought you were dead, and he was still breathing after everything he'd done to me. Done to us. I couldn't." Her head shakes, hands wobbly with adrenaline. "I couldn't control it. It was easier to feel the urge than deal with the sadness. So yes, I killed out of emotion. But that's not my fault."

Oh, spare me.

My fingers tighten on her chin, showing my disapproval of her answer.

"Whose fault is it, Lyra? His? God? Are you back to not owning what you are? What you like to do to people?"

"Yours," she accuses. "It's your fucking fault."

I scoff, shaking my head at the response. I open my mouth to argue, maybe to say something harsh so that maybe she stands a chance of detaching from me before it gets her killed, but she beats me to the punch.

"You left." Her voice shakes, sadness and grief rippling from every single word. "You left Alistair. You left Rook and Silas. You left *me*." Her small hands hit her chest at the words, as if she feels each of them like a knife to the heart.

I feel her emotions like every drop of rain.

How easily she shows every ounce of feeling on her face. Always real, too raw.

"We had no idea where you went or what happened. We thought you were fucking dead! You let your best friends believe you'd fucking died, and you expect me to be fine? To be okay!"

The storm bashes against my skin, and the thunder echoes loudly, shaking the trees. Elements of nature in tune with the havoc brewing beneath our skin.

"Are you so out of tune with humanity that you can't possibly fucking understand what you've done? We looked everywhere. I couldn't find—"

"Did you ever stop to think I didn't want to be found? By anyone?" I interrupt her screaming. "Did you think about that before slitting a man's throat in the back seat of your car like some ama-

30

teur?"

"I'm not anyone."

Her reply is instant. Resolute. So confident in the words that even I believe her for a moment. The wind blows her hair across her face, and I gently tuck the strands behind her ear.

I tilt my head, stroking her cheek with the back of my hand.

"Aren't you though?"

Lyra's body jerks, and she flinches as if I'd smacked her across the face with the hand still brushing her skin. She pulls from my touch for the first time since I've met her. Darling phantom is the one to remove herself from me.

She's drowning in the storm, the gusts of harsh wind making her hair fly around her head. Her shoulders straighten, and all remains of emotions floods away, washed by my words.

I can see every single brick being laid as she builds those walls right in front of me. So, I help with the construction.

"Do you feel that?" I ask. "Knowing how easy it was for me to leave you?"

Those walls are a defense from things that scare her. A stress response, thanks to my father. I've seen them before, but those shields aren't standing tall due to fear tonight.

It's because of pain.

I lean close, lazily swiping my thumb across her bottom lip with a predatory grin on my lips.

"Remember that when you try to love me again."

I'd told myself for years that all I'd wanted was to shatter the light in her eyes. Smother it out with my hands around her throat. Who knew this was what would do the trick.

It flutters away into the darkness, and I want to keep it. That last good piece in her, tucked away inside of a jar. But it's gone before I have the chance to savor it.

Even though this is exactly what I wanted, had been wanting, I don't feel triumphant. Power doesn't lace through my veins.

I just feel damp.

And I despise the look on her face, the one I'd purposely put there.

Vacant, unmoving, hiding.

But I was left with no other choice.

She shoves my hand out of her face, her jaw grinding, eyes slit and narrowed, glaring at me like prey. Her hands are balled up into tight fists at her sides, and I think she might actually try to kill me.

Good, I want to praise. *Protect yourself from me—you need it more than anyone.*

"Then why come back? If not for us, then what, your ego?"

My laugh is cold, lacking humor.

"Don't act so surprised, pet. You know who I am. It's all about my ego."

I'd thought Colin here was her final cut for the night, but she quickly shows me that she isn't finished making others bleed.

"After all these years, you're still chasing your daddy's approval."

I feel the sting immediately, her knife hitting right on target, and she knows it, standing in front of me with a stilled spine. I'm standing toe to toe with my mirror.

Gone is docile, loving Lyra Abbott. She is tucked away, and in her place stands something far more bloodthirsty. I doubt the little girl who once went by Scarlett even exists.

I want to tell her that if Henry saw me right now, he'd deny my genes. He'd know exactly why I'd gone off the grid to hunt his copycat killer, and it sadly had nothing to do with my ego.

My father would be disgusted by me.

Yet, I remain quiet, even as she begins digging a hole in her backyard for a body to fill.

I stand there in silence, holding on to the acceptance that, yes, Henry gave her the trauma that birthed a curiosity, planted the seed of morbid desire. A hunger. A craving.

But it wasn't my father that turned Lyra into a monster.

It was me.

FOUR
Traitor

Thatcher

Alistair Caldwell is known to think with his fists first. Fighting is a calling card for a neglected boy who turned into a vicious man.

As his fist collides with my jaw, delivering a solid blow to the side of my face, I almost feel empathy for all the people who'd taken beatings from him in the past.

Almost.

A dull throb ricochets across my face, the rush of metallic filling my mouth. I stare down at the ground for a second, accepting the violence he'd just delivered before dragging my thumb across my bottom lip as I turn my head to meet his dark eyes.

I've known him a very long time but have never once been on the receiving end of his physical violence. Not once.

"Miss me, Ali?"

He doesn't say anything, just stands in silence. I can see the words in his eyes, all the ones he won't say out loud. History lingers in the room, memories.

If he was different, if he wasn't born in the shadows and raised to be forgotten, he would've said something like,

"You left me."

And if I was different, if I was able to feel and I wasn't robbed of humanity as a child, I might've replied,

"I would have come back for you. Always."

But that isn't our reality.

We are simply sharpened weapons created for destruction, desperate for peace and given only endless war.

"That's it?" Rook grunts, slamming his shoulder unnecessarily hard into mine as he comes storming into his father's empty office, shutting the door behind him. "You hit me harder when we were fucking twelve. You knocked out a molar."

He taps his jaw for emphasis, looking at Alistair but refusing to give me anything but his back. Afraid to meet my gaze, scared I'll see everything he tries to bury.

"You're the one always screaming harder, daddy," I bite, slitting my eyes. He turns his head, looking at me over his shoulder, a sick grin on his lips as he twists that match between his teeth.

"How the fuck he's your favorite will never make sense to me," Rook mutters, slapping Alistair on the shoulder as he walks past. "God forbid we hurt the perfect one. Can't have him bruised and wanted for murder."

He walks lazily towards his father's desk, sitting in the chair and propping his feet up on the wood.

"I hope your father is at work and not due to return anytime soon? He'd love nothing more than to watch me get shoved into the back of a police car."

"He's at the office all day, won't be back until late. Probably be too drunk to tell the difference between your face and my pale ass."

I look at both of the people I'd grown up with, knowing the loyalty that kept us threaded together is heavily frayed with my choice to leave. It will only get worse once they figure out I can't tell them why.

Not the real reason anyway, and they are bloodhounds when it comes to the truth. They'll see right through the lie but never figure out the truth.

They'd need to trust me. Blind faith.

Which they have little of at the moment, and that does something volatile to my insides. Never once had I put any of them in danger; never once had I risked them.

Why question me now?

"Let's get this over with," I sigh, working my sore jaw. "It was in everyone's best interest that I leave. Telling any of you would have only put you in the way."

Alistair scoffs, his fists tightening at his sides. I know he wants to hit me again, but he refrains, choosing violent words instead.

"You left us to find your grandmother in pieces. Try another answer. This time, cut out the bullshit."

Regardless of what either of them says, they feel. Each of them feels emotion in various ways, Alistair on a more drastic scale. He's either angry or content, categorizing all his feelings into those two boxes, while Rook feels them all on a secret sliding scale.

I know the loss of May hurt them, that their grief is real—I just can't understand it. She is—was—one of the only parental figures that showed them genuine kindness. They spent holidays at my home, gotten to know the only healthy adult in my life.

Her loss was a ripple effect through each of us. We all felt it, we all handled it differently, but we still felt it.

"I didn't have another choice. The police would have seen the crime scene, and I would've been charged for every single one of those girls' murders. A done deal—I wouldn't have made it out of Ponderosa Springs before there were cuffs on my wrists."

"You could've fucking told us. Warned us." Rook speaks up, lighting the end of his blunt and taking steady puffs.

"The FBI has a warrant out for my arrest. How did you expect to dig up any more information on Stephen and the Halo with them sniffing around like hungry dogs?" I counter. "I needed to disappear. This was our best bet."

"For you," he says around the smoke floating around his face, eyes hardened in my direction. "It was best for you. Telling us, including us in your hideaway plan, would have been best. Disappearing without a trace was for you—don't get that twisted, selfish prick."

There are many days out of the year that I question how Rook and I are still friends. It's rare we agree on things and even more rare that we actively get along.

But for some reason, I still protect him. All of them.

It had been the only thing on my mind after I found May. Making sure that they were protected, unscathed from whatever blowback this copycat murder was trying to cause.

"They would've found me if you knew."

"Yeah? How? Because you don't trust us enough to keep that secret? Your god complex is unreal—you expect us to trust every motive you have without question, and the most insane thing is we fucking do."

"Don't question my—"

"Why'd you come back?" Alistair interrupts, crossing his arms in front of his chest. "If that was your plan, why are you here?"

The question hits harder than the punch, the...disbelief in his tone. As if no matter what my answer may be, he won't believe it, already counting my words as a lie.

Contrary to Rook's statement, I've never questioned them. Their methods? Sure. But not their motives, not their fragile fucking feelings. Never once.

I look at Alistair, eyes cold.

"I never questioned you when Briar got involved. I didn't like it, but I let it happen without so much as judgment. It was me who stayed in the hospital when she was sedated while you handled Dorian and your parents. I've followed you blindly for years," I spit with hateful venom.

If they want to play, we can play.

"And you." I turn my gaze to Rook, hiding behind his smoke. "Who never questioned your need to hurt? When you showed up at my door, begging me to slice you open, I gave you what you needed. Put my life on the line to kidnap a cop for you to exact revenge for a girl, and you didn't even have to ask me."

The words settle into the air like particles of dust, swinging between all of us like a pendulum, and I'm just waiting to see which one of us gets cut the worst.

I'd been loyal to them for almost my entire life, and this is their repayment?

"I'm surprised you haven't asked me if I did it. Slaughtered my own grandmother. I mean, could you put it past me? It's not like you trust me."

"Thatcher—"

"I'm the villain now. How very interesting. Here I thought we were all on the same side," I hum. "Maybe you do take after your father, after all, Caldwell. Traitor seems to run in the gene pool."

Rage, molten and hot, pours from his eyes. I can feel it burning in the air. That's the thing about being close. You know which cut hurts the most, which words will slice the deepest.

I hear the chair squeak and smell the weed as Rook walks closer, prepared to be the buffer between the two of us. His hit earlier was a warning. There's no doubt Alistair would break my face if given the chance. I've watched him fight men twice my size and leave without a scratch.

But I don't even need to touch him to inflict pain. That's not how his mind works. It never has. He'd deny it, of course, but if I walked away from him, from them? It would destroy him.

Because I'm the ice that chills the fury in his veins. The one who let him sneak into my window when his parents were home. I'm the one who showed him how to bandage his wounds. I'm the person that let him sleep on my floor, the person who stayed awake until he fell asleep.

I didn't do it 'cause I cared.

I did it 'cause he needed it. I'm always handling the things they need but don't have the guts to do for themselves. Alistair's rage, Rook's pain, and Silas's demons.

I'm his—he knows it—just as much as he is mine, but the difference? I don't need him.

I don't need any of them.

"Just answer the fucking question, Thatcher."

Tilting my head, I hear the satisfying noise of my neck cracking before I reply.

"I was tracking a lead. Thought I'd handle the copycat killer while you two finished the rest. But it went dead." Literally, I think. "Ran out of options after that."

In my defense, it's all true.

I was tracking Colin—he was my only real lead when it came to finding information about who is stealing my father's spotlight. They don't have to know that slaying other serial killers is a biannual ritual of mine. That the existence of this wannabe is a direct insult to all I do.

They also don't need to know I had to come back because Lyra snapped and I had to make sure the security footage in the grocery store was cleared. Explaining to them something I can't explain to myself feels unnecessary.

It's my secret to keep. They all have them. I'm allowed to keep a few things to myself.

"Would've been nice to know you were alive," Rook mumbles, probably assuming that's all they'll get from me in terms of this subject.

"What do you want, Rook?" I snap. "An apology?"

He pinches the blunt between his fingertips tightly, grinding his jaw before he breaks.

About time. He was being far too calm to be considered normal.

"You're my brother. I hate you—I hate you so fucking much, but you're my brother," he hisses, flashing the coin tattoo on his inner bicep that mirrors the only one I own. The same one Alistair and Silas bear. "You're his brother! Silas is locked in a goddamn ward. I buried someone I love without you and thought you'd be next. I'm not losing any more of you, regardless of your frigid personality."

Brother.

I've been labeled by other people's names my entire life.

Killer. Psycho. Son.

But *brother* hadn't been one.

"I—"

A knock at the door steals my voice, even though I'm not even sure what I was about to say. I turn to look over my shoulder, seeing a head of red hair popping in.

"Bad timing?"

"Perfect as always, TG," Rook breathes, like he hadn't been able to until she was around. "Come here, baby."

Sage glances around the room sharply before walking fully inside with two more people in tow. She sinks into Rook's side calmly while Briar has nothing better to do than open her mouth.

"Ouch," she says with a bit of a smirk. "You look like you could use this."

A frozen ice bag flies from her hands and lands against my chest, and I'm quick to grab it so it doesn't fall. They very well could've been eavesdropping, and that's how she'd known her boyfriend had socked me in the jaw, or maybe she knows him better than I thought.

Briar holds another thing of ice, carefully placing it against Alistair's knuckles with a shake of her head. But he simply lays his lips against her forehead in thanks.

Lyra is the last girl inside, still standing behind me and tucked against the door. I shift so that my entire body is in front of her, shielding her behind my frame.

I can feel the anger rolling off her small body in waves. It's probably silly of me to stand with my back to someone so prone to stabbing men out of emotion.

"Glad you're not dead," Sage says to me. "Would've only been me giving Rook shit, and that's incredibly boring."

"Well, now that he's alive, we need to find somewhere to put him. He can't stay at any of our places; it's risky having him here now. They know we'd hide him."

"Which is why I should've stayed dead a little longer," I say to Alistair, already knowing this would be an issue.

"You're richer than God. Can't you buy a place? Fly out of the country?" Briar adds, as if it were that easy.

"All I can use is the cash I got from my grandfather's safe when I left. Using my credit cards, trying my passport, anything short of under a rock will have Odette Marshall arresting me on national television."

"So we can—"

"My cabin." Lyra's quiet voice drifts past my shoulder. "It's deep in the forest, way off the radar. Even if the police did show up, there's a bunker beneath the foundation. They'd never find him."

My spine goes stiff.

"No."

I turn around slowly, staring down at her. I notice that her hair is

THE BLOOD WE CRAVE

pulled into a bun, and for some reason, I want to take it down. I don't like the idea of her containing those wild curls.

"Why? It's not an estate. There's no butlers or private chefs." She lifts an eyebrow, full of attitude I don't appreciate. "But you'll be hidden. You'll be safe."

"You won't be."

I hate that I said it out loud. That I couldn't stop myself from saying it.

A deep V forms between her brows, so I slide my hands into my pockets to keep from slipping my thumb across her forehead to soothe the wrinkles. Touching her, being inside of her—God—had been a horrible mistake.

I told her if I had her once, I wouldn't be able to stop, and I meant it.

It's all I can think about when she's around. How she felt, what she sounded like, that my blood flows through hers, and how well she'd taken everything I'd given.

I want her, I won't deny that to myself. She's the only person I've had any form of physical pull to, but that is all it is—a physical, biological response. That's all it can be.

Eyes are on my back, all with different questions, but none of them will get an answer. I can barely admit it inside my own mind that the reason I'd left, why I disappeared and why I came back, was because of her.

All because of Lyra. To protect my bloody, cherry-flavored girl.

If the copycat went after May, she is next on his list. If Odette Marshall figured it out, it won't take him long. I can't risk her. The closer I get to her, the more danger she falls into.

"From you?" she asks, crossing her arms in front of her chest. "What are you going to do, kill me in my sleep?"

"Don't flirt with me like that." I smirk, watching the color of her cheeks turn pink.

Her anger doesn't take away her desire for me. It's embedded in her, and nothing I do will change that. I know because it works the same way for me. Our connection is a major inconvenience.

"You don't have another option." She chews the inside of her cheek but stands a little taller than normal. "It's my cabin or jail. Be thankful I'm offering it in the first place."

A smile tugs at my mouth. "Impressive backbone you've developed, Miss Abbott. Let me know who to send the thank-you card to."

Maybe she did learn something from our lessons.

I like the way she stands in front of me, even if the confidence is fake and it's fueled by the pain I caused. Lyra's becoming more comfortable with the creature that lurks beneath her skin, no longer hiding from it.

All that to say, it doesn't change my mind.

I can't let anything happen to her. I especially can't let an unoriginal serial murderer have her. She doesn't deserve my hate, but she deserves to live more. I won't put her at risk.

"I don't want to share my space with you either, Thatcher. But it's all you've got."

"No."

She lets out a little sigh, rolling her eyes. "Jail it is, then. Rot for all I care."

"I—"

"Did something happen between you two?" Briar interrupts me, calling Lyra out for the false narrative she is painting.

Looking at me and spewing words she thinks will affect me. Pretending that little heart inside her pale chest isn't beating for me. Like my ghost doesn't exist just for me. Like she doesn't bleed for me.

However, the rest of the people in this room don't need to know that.

"Yeah, like fucking?" Rook adds.

My jaw tightens.

I don't want to move in with her, but I definitely don't need anyone asking questions regarding myself and Lyra. Giving in to this feels like signing her death certificate, but maybe if I can stay with her a few days, I'll find another arrangement quickly.

Just a few days.

"Funny," I muse, "but no. Jail and extended time spent with Lyra feel very similar right now. I was hoping for a third option."

Hurt flashes across her face, and I want to grab her. Shake her shoulders and tell her that this is for the best. That I wish she could see how dangerous being near me is, that all of this is for her. Make her understand that, for whatever reason, my brain can't handle the thought of her youthful corpse.

But I keep quiet, let her believe all the worst things about me.

"Are you sure you're okay with this?" Briar asks her friend, worried.

If Briar knew just how scary Lyra Abbott could become, she'd never be concerned for her safety. She herself would be fearful of this little killer. Her best friend would stand in front of her and think, how did this sweet girl turn into such a horrible creature?

The wall slams down in front of her eyes, protecting all emotion behind it, flicking her gaze to the people behind me with a tight-lipped smile.

"Yup," she hums. "I just have to cancel my plans with Godfrey this weekend. He was coming over to help with a spider display I'm working on."

My jaw tightens, hands flexing inside my pockets. I dare her with my eyes to let her invite him to her home. She'll spend the evening weeping in a puddle of his mangled body parts.

He's not allowed to have her either.

No one is.

Because even though I can't have her, she's still my ghost.

She still haunts me.

And every single murderous inch belongs to me.

FIVE
snow white

lyra

Pulling the door open for Thatcher feels like letting him further into my soul, as if he wasn't embedded there enough. Seeing his lean frame step into my home, my very own forgotten world, makes my chest tighten.

Everything inside was curated by my two hands. From the Nevermore collage pasted on the living room walls to the deep purple kitchen. A gothic, cozy, dim masterpiece. Taxidermy items littered across every space, the smell of lavender—it is me, and he is seeing all of that.

"There are four rooms," I hum, hearing his footsteps follow me up the steps. "Two bathrooms."

This does not pull any sort of response. It's not as if I thought it would, considering when he walked inside, he barely nodded in recognition when I greeted him.

I'm not stupid, nor am I naïve, contrary to what he probably believes in that thick skull.

A person who doesn't know him might chalk his bitter behavior towards me up to the fact his grandmother had just died, which is partially true. Another might think it's just how he is, that he never really cared to begin with and he's only been toying with my measly feelings.

But neither is accurate.

Thatcher's wedge of distance he'd shoved between us—him leaving, all his ridiculous behavior—was the result of fear. Now, he'd never admit this to himself or out loud, of course, but I can see it.

He's afraid.

This copycat killer went after his grandmother, the last living relative that cared for him. It doesn't take a rocket scientist to know he's scared of the same thing happening to the guys. To me.

Space, cruelty, distance. It was the only option he thought he had. Push us away, and we'd stay safe. While it hadn't been obvious when we were burying Player One's body, who I'd learned was named Colin, it became clear when we were at Rook's yesterday.

He wanted me safe, all of us, and for him, that meant pulling away.

"This is my bedroom." I wave my hand towards the first door across from the balcony that overlooks the living room. "You can have the one next to mine."

"Why not that one? Or the one downstairs?"

I don't hold back my eye roll at his attempt to get the furthest away from me as he possibly can.

"The one downstairs is my workspace, unless you're cool sleeping with my pet snake and all the dead bugs."

He shakes his head, tightening his jaw. "Aren't people supposed to have pets that are fluffy and not likely to eat you?"

"Where's the fun in that?" I arch an eyebrow, opening the door to the clean spare room. "Plus, Alvi is quiet and minds his business."

"And what's in that room?" He motions his hand towards the door at the end of the upstairs hall. "Safe haven for the rest of your slithering pets?"

I chew the inside of my cheek, glancing at the room hidden away in the dim light. Heat blooms on my face, and I clear my throat, looking at him.

"It's storage and still needs to be remodeled, so it's locked." It's a seamless lie, one I hope he leaves alone. "There's an en suite bathroom, bed, and dresser. It's not a lot, but it will do."

He stares at the door down the hall for a moment longer, making my palms sweat before brushing by me in order to enter the room. I take a breath of his familiar cologne, savoring the closeness for the second he allows it.

Thatcher lays his things on the bed, then slides his hands into his pockets and looks around. I trace the veins in his arms with my eyes, fingers itching to run along the bluish lines. Tailored slacks frame his lean legs, and the simple starched button-down doesn't hide just how toned his stomach is beneath. Not a hair out of place nor a single imperfection.

The light shines in through the blindless window, casting an evening glow against his skin.

He looks so out of place. A high-priced marble statue that a relative bought for the impressive price tag without actually knowing what I like. Thatcher looks far too clean, too expensive to be staying on my spare bed that I bought on sale in a department store.

His footsteps echo across the hardwood floor as he walks to the nightstand next to the bed. I watch as he scoops up the black leather-bound book, one I'd forgotten in here a while ago, his hand running down the spine before pulling it open.

A piece of fabric rests as a page marker. It's almost intimate the way his fingers run along the edges of the pages, reading the words along the page with innate curiosity.

"Skin white as snow, lips red as blood, and hair black as ebony wood," he reads aloud, lifting his gaze to mine with a knowing smirk. "Is this page marked 'cause it's where you stopped or because it's your favorite Grimms' fairy tale?"

"It was my mother's favorite," I answer softly, pinpricks running along my spine. "She used to read those to me as a kid."

"Smart woman to raise her daughter not to believe in happy ever afters."

I furrow my brow, walking further into the room, plucking the book from his hands and tucking it against my chest as if I could protect the memories inside.

"Wicked people dancing on hot coals and kings dying from their greed is happy. Not for those who watched Disney classics, but for people like me."

"People like you?" He arches an eyebrow.

"Those who know happily ever afters don't always come with the promise of sunshine or midnight kisses." I tighten my grip on the book. "The night can be cold, cloaked in bitter darkness, and even then, you can still have your fairy-tale ending."

Like a story about a boy called Jack Frost, who saved me from a monster.

There is a question in his eyes, but he keeps it to himself, dismissing our conversation to continue looking around the room. I walk back to the doorframe, letting him get comfortable, ready to leave until he speaks again.

"It's cleaner than I expected it to be. Chaotic with no sense of design structure, but clean."

How sweet of him, insulting me. I wonder, is this him trying to remind me of my place in his life so I don't get attached to having him under the same roof, right next door? Or is he trying to remind himself?

I don't bother looking over my shoulder at him, just stand in the doorway with my back to him.

"Woah, how nice to have your approval of *my* home."

It's unfortunate for him that I know how his mind works. How he plays games.

I'm not angry at him, not really, even though I wanted to be the other night. I love him, understand him far too much to be upset at him for behaving the only way he knows how.

Cold. Distant. Sharp.

But I am no longer going to be meek. Not when my hands have been responsible for three deaths. The barrier keeping who I was and who I am snapped open when he left, while I was wondering if he was alive or dead.

If Thatcher is going to cut me with his words, I'll return the favor. I know what we are to each other, but I'm done letting him hurt me with no rebuttal. We were made from the same blade; it's not hard to know which spot bleeds the most.

Maybe he'll get a taste of his own medicine for once.

All I know is I don't want to be beneath him. I want to be his equal. Mirror images of one another. He reflects all I am inside, and I reflect what's inside of him. Two pieces on level playing ground.

It's us at the end of this, and deep down, he knows that. That there can't possibly be anyone else for either of us.

"Having me here makes you uncomfortable, doesn't it? Puts you on edge? Or is that just your new personality now that you've accepted being a killer?" I know when I turn around, he'll be smirking. That stupid smirk that makes my insides curl.

"Does it matter?" I offer in return, turning slightly to face him, leaning against the doorframe with my arms crossed in front of me, book tucked tightly. Trying to ignore the way my heart is screaming. *He's so close. Touch him. Touch him.*

I wish she understood how hard he makes that for us. That she picked the most difficult man to love.

"No." He clicks his tongue. "But I can't help but wonder how the person who has invaded my space since we were teenagers has a problem sharing hers."

I tighten my jaw, grinding my molars, fighting the blush threatening my cheeks. "You love knowing that, don't you? That I followed you? Does it fuel your already massive ego to know you had a stalker?"

"That doesn't answer my question."

"You aren't owed a reply just because you ask me something."

He smiles, pressing his tongue to his cheek, a piece of his hair falling in front of his face as he replies. "Are you keeping secrets from me now, pet?" His eyes turn hard. "Considering I didn't tell anyone about your recent homicide or how I helped you get rid of a body, I would think that warrants a little trust, does it not?"

The threat is laced within his words. I decided to keep things to myself because of the wedge he drove between us, and now I'm getting blackmailed to share?

He can never deny being a Pierson, that's for sure.

"It's nothing to do with trusting you, Thatcher," I say with bitterness in my voice. "I'd be uncomfortable with anyone being here. This is my home, my space, the place I don't have to hide. Which means it's—"

"Easy for people to see you," he finishes for me. "All of you."

I swallow the knot in my throat, my mouth dry because of the heat in his gaze. How his eyes don't move from mine for even a second. I hate when he does this, looks at me like he sees everything and it doesn't scare him.

My skin pricks with goosebumps as I nod.

"That's not something I'm used to. The world seeing me." I pick at the edges of my sweater, pulling the thin thread at the hem. "We can't all be built for the hustle of political conversation and media presence."

Every room he steps into, he owns every single stare. Revels in their fear and smiles because of it. I've watched him talk his way through a room effortlessly. This town condemns him, but there is respect for who he is, and he knows that.

He laughs, humorless and rough. A black hole of a sound, sucking up all the light in the room.

I wonder if he knows what it is to truly laugh.

"After Henry was arrested, I stayed locked inside the estate for months. This version of me? It didn't exist yet." He looks around the room, probably picturing his childhood bedroom. Then he's back to staring at me, his long legs bringing him closer and closer to me.

"I refused to leave the grounds, barely spoke to anyone, including my grandfather, which drove him mad. So, to put him out of his misery, May took me out to the gardens, and we sat in silence for hours. I watched while she tended to flowers and spoke to the staff. It wasn't until it started to get dark that she spoke to me."

I try to imagine Thatcher hiding from the world, and every time I do, it feels wrong. Somehow, I had forgotten that his life had changed that night too. I'd lost my mother, but he'd lost his father. Regardless of the monster he was or what he did to all those women, he was still Thatcher's father.

It's weird, odd, to think that he was lonely too. Surrounded by people but so very alone. Just like me.

He stands just in front of me, keeping an inch or two between us, just enough for me to feel him. Just enough to want more.

"She said to me, 'A child is said to be two parts of a whole. One belonging to the father and the other its mother. But,'" he says, a ghost of a smile on his lips, "'it's forgotten and often never mentioned that children are three parts of a whole. There is a large part that belongs to them. This piece, unlike either of their creators, is wholly oneself.'"

I feel his fingers reach for the book in my hands, pulling it from my grip with ease before continuing. "She said that part, the one I own, is what matters. It's that piece that doesn't deserve to be hidden from the world's eyes due to my father's mistakes."

He thumbs through the pages absent-mindedly, running his tongue along his dry lips. "I don't kill people because my father did. I do it because the piece of me, the one that's all mine, feeds on it, lives for the power. May gave me perspective, strength to no longer care what this town whispered or what they thought. It was my father who made the silent boy, but she made the man."

My eyebrows furrow, pain lacing my chest. Hurt for the version of Thatcher that was once a little boy. One that didn't know who he was other than his father's son. A young mind who believed the sum of all his parts equaled evil.

I hurt for the little boy who hid away because everyone who laid eyes on him after his father's arrest saw him only as a ticking time bomb. A killer in the making. A future terror.

He never stood a chance at being anything other than jaded.

"Why'd you tell me that?" I ask, unsure if it's the grief of losing May or nostalgia, but he never just willingly shares things.

Thatcher's eyes skim the pages. "Because it's obvious you haven't shared with your friends the details of our...situation." His eyes look me up and down, a flash of remembrance from the night his hands had been all over my body, searching with no end. "Now we're even for secrets."

Unable to stop myself, I reach out, touching the back of his hand and feeling the cold immediately. "I don't want to be even. I just want—"

With practiced ease, he pulls away as if I've burned him, taking a step back further into the room, book tucked beneath his arm.

"Oh, to answer your earlier question," he interrupts, looking down his nose at me. "You fuel more than my ego, knowing how far you'd go for me. You'd give me anything. You and that pretty, dark heart."

That glimpse of vulnerability disappears. The mask of a villain comes slamming down over his face, and he smirks.

"If I asked, you'd die for me, darling phantom. Wouldn't you?"

I know they call him a psychopath. That he is the darkness that eats the light and nothing about him is remotely human. He can't feel.

But I've felt his heart beneath my hands, committed the steady rhythm to memory, and I know it matches my own. It's a pair, his and mine, created from the same flesh and muscle, cleaved into two separate bodies.

That's the thing about love. It doesn't care if you're toxic. If their parent murdered yours, or he's incapable of feeling. Love doesn't care because it takes you over. It consumes you, eats at you, and leaves you barren.

It does what it wants. It takes what it needs, and it doesn't care what it does when it leaves.

"Maybe I'd die for you, Thatcher Pierson," I mumble. "But death is inevitable for us all. It's what you'd do for me that matters."

His eyebrow arches in question.

"You'd disappear again, just like you did when you were a little boy, just to keep me safe." I push off the doorframe, turning to walk down the hallway with his eyes still on my back. "And I didn't even ask you to."

SIX
alone with you

Thatcher

Everything smells like her, and I hate it.
It's difficult to keep my mind focused on the task of shutting her out when my body, my flesh, is so weak.

I am surrounded, and there is no escaping her.

A week I've been here. In that week, my sanity has reached an all-time low. The four walls of this room I've trapped myself in aren't enough to keep her out. Book after book, page after page, with hopes of distracting myself from my settings, but I can feel her.

Just outside the door, existing, living, *fucking* humming.

Solitary confinement has left me with irrational behaviors. Like creating a growing list of things I've learned about my new roommate.

Lyra is a night owl.

I hear her waltzing across the creaky floorboards until the late hours of the night, humming and playing soft, melancholy music in her room. The walls are too thin; they let every sound pass through. When I lean against the headboard of the bed and close my eyes, I'm practically in her room.

So I've picked up on her habit of fixation. When she finds a song she likes, it's the only one she listens to for hours. Over and over again until she's tired of it. It's an endless process that my headphones struggle to block out.

Birds chirp outside my window, and a heavy breath heaves past my lips as I run a hand through my hair. Morning has arrived, which means the night crawler of the house is sound asleep.

My shoulders are tight when I slip out of bed, legs heavy as I grab a pair of black sweatpants from the dresser and a white shirt. I'm tense beyond measure, from the fact my face is plastered on wanted posters to the disruption of my routine.

I have lived my life according to a strict schedule since I was young. Not being able to continue that has set me far too close to the edge. I feel more like a caged animal every day. No place to go, no choice but to pace within the bars of my cell.

I'm careful not to make noise, knowing the early hours of the morning are the only time I venture out into the cabin. I have until noon until the creature wakes from her slumber.

Snow coats the ground when I open the door, and the freezing cold weather makes my body shiver. Running has been the only part of my normal schedule I've been able to maintain.

Lyra's cabin is outside Ponderosa Springs' limits, hidden away in a small coastal mountain range and tucked within the forest. It's secluded, void of neighboring homes and traffic. I don't need to concern myself with anyone seeing me and calling the police.

The frozen ground crunches beneath my steady footfalls, my breath coming out in visible puffs. I reach behind my head, tugging my shirt off and tucking it in the waistband of my sweats. The chilly air bites into my fingers, a familiar ache settling into my body.

"You are my masterpiece, Alexander. Look at what I've created in you. Structured. Controlled. Perfection."

I stand in the snow in nothing but a pair of boxers, and my tiny bones rattle. The sound of my teeth clacking together rings in my ears.

"Pain is a feeling. What do you do with feelings, Alexander?"

"Kill them."

I run a little faster, physically yanking myself from the memory inside my mind, and I shove it back into the dark where it belongs, this pit in my brain that holds everything I don't care to remember.

I run until I'm no longer cold, until the craving for structure settles and the oblivion inside me absorbs all the thoughts I don't need.

The warmth of the cabin blasts across my face, the smell of lavender candles that crackle on the windowsills. I place my wet shoes by the door and continue my *new* morning routine.

Snooping around her things.

It's an even trade, I think. She's been sneaking around me for years; it's only fair I return the favor now.

Leaving the doorway and sinking further into the cabin, I see her taxidermy hobby has taken up most of the living room. It's a mess, and my mind almost splits in half at the disorder, tools scattered across the floor in front of the empty fireplace. A medium-size glass frame sits on the table, and it's filled with purple thread to mimic a spiderweb, I assume.

I walk into the disaster zone, picking up the journal lying on top of a pile of homework. Her handwriting is exactly as I imagined it'd be—chaotic. As if her pen can't possibly keep up with all the thoughts in her mind. There are scribbled words across the entire page, forgoing the straight lines, a mix between cursive and print.

Poecilotheria metallica, Nephila inaurata, Chrysilla lauta.

A list of spiders she's currently interested in takes up the pages. I shake my head, biting back a smile as I stare at her horrible drawings of them and what she envisions for this final piece. Setting the journal back, I make my way through the house.

The odd contrast of healthy plants and animal skull decor is fitting, representing her balance of life and death. I run my fingers along the golden-framed landscape pictures, curious about how long it took her to put all of this together.

There is a stack of books on one of the end tables on my way to the kitchen, and I stop to look through them. The pages are bent, worn, and give the impression that they've been read through.

Lady Athlyne, The Island of Doctor Moreau, At the Mountains of Madness.

It's clear Lyra has a fetish for horror novels. I can at the very least commend her for enjoying classics.

In the middle of the stack is a leather-bound book, black and gold-leaf designs swirling along the front. Curiosity gets the best of me, considering it doesn't have a title, so I flip it open.

My dearest Scarlett, my beautiful, wonderful Scarlett.

I hope these memories remind you of how special your addictive heart is. How the way you love is a gift to be cherished.

I love you across oceans and mountains, my strange girl.

Xo, Mom.

Beyond the dedication, there are several pictures of Lyra through the many stages of childhood. A scrapbook of her youth. I thumb through her as a baby, stopping to run along the edges of a particular one of her as a toddler.

Lyra's small, barely five, in a dress covered in stars. Her hair is twisted up into two high buns, and the smile across her young face is blinding. If someone asked me what I thought pure happiness looked like, I'd show them this.

Her mother, Phoebe, is sitting on the ground next to her, holding the tail end of a snake while Lyra holds the upper half. They look so similar, especially now that Lyra has grown into her features.

It's these moments where I can quietly admire all she is, not having to worry about hiding my appreciation of her peculiar ways. It's in these hours of the morning that I give myself some leeway, and I am soft.

Weak for her.

A noise coming from the kitchen disrupts my snooping. I'm quick to snap the photo album closed but not before slipping the picture into my pocket. My brows are furrowed as I reach into my pocket for a knife, but I find them empty.

I flex my fingers, anger sinking deep into my gut. Would that measly copycat killer just waltz into her home? Did he know I was here? Lyra would have screamed if something happened, right?

This amateur is starting to irritate me, toying with me like he had the right or ability to stand toe to toe with me. I'm not sure who he is, but I do know when I find out, I will take immense pleasure in him watching how a master works.

His flesh seared by my blade. Body chopped into pieces, slowly.

I'll clean and cauterize the blood vessels so he lasts longer. A chill runs down my spine as I think about setting up a mirror so he can watch as I cut him up. Bury my hand into his gut and use his intestines as decoration.

I miss killing, long for the power.

Have gone far too long without making sweet, deathly music.

I can already see the notes on the page for the concerto I'll create for him.

When I come around the corner to the open kitchen, my torture plan fizzles out because instead of a cold-blooded killer, I find a warm-blooded one in its place.

Lyra is humming.

"Salt and the Sea" by Gregory Alan Isakov. Originally sung by the Lumineers, and a song I know without my consent. Her latest fixation, it seems.

She sits crisscross on the island, a blanket pulled over her shoulders and a book tucked in her lap. The dim light of a lamp nearby casts a glow across her face, showing off her cherub face and a few curls that poke out from the hood pulled over her head. I lean against the entryway, biting my tongue as I catch a peek at the faded tattoo across the front of her ankle.

Nevermore.

The perfect wicked concoction of macabre and beautiful. It's easy to stand out amongst the world of the living, but Lyra, sweet Scarlett, she is life that spins through graveyards. A face that echoes across the dead. Beauty so divine death can't bring himself to touch her.

My hands buzz with an itch as she picks up a cherry, staining the tips of her fingers before turning the page, transferring the sticky substance to the page.

A drop of red juice slips from her lips, dripping down her chin.

I've never been so hungry for cherries. I crave the taste of them on her tongue, her skin. My groin tightens with desire, and these loose sweatpants do little to conceal how starved I am for her.

"If this was a horror movie," I say, "you'd be dead."

"I was being nice and letting you finish staring." She yawns, stretching her arms above her head and exposing the skin of her lower stomach.

My jaw tightens, and something warm burns my face. A knowing grin tugs at the corner of her lips as she lazily pulls her eyes from the book, unshaken by my arrival.

The smile fades once she sees me, drops as quickly as it arrived, and I can feel the heat of her gaze tracing my naked upper half with a look of unashamed attraction. Lust glazes over her eyes, and she does nothing to hide it.

Owns it.

It's a special kind of torture being this close and not touching her. If there was a way to go back and take back every touch, every kiss, every cut, I would do it. Because now, it's all that lives in my brain when she's around.

"Should I return that favor?" I arch an eyebrow, smirking.

A cat must have her tongue because she keeps her mouth closed as I walk to her coffee machine, needing to move before she does something stupid like touch me and I do something reckless like let her.

The lingering smell of a freshly brewed pot soothes the tiredness in my bones. I open the cabinet above me, rolling my eyes at the litter of mismatched coffee mugs. From *Hex the Patrichary* to *Poe Me Another Cup*, they range in color and size.

I pick a solid white one, pouring the brown liquid inside and moving towards the fridge. I expect to be putting milk inside, but when I open the refrigerator, I find the coffee creamer I've been using for years nestled on the top shelf.

"You watched me drink my morning coffee?" I ask, grabbing the creamer before looking at her.

She swings her legs over the edge of the island, shrugging. "It's a common brand."

"Sure it is." I run my tongue across the front of my teeth. "I'm curious, how much do you know about me, pet?"

"You're an asshole."

"And you're a stalker. My stalker. I think I'm allowed to ask what boundaries you've crossed for the sake of following me." I place the coffee cup in front of me, leaning my forearms on the island several inches away from her.

This is the most we've talked since I've been here. Well, she's talked—I've stayed silent and done my best to avoid her. Because somehow, I always know how conversations end with us.

Her face is a light pink as she softly fiddles with the hem of her Hollow Heights sweatshirt before she speaks again. "I wasn't doing it in a creepy way or for some sick gratification that they show on the news."

"No, you did it for love, right?" My voice is harsh, pushing her towards the answer I want. "That's what every stalker says when they get caught. It was all for love."

Fire burns in her gaze, the switch flipping inside of her. "You were there on the most traumatic night of my life. The last good thing in a room filled with so much bad. You were there, and I clung to you."

No one has ever called me good before.

Not a single person. Not even as a child.

"I didn't even know what love was then. But I was alone. I had no one else except the memory of a boy who saved my life, a boy who had chosen kindness, and it was all I had. All I had inside foster care and group homes." Her voice cracks a little, and she chews the inside of her cheek. "You were all I had."

A tear rolls down her porcelain face, followed by another.

I despise myself for the way I've broken my vow of silence and for the way I'm about to break another rule. The word "control" seems to hold no weight when I'm around Little Miss Death.

A piece of me that's stronger than the rest demands to fix what I'd just done, to comfort her in some way. I have no choice but to be pulled towards her.

She was a broken girl who grew up alone, disappeared within the cracks of the earth, and existed in the void. I wonder what she could have been without the trauma, with her mother still alive.

She'd lived through so much pain that I had been her only place of comfort.

Me.

I step in front of her small body, her legs spreading to make room for my waist between them. Chill bumps scatter up her thighs as she touches my cold skin. She lets out a gasp as my hands slide across her cheeks, holding her face.

My thumb catches a few of the new tears, sliding them away with gentle strokes.

Do you know what it's like to go your entire life and never know gentle? How to be kind? Then you meet someone who is overflowing with it, and suddenly, you can't be anything but soft just for them?

Touching Lyra is the same as stroking ivory keys.

Everything stops spinning, and my mind goes wholly still. There within the black-and-white of her soul exists a solace. My fingers beg to hear the music she'd make for me.

It's simply her and the piano.

They know my secrets, the things the rest of the world will never.

"No tears, Scarlett. Not for me," I say. "Save those for someone who deserves them."

Lyra melts into me, the cold of my touch a comfort she seeks instead of tugs away from. It's quiet for several seconds while I wipe the tears from her face and she falls into me.

"I never got to thank you," she whispers. "For that night. That's how it started, the stalking. I just wanted to thank you for saving me, and I tried a few times. You were just…" She struggles to find the words, chewing the inside of her cheek to help gather them. "This intangible person. Alluring and so overwhelming. You are so beautiful that people were terrified yet refused to look away. Every time I thought, 'This is the moment to say something,' nothing ever came out. I was this little orphan girl that no one ever noticed, and you were infamous. I never meant for it to turn into what it did. I never meant for you to hate me."

Beautiful.

What a silly word to describe someone who has been quietly rotting inside for years.

No one had noticed her, that was correct. But I had.

I'd noticed her long before she started following me around.

We were maybe ten when she came back to Ponderosa Springs. It was everyone's first day back to school, and I remembered her the moment she stepped into class. And I remember that day because I heard music when she walked in.

Music I'd created after the night we met.

The unfinished piece, my very first.

Lyra is the reason I make concertos for my victims. She's the initial inspiration for my uncommon trophy. She's why every murder I'd ever committed was inscribed into notes on sheet paper. Why every kill has three forms.

The Selection, The Hunt, The Kill.

Scelta, Caccia, L'uccisione.

Music is the only way I can remember in vivid colors, with no black spots or blurry images. A way to relive those horrifyingly beautiful, powerful moments. And Lyra had been my very first muse.

Yet she is the only one who doesn't have a final piece, whose file has empty sheets for the L'uccisione.

"My dislike never had anything to do with *you*, darling phantom. You were a reminder of what my father wanted me to become," I tell her candidly. "Until one day, you weren't."

"And now? What am I a reminder of now?"

"All the things I can never have."

Secrets I never wanted to share linger. All of these words I wanted to keep to myself, with the hope of taking the look of sadness away. She forces me to be someone I don't know just to prevent her pain.

Her pointer finger traces the line of my collarbone, working down until she is painting the lines of my tattoo, her amber ring burning in the light of the kitchen. I can feel her warmth drip along my skin. The tips of my fingers dig into the back of her head.

"Your favorite artist is Henry Fuseli, and you've always been partial to the Dark Art movement, even though May tried to get you to love Monet. I know you accidentally broke Silas's nose trying to get down from the school's roof after senior prom. You write with your left hand, even though your right is your dominant side."

Her words match the smooth lines she draws on my skin. I feel the way her legs tighten against my hips, wanting me closer, but she's afraid I'll pull away.

"You stay for hours after weekends at the Graveyard so you can clean Alistair's hands. And you let Rook think you hate him so he never knows that you pulled a knife on Theo Van Doren after graduation and threatened to cut off his fingers if he hit him again. I know you don't drink or smoke, you're allergic to shellfish, that you hate warm weather and the color yellow."

"It's a horrible color," I mutter, my throat constricting.

My thumb drags across her bottom lip, and I want to sink my teeth into the soft pink flesh but am clinging to the last of my control. She scoots closer, so carefully that I don't notice until I feel the heat of her core pressed against my groin.

I press a little harder into her, wanting to sink inside of her and live there for the rest of eternity. I can't help myself, not when she's so close. I give in just an inch, just enough to curb my hunger.

I drop a hand, trailing up and down her milky thighs, aching to see them dripping red. My blade slicing a pretty line right across her soft flesh and watching as she bleeds. Running my tongue along the seam of the wound and drinking down every ounce of her so she'd melt in my veins.

Despite myself, I anchor my fingers around her waist, rolling her hips against my cock. It's misery, pure agonizing misery, how badly I crave her. Tilting her head up towards me with my other hand, I make her look at me.

Lust drowns her eyes, luring me further in.

"Those are all the things you are, Thatcher Alexander Pierson. All of that and so much more." Her hands wrap around the sides of my neck, pulling herself towards my mouth. "Things he can never take away from you."

The smell of cherries on her breath is overwhelming, and my tongue leisurely swipes across her bottom lip to get a taste. A groan rumbles in my chest, and her legs tighten around my waist.

I never thought there would be anything stronger than the urge to kill.

Until I tasted her.

I'd die to be inside of her. Consuming her. Beneath her fucking skin. To feel her clench around me in ecstasy as her blood poured into my throat like ambrosia.

Which I have every intention of doing, regardless of the consequences, until her phone starts ringing. The loud, piercing ringtone clears the fog of desire and flicks the switch back off inside me.

I jerk back from her tightly wound body, pushing a frustrated hand through my hair as I release a heavy breath. Her face is flushed, and her teeth hold that bottom lip hostage.

"Why won't you—"

"You should answer that," I interject, not trusting myself to fall into conversation again, seeing Briar's name light up the screen. "Could be about the Halo."

I turn on my heel, forgetting my coffee. Nothing is more important than putting distance between the two of us.

"Thatcher, wait," she tries, and I hear her slide off the counter, but I don't turn around.

I can't turn around because I will regret what happens after.

So I keep walking. I keep moving forward until I'm back inside my room and the door is locked. My head throbs as if my brain is splitting in two. It's too much—all of this rumbling inside is too much.

I know who I am.

What I am capable of.

Yet my mind is always left spiraling when I leave Lyra. She does this to me and always leaves me with the same question.

Who am I when I'm with her?

SEVEN
girls' night

lyra

"Why do they always make it so obvious who's going to survive at the end? And why can't everyone live? Makes no sense."

Sage pulls the throw pillow tighter to her chest, half covering her face with it, tucking her feet underneath her on the love seat, as if hiding herself will prevent the creature in the film from jumping through the screen.

"Someone has to die, but they want you to have someone to root for. If not, the horror aspect is pointless." I bite into a Twizzler, chewing on the gummy candy. "There is no fear without a little hope."

I stretch my feet out in front of me, wiggling my toes towards the roaring fireplace. While I sit on the floor atop a pile of blankets, Briar lies horizontally behind me, curled in a blanket on the couch.

"It's not even that scary," she murmurs behind me, and I lean my back against the couch, looking over at her face.

I snort. "Your boyfriend tried to kill you. Of course the demon in the forest doesn't freak out the girl with a fear fetish."

Briar gasps, a grin on her face as she playfully nudges the back of my head with her foot. "Low fucking blow, Abbott."

"It's true," I mutter, taking another bite of my candy.

She just smiles, rolling her eyes, because a part of her knows I'm right. But that doesn't matter. It's her happiness, genuine and light. Lately, we all walk around with this weight, constantly waiting for the other shoe to drop. Someone to go missing. A friend to die.

Even though we're more than aware tonight was a ploy set up by Rook and Alistair to have us all safe, in one place, while they spent the day twenty miles from Ponderosa Springs.

Today had been marked on the calendar in Stephen's office, the one I'd stumbled upon. The guys felt like this was our best bet, and even though my friends were nervous for them, we all agreed. We've yet to hear anything from them besides updates on their safety, but so far, terminal thirteen, the shipping port on the coast, hasn't brought any proof, nothing solid enough to hand over to the police.

As if that alone wasn't enough, another girl had shown up at Black Sands Cove. A tourist found the severed arm resting in a lounge chair, with a single rose, a neat little bow, and a message carved deep into the flesh.

Can you catch a ghost?

This killer is good. They've successfully avoided arrest, possibly due to the fact the police are too busy pinning it on Thatcher, but it doesn't take away from the facts.

That they are good.

Smart. Precise. Clean.

An eerie chill snakes down my spine, and it has little to do with the movie. I know it's physically impossible for Henry Pierson to return to Ponderosa Springs. That it was someone else, someone involved with the Halo.

But I know everything about the Butcher of the Spring. Leaving roses was not from the original killings, but everything else has been. The body parts left in the open with bows and messages for the police to find. No other remains recovered. Women of all ages and backgrounds.

I know it isn't him. But sometimes, my mind likes to tell me it is. Late in the night, this overwhelming feeling of déjà vu would overtake me. Like he was coming for me, and just like my mother, I'd be his very last victim.

Fate tying up loose ends that should've been cut years ago.

"Shit!" Sage lets out a tiny scream, making me jump, and I turn towards the screen to see one of the side characters being dragged off-screen by something very large with nasty claws.

I let out a breath, reminding myself that tonight none of the other stuff matters. Tonight, it's just this. The unhealthy snacks and scary movies. Jokes and laughter. It feels like a balm against our tired souls.

We aren't victims. There is no debauched sex ring or killers running amok. We're just girls in college, experiencing life the way so many others do. It's these moments, just like this, that make it all worth it. That remind me how badly I want us all to make it out on the other side.

So that these moments turn into a lifetime.

"You're such a chicken shit! You picked this movie," Briar laughs, throwing a jelly bean in her direction. "I thought weed was supposed to mellow you out?"

"I told Rook that new stuff makes me paranoid as fuck." She hides behind her hands, giggling as her red hair falls in front of her face.

The high from the pre-rolled joint (thank you, Rook) still lingers in my bones, making me feel heavy yet weightless, as if my limbs weighed a ton but could still take flight if I jumped.

I'm not a huge drug or alcohol user, but weed is nice for nights like these. A way to forget, to put the world outside on pause and exist in the now.

The sleepy phase starts to trickle into the back of my mind. All the euphoria and laughter from earlier, the random food cravings, are starting to catch up, and my eyes grow heavy.

We only return to the movie for a few silent seconds before Sage is speaking again, probably in hopes of breaking the ominous vibe the movie is throwing across the room.

"Sooo," she hums, scooping the bottle of strawberry vodka up from the floor, "I know we said we wouldn't talk about the elephant in the room. But I'm a nosey bitch."

Briar perks up from the couch, like she's been waiting for our bold friend to make the first move towards this conversation.

"What do you mean?" I ask dumbly, spinning my candy between my fingers.

"She means, what's it like living with Count Dracula upstairs," Briar answers, wiggling her eyebrows suggestively. "Does he sleep in a coffin?"

Warmth spreads to my face, and suddenly, the burning fire feels a little too hot. I've always been fine chatting with them about Rook and Alistair—it's fun, but I'm not the girl at the slumber party with boy gossip.

I've never even been the girl at the slumber party.

"It's not really that different from living alone," I say, trying to sweep the situation beneath the rug. "He doesn't come out much. We barely see each other."

He has nightmares, I want to say. Horrible nightmares that I can hear from the hall, in my room. The bed creaks beneath his terror, and he shouts nonsense into the night.

But I don't think he's even aware of them.

"I don't blame him."

"Hey!" I laugh, smacking Briar's leg.

"No, not like that," she corrects. "I mean, listen, I'm not exactly a member of the Thatcher Pierson fan club."

"Oh, really? I never would have guessed. You two seem so friendly," Sage says, giggling as she takes a drink out of the bottle before handing it to me.

Briar flips her off with a smug grin. "I just feel for him, is all. He's lost a lot recently, including his home. Nothing is familiar anymore. I'd probably lock myself in my room too."

"Trust me, he's not here 'cause he wants to be. This is just his only option besides jail."

I should tell them a little about Thatcher's and my relationship. But I don't think I'm ready to talk about it out loud, not when everything is so messy.

I mean, what would I say?

He'd been teaching me how to kill people so I didn't go on a murder rampage, we fooled around a handful of times—oh, and we had sex in the house my mother was murdered in just before everything went to shit?

There aren't words to describe what we have. It's futile to try, at least right now. I'd like to think one day, when we've navigated what this is, I'll be able to share it.

"Come on!" Sage pouts a bit. "You're locked in this cabin with a guy you've liked since middle school, and you haven't even *thought* about fucking him?"

"Oh my God," I groan, feeling the burning liquid running down my throat. I wipe my mouth with the back of my hand. "I am not talking about this. He's right upstairs, and you're loud!"

I throw a pillow at Sage, but she catches it. "Lyra, I know you're shy, but you're hot as fuck. If you made a move, he's an idiot to turn it down."

My face burns with a mixture of alcohol and embarrassment. I hide it with my hands, not exactly used to having this much attention on my love life. I quite like being the friend in the background. I want to go back to that.

"I don't think finding you attractive is the problem for Thatcher," Briar adds.

"Huh?" I ask with a huff, passing the bottle in her direction.

"He looks at you like he wants to be beneath your skin."

Too late for that. Far too late.

He's already there, even if he doesn't want to be, buried deep within the cords of my veins and constantly moving through me. He's always there.

"So what's your plan of seduction? Are you going for an innocent school—"

"Alright, you're done." I stand up abruptly. "I'm going to sleep. Are you guys okay down here?"

"Wait, wait!" Sage jumps up far too quickly for someone who's been drinking all night. "One last cheers before bed."

Briar nods in agreement, joining us in the middle of the room, holding the neck of the vodka bottle. We stand in a circle, the fire glowing on our smiling faces.

The joy from tonight hangs in the air, wrapping me in a warm hug.

"To the Loner Society." Briar lifts the bottle before pressing it to her lips and taking a drink, her throat working to swallow the liquid before she passes it over to Sage.

It had started as a joke, the Loner Society, but slowly, over time, it became real. A group of people shunned by those who control the social food chain. Three unlikely girls in an unlikely situation.

"Cheers! To sleepovers with friends who aren't backstabbing bitches!" She gives a little wink before taking her drink and giving it over to me.

I look at both of them waiting for me, and I can't think of many other places I'd want to be than right here, surrounded by two people I'd never planned to meet but can't live without.

The kind of friends you dream of as a lonely kid.

I lift the bottle up. "To all of us surviving."

EIGHT
hush

lyra

There is a lingering smile on my lips when I leave the bathroom, my fingers clicking off the light and submerging upstairs in darkness. A cloud of steam from my shower billows into the hall. My sock-covered feet slide across the floor as I walk to my room.

The lingering effects of weed and alcohol still fizzle inside my mind. Tonight had been exactly what we needed. A little break from the anarchy. A pocket of peace.

It's late, and the house is quiet. Sounds of rest echo between the walls. I can hear every creak of wood beneath my steps as I make my way into my bedroom. My bed frame squeaks when I lie down on top of the covers and stare up at the white ceiling, curious if Thatcher is doing the same thing.

Both of our beds are pushed against a shared wall, several layers of wood separating us. I sit up on my knees, pressing the side of my head to the wall, closing my eyes, and trying to listen for him.

Eerie silence greets me, a huff of disappointment expelling from my chest as I lie back down, going through my normal night routine of wondering. Dreaming.

In my mind, the wall isn't there. When night falls, it's just us lying adjacent and breathing in the world. No words, just existing with each other, because sometimes that's enough.

I think about how he lies in bed, suspecting he sleeps on his stomach, but when he's restless, he rolls to his back. Only a sheet covers him because he enjoys the cold.

Most nights though, I wonder if he thinks about me. About how difficult it is to be this close to one another. A thin veil of separation that he slammed between us.

"He looks at you like he wants to be beneath your skin."

Does he remember how that felt? To be buried within my skin?

My nipples stiffen at the thought, rubbing against my thin cotton tank top.

When it's late and the house is still, does he let himself remember the way we looked decorated in blood? Our bodies were a mirage of liquid death and vitality, hands greedy to discover all the ways for us to connect. Can he hear how I moaned in his memory, in a beautiful blend of pain and pleasure, while he molded my body to his cock?

Thatcher was perfectly made, but *I* was made perfect for him.

I let out a shaky breath, my hands gliding down the front of my breasts. A dull ache thrums between my thighs, caused by emptiness. I crave to feel full of him again.

Does he close his eyes and feel himself taking my virginity, forcing his way into my tight walls in the midst of my orgasm? The way I tensed around him, refusing to let him leave?

I grab a pillow from behind my head, shoving it between my legs to aid the throbbing. A whimper tumbles from my lips as I grind my core against the material, and it's painfully disappointing.

It's too soft.

I need firm. I don't need soft or gentle. I ache for the sharp edges and hard weight, the force of his waist to spread me wide.

My tongue swipes across my bottom lip, chasing the flavor of metallic. I just need a little relief from the tension that's built since he moved in. He's not just living in my mind now; he's in my home.

In my life.

Before, I could picture a moment, imagine all the things he would do. Now, I've had the real version. The unbound version of him that claimed my body with feral hunger.

Frustration burns my eyes as I lift my hips again, the fabric of my panties scratching against my clit. Underwhelming sensations coast through me like a dull lighter, sparking over and over with no chance of producing a flame. My chest heaves, quiet moans tickling my ears.

"*Thatch,*" I whisper in the dark for no one to hear but me.

Pretending feels like torment, a sick tease to build me up and leave me dangling off the edge. It's pointless when my dream has become a reality I can no longer grasp.

I flip my body over, folding the pillow in half before shoving it against my pussy, straddling it. I try to lose myself in my mind, chasing his memory. My hips rock forward, and I lift my hands to palm my tender breasts, stomach tightening as I roll my body along the seam of the cushion, trying to trick myself into imagining it's his finger I'm riding. Mouth. Cock. Anything.

But it's futile.

The coil is wound so tightly in me I'm on the verge of tears, simply scratching everywhere but where it truly itches, working so hard towards an unsatisfactory end.

A sad whimper shakes my chest. My teeth catch my bottom lip, sinking into the flesh with enough force to bring blood. A calming hum hits my throat as I taste it on my tongue.

"My, my." The click of his tongue rings in my ears, making me gasp. "Can you not get yourself there, pet?"

My body wakes up, curling out of its slumber with a vengeance. My hips rock accidentally, a zap of raw pleasure thrumming from my clit that makes me shake.

His arrival is a lightning strike.

Electric. Dangerous. Tempting.

I open my eyes and turn my head, finding him there.

Staring.

Thatcher leans against my door, arms crossed in front of his bare chest. My heart pulses all the way to my toes.

"How pitiful." His voice is steady and passive, unaffected by the sight in front of him. But his stare, even in the darkness, is anything but passive.

Thatcher's eyes are always sharp, always studying his surroundings as if waiting for something to happen. What that is? Who knows. But he's always watching, and right now, that razor-edged gaze is on only me, slicing me to pieces as he takes his time tracing the lines of my body. Up, then back down, pausing at the apex of my thighs before traveling back up.

A shiver bolts down my spine, and the place between my thighs quivers. I wet my dry lips with my tongue. Those dark slacks rest wickedly low on his hips, unfairly showing off the two shallow grooves that run diagonally into his pants.

He's marble made, sculpted, and carved with brutal strokes but still somehow carrying the soft tenderness of a human.

My fingers curl into the blanket as I scramble off the pillow and press myself into the opposite wall with my knees against my chest. But unfortunately, my heart isn't the only thing that calls for him, not anymore.

My pussy screams for him, knowing he's the only one who can satisfy her, the only one she wants.

"What are you doing?" I huff, swatting at my damp curls to tame the frizz.

"I was trying to sleep," he says, pushing off the door. "Which is impossible with all the noise coming from your room."

Blood rushes to my cheeks.

"I didn't realize—"

"You didn't realize your bed was thumping against the wall? Or that you were practically in my ear with those deprived moans?" A smirk appears just before he sinks his teeth into his bottom lip. "I'm disappointed, pet. I was hoping to find a man between those pale thighs. I've been itching to kill something."

An image pixelates behind my eyes.

A taboo portrait of a disturbingly erotic fantasy I'd never speak out loud.

My knees knock together as I squeeze them towards one another, my heart banging against my rib cage. The heat between my legs has grown unbearable since his arrival.

"You're thinking about it, aren't you?" His grin is a threat.

My favorite kind of warning.

He walks forward, delving into the depths of my mind without my permission.

"What I would do if I caught another man touching you. Are you picturing me slicing him to pieces while he begs for his life? How I would make him apologize to me for ever laying his eyes on you. For stupidly thinking you belonged to anyone but me, pet."

I swallow roughly, digging my fingers into my legs as I shake my head, denying the truth for my sanity. Needing him to stop because I hate myself a little more every second. Knowing his words are causing the rush of warm arousal to leak down my inner thighs.

When his knees bump against the edge of the bed, I look up at him.

Thatcher looms, veiled by the night. A tower of regal destruction and the center of my pleasure. It's an alarming delusion we've created. I know it's wrong, but I can't bring myself to care when it feels this good.

Regardless of how heinous it may be.

"Or is it the aftermath you crave?" He plants a knee on the bed, his strong thighs flexing. My mattress groans with the weight of him. "When I shove my fingers into that pretty cunt of yours while he bleeds out? He'll die hearing you scream my name. Take his very last breath just as your whiny little pussy clenches around my cock."

The moonlight throws a silver hue across the harsh angles of his face, putting that volatile gaze on display for me. One wrong move and we will be stripped of our base instincts.

Prey and predator.

"You'd kill someone for simply touching me?" I breathe, asking a question I know the answer to but still wanting to hear the reply on his lips.

A whoosh is expelled from my lungs as his fingers curl around my ankle, yanking me towards his body. I moan as my center collides with the leg that is still on the floor, his muscular thigh spreading me open while the other kneels just outside my hip.

The move has made my tank top ride up just beneath my braless chest, exposing everything below it, including the simple pair of black panties I'd picked for bed.

"Darling." He traces the front of his white teeth with his tongue, a starved animal ready to feast. "I'd rid the world of men who breathe the same air as you."

I wither beneath him, uncomfortably hot. The slightest breeze makes me arch forward. Unable to help myself, I grind my hips against his thigh, creating the perfect amount of friction and pressure to aid my throbbing center.

"You'd like that, wouldn't you, pet?"

I nod, unable to speak, incapable of doing much else but chase relief. I'm begging him silently to help the wave inside of me hit its crest.

"What a bloodthirsty little slut," he says curtly, pushing his cold hand flat against my bare stomach, forcing me to keep still. Torturing me. "What will you do if your friends find you like this? Spread open and wet for me?"

I should be embarrassed by the way I whine, how I nearly shed a tear as he pauses my grinding against the muscle on his leg. But this is too painful—I can feel my pussy clenching around nothing, aching for him to fill it.

I should be afraid of Sage and Briar catching us, but I'm too far gone to care. The world could burn down, but I wouldn't care as long as he kept touching me.

"Yours," I whisper, making him furrow his brows in a silent question. "I'm your slut. There is no one else for me."

"Yeah," he murmurs darkly, allowing his hand to drift upward. "You are, aren't you?"

His long fingers span across my torso, tickling my rib cage with gentle strokes that do nothing to ease my desire. Lewdly clamping my thighs around his leg, I can feel myself soaking a spot in his pants.

The derogatory name should sting with the impact of an insult. But it's true, and I like it. I like that he knows my body is so open for him, that I crave him so deeply I don't care about looking desperate.

Every inch of movement is agonizingly slow, the way he works up until his hand is resting just beneath my breasts. I squeeze my eyes, sucking in a breath when he flicks my pebbled nipple through my shirt.

Bliss lasts only a second because as quick as it's there, it's gone just as fast. I groan in disappointment when he pulls his touch from me.

My eyelids are heavy with lust as I look up at him through my lashes. There's a smirk on his face because he knows exactly what he's doing to me. Thatcher is purposefully cruel, enjoying every second, knowing no matter how much torment he puts me through, I will only beg for more.

Ignoring my body, he scoops up the pillow I was using earlier, making my stomach clench. His gaze is heated, darkened with lust and unmoving from my own when he raises it to his nose, pressing to the wet spot in the center and inhaling deeply.

"How sweet," he purrs. "I can smell how desperate your cunt is for me."

I feel his body sway forward, giving in to the heat between my legs just enough. Placing one of his large hands next to my head, he uses the other to palm my breast above my shirt, no longer teasing as he lifts and squeezes, rolling my delicate nipples between his fingers.

"Touch yourself for me."

"But—"

"I won't ask again," he orders, sliding his hand corded with veins to the base of my throat, giving it a warning squeeze.

We are so close that I can feel the desire rolling from his body. I can smell the woodsy citrus scent wafting from his skin, the forest after it rains—so close that I can see just how pure the blue in his irises is. There is no other color; they are a frosted lake with arctic water running beneath.

His breath fans across my face, fluttering across my eyelashes. I preen beneath his gaze, unashamed as my shaky hand slides down the front of my drenched panties.

I gasp at how slick I feel, and Thatcher is right there to inhale it into his own mouth. That's how we move, my hand playing with myself while he swallows every breath before breathing it back into my lungs.

A moan rattles my stomach, and feeling light-headed, I brush a finger over the aching bundle of nerves, massaging with frantic need.

"It's cute how clingy you are." He drops his mouth to my breast, sucking my nipple between his teeth, biting down before apologizing with his tongue. "You can't even come without me."

Fuck.

"Thatcher," I mumble, rubbing tighter circles around my clit, "I need more. I need *you*."

"You're so weak for me, aren't you? So desperate and fucking needy." He lowers his lips to my ear, a breathy growl. "I could slice you open right here and give you a pretty ruby necklace. Would you like that, darling?"

He thrusts his knee against me hard. Demanding my fingers to move quicker, he pulls back briefly only to return with a bite of icy metal.

It runs along my throat, and I don't need to look to see it's a knife in his hands. Warm juices drip through my panties, leaking down my thighs.

I want it. Almost as badly as I need to come.

I need to feel the sting that comes from his cutting. The delicious burn soars across my skin just before a fountain of red nectar pours from the wound. There is immense pleasure that comes from trusting someone like this.

He could kill me if he wanted, and the adrenaline from that possibility makes butterflies flutter in my pussy.

I don't answer him with words. Instead, I grab the neckline of my top with my free hand, jerking the material down to expose myself, giving him ample access to cut me where he pleases.

I'm an open canvas for him to divulge in.

"How very sweet of you, pet." He grins, the tip of his tongue touching his upper lip. "You're so very good, baby. So sweet to me, aren't you?"

He toys with me, rocking his muscular thigh into my cunt while he drags the knife from my throat, dancing around my skin until he stops on my supple breast.

Applying just the right amount of pressure is all it takes. I cry out, bucking my hips wildly against my hand, listening to the sloppy, wet noises my hand is creating in order to distract from the inevitable pain.

The sting rushes through my veins like a drug, and the tickle of blood dripping down and coating my nipple is the high. It's an addictive cycle, and I never want it to stop.

Thatcher drops his head to the crook of my neck with a guttural groan. So raw and animalistic I feel it vibrate my bones.

"Let me see how soaked your cunt is. How badly she craves me," he orders, leaving a trail of searing kisses along the column of my neck, swirling his tongue along the sensitive skin.

I'm so close to the edge that I can't imagine pulling my fingers away.

"Baby." He flicks his tongue just behind my ear, nipping gently. "Show me how wet bleeding for me made you, Lyra."

The edge in his voice disappears. That softness inside of him appears, just enough of it to sound like he's begging. As if the sight of me leaking crimson is enough to bring him to his knees.

I have no choice but to pull my hand from between my legs, squeezing my eyes tightly at the pain of losing my orgasm. The moonlight catches the liquid coating my fingers and palm as I place it between us.

He wraps a hand around my wrist, leading my fingers to my breasts, forcing me to swipe at the liquid trickling down my chest.

Only when I'm coated in both my arousal and blood does he bring my fingers to his mouth, wrapping me in his warmth. Our eyes connect as he swirls his wet tongue around me, sucking at them. I rotate my hips against his leg as his lustful gaze burns me, and this action alone is enough to make me come.

He hums before removing his mouth, licking his lips as if he can't get enough.

"Such a good fucking girl for me, pet," he praises. "You taste like my favorite nightmare."

"Thatch—"

I'm rewarded with a punishing kiss that tastes of all things wicked. I mewl into him, and he eats it up with flicks of his tongue. It feels like we merge into one person, my toes curling when he licks the roof of my mouth. I curl my arms around his neck, pulling him into me, tugging until I feel the weight of his hips spreading me open.

His groin meets my ruined panties, causing us both to gasp in joint pleasure. I never feel more complete than when I'm with him like this. When our skin is connected and our bodies crave nothing but what the other gives.

Thatcher grinds into me, rubbing his pant-clad cock against my cunt. We grab and grope at each other's bodies, pulling and tugging, running towards our own releases that are only found within each other.

All I can hear is his name on my lips, pleas for more, and his erratic breath in my ear while the bed creaks under the weight of his thrusting.

Blood continues to pour from my wound, and his tongue is there to catch it, sucking it into his mouth and devouring it. Licking it between my breasts, savoring every drip. Swallowing me so that I'm inside of him in a way no one will ever be.

"Thatch," I beg. "More, please. I need more. You have to give me more."

Teeth sink into the junction of my shoulder and neck, and one of his hands hooks on my waist, helping move me against his throbbing dick. Even with the clothes, I can feel how hard he is, how hot. Every pulse.

"Oh, so needy. Your poor cunt having nothing to fill it," he teases, edging me on. "You want me inside of you, darling? Are you aching for me to stuff you full?"

I nod, tears streaming down my cheeks from exasperation. I would do anything for release, to come, for him to be inside of me. Anything to curb this hunger.

The coldness of his fingers curls against my hip. He's gripping me so hard I'm certain when I look at my body in the mirror tomorrow morning, his hold will be immortalized in the form of bruises.

"Beg for it."

Another torturous thrust, his mouth hovering just above my own. I can feel every word from his lips against my own. "You want me that badly, this pathetically. Then fucking beg me for it."

"Please, Thatcher. Please, I'll be such a good slut for you, please," I cry, my nails finding a home in the tops of his shoulders, marking him. "*Angel.*"

The nickname is a sigh, a sign of my will breaking in half.

I'm delirious, trapped in a wormhole of agonizing ecstasy, but I still see the way his gaze softens. How his eyes seem to brighten, and the edges of his lips tilt up just enough that I notice through the haze of tears.

Lifting his weight from me, creating enough distance for him to slip his fingers between my thighs, he tenderly strokes me through my panties, pressing his thumb into my clit just before he jerks the material to the side.

The cold air makes my nails sink further into his skin, my hips jumping from the bed, seeking his touch. I arch into his hand, biting down on the inside of my lip to keep from screaming when the heel of his palm rubs against my clit.

"God," he curses. "You're drenched, fucking soaked. It would be so easy for me to slide my cock into your tight little hole, pet. Have you let anyone touch this pathetic pussy?"

I shake my head in distress. "No. No. Never."

"That's right, because it's mine, isn't it? I ruined you for anyone else, didn't I? I warned you." He uses one finger to caress through my slippery folds, taunting me with pleasure that's within reach, dangling it in front of me just to see how hard I'll work for it. "I own you, Lyra Abbott. Your body, your soul, your heart. Even if I can't have it, I *own* you."

He's owned me far before he took a claim on my body. Far before we knew each other. Far before this life or any life before. When the stars were dust and the universe a black, endless night.

There is no real beginning for us, and there will never truly be an end. Not when the threads of fate have woven us in a never-ending loop. A love that travels lifetimes.

We are a divine connection that can never be touched. Not even by the hands of death.

"Yes!" I say louder than I'd anticipated.

When he finally takes mercy on me, I clench around him. I feel his middle finger sinking into my tight hole, my walls sucking him in like a vise. His lazy pumps, mixed with the pressure on my sensitive bud, are enough to get me there.

The buildup starts in my stomach. I tighten up, pushing my hips against his hand to meet him halfway, chasing my orgasm with a feral desire that completely takes over.

"Hey, Lyra." A knock at my door makes me freeze. "Do you have an extra towel? I can't sleep, so I'm gonna shower." Briar's voice rings through the room.

My eyes widen, not only from the shock but because Thatcher slides another finger inside of me with no care for my friend outside. He continues to drive in and out of me, petting that spot deep inside that has me close to seeing stars.

He drops his head to my ear, his hot breath on my neck. His voice is low and secretive, but I hear every word. "Better be quiet, pet. Don't let your friend know how good the hands of a killer feel inside your pussy."

I grab at his wrist, a feeble attempt to stop him, but it just spurs him on. He speeds up, forcing my pussy to make obscene noises from how wet I am, using my lewd juices to shove in and out so easily.

His bloodstained lips pepper kisses along my chest and neck, painting me in his favorite color. My thighs lock, my knees go weak, and I know there is no stopping the inevitable crash.

"Answer her." He curls his fingers inside of me, pushing harder on my clit with his palm. "Do this for me, and I'll let you come."

My fear of getting caught is nothing compared to my desire for him.

I want to be good for him. Even when he was just teaching me, I still wanted to please him because his praise makes me feel like I'm walking on clouds.

"Beneath the—" My toes curl as the coil in my stomach starts to snap in half. "—bathroom sink!"

I meet every thrust of his hand with a snap of my hips, securing an arm around his shoulders and arching off the bed as I push myself against him with reckless abandon.

She calls back in thanks, but I barely hear her. My ears are thrumming, blinding white heat soaring through my veins. It dawns on me that I don't care if she knows or she sees. All that matters is him, is this.

"That's it, baby. Come for me. Soak my fingers," Thatcher coos in my ear. "You're such a good girl for me."

For a split second, my vision turns white. The room spins as my toes curl into my mattress. I cling to Thatcher's shoulders for dear life as I convulse around his hand. My teeth find themselves buried just above his collarbone in order to muffle my screams.

Every breath makes me shake, my orgasm ebbing through me like crashing waves, washing over me again and again, an endless ripple of bliss. My skin buzzes, humming with the aftershock.

He strokes my hair with soft pats, consoling my body until I'm pliant in his arms. I let him rest me on the bed, feeling the blanket being pulled up towards my neck.

I reach for him or try to reach for him, wanting to keep him close as the tidal waves slow. But exhaustion wraps me up and pulls me beneath the surface. I'm not even sure if I lift my arms before snuggling deeper into the comforter.

A shiver tickles my spine when I feel Thatcher's lips graze my damp forehead. It's a whisper of a kiss, and I want to reach out for him, pull him in and force him to stay in my room, but my eyelids grow heavy.

Darkness is quick to pull me into slumber, but just before it all fades to black, I hear his voice in my ears.

"I wish you'd stop me from hurting you, darling phantom," he whispers, "because I cannot stop myself."

NINE
winter rose

Thatcher

It's my third shower today, and I can still feel her in my skin,
crawling, rippling beneath the surface, and finding a home deep
in my veins. I could blame it on the fact she's a parasite of a
woman that doesn't want to leave anytime soon. But that would be
a lie.

I don't make it a habit of telling myself those.

I'd been the one to seek her out Saturday night. There were plenty of opportunities for me to leave. She hadn't even noticed when I
opened the door—it would have been easy for me to slip away back
to my room unscathed.

But.

I couldn't *not* touch her.

Not when she looked so tormented, her face twisted in pain from
frustration. The moon was her spotlight, the bed her stage, and she
was a breathtaking performer. I stood no chance the moment I saw
her. The nail in my coffin of control had been my name coming from

those lips.

How could anyone walk away from that? From her?

Since she'd snuck quietly back into my life, I'd been at war with myself. A battle that left no winner and my insides shredded with confusion. But last night, I'd raised a white flag.

Maybe it's the isolation, the lack of human contact, or maybe I'd just accepted that I am, in fact, weak for one dark-haired girl with eyes that tell stories of the dead. That someone had found a way inside, and I don't want her to come out.

I can feel my father's disappointment as if he somehow knew of my transgression. His voice lives in my head.

"How could you be so pathetic, Alexander? How could you be so weak? You've failed."

But he hadn't seen the way Lyra looked at me. Hadn't been in that room, hadn't smelled her skin or tasted her lips. I hate myself a little for giving in to it, but I would've hated not making her come more.

I'd wanted her and don't yet feel guilty for indulging in that desire. Not when she feels like an angel to a touch-starved demon. I might have made it my entire life not needing to touch another person, but now that I've had her skin against mine, it feels painful to go without.

It's Monday, and like a coward, I've hidden away in this room, avoiding her and the conversation I know she's desperate to have with me. I'm hoping it'll be easier for us to separate now that classes have started back.

My distance isn't because I don't want her.

It's because I want her too much, and living in this house with her is hell.

I'm incapable of denying her. It's easier just to avoid temptation when you're not directly faced with it. I know the closer she gets to me, the more danger she will find herself in. I can't focus on catching a killer if I'm constantly thinking about her safety.

Buzz *Buzz*

I walk towards the burner phone on the bed, rubbing a towel through my wet hair. The caller ID reads unknown, but I recognize the number immediately.

"Caldwell," I clip. "To what do I owe the pleasure?"

"Have you read the newspaper?" he asks.

No pleasantries, forever blunt and straight to the point.

"Can't say I have. Haven't found the time with how busy I've been pacing a hole through Lyra's floorboards."

I hear him scoff as I tuck the phone between my ear and shoulder, dressing while I listen to him speak.

"They named our copycat"—the tone in his voice lets me know I'm not going to like it—"the Imitator."

My eyes roll, even though I'm the only person here to notice. "How painfully unoriginal."

Serial killers have a plethora of differences from age to gender, motivation, and technique. But there are a select few traits we all share. Our ego, lack of remorse, and need for control.

Being one myself, I know for a fact this moniker has done nothing but inflate his already-boosted self-image. Naming a killer makes us real, which does nothing but inflict fear on those we prey on. Fear that is feasted upon and used as fuel for our next kill.

However, being named and compared to another is insulting, at least it would be for me. But apparently, this person cutting up body parts has no issue with his lack of creativity.

"According to this, the FBI is certain it's a guy and has set a mandatory curfew for all residents."

"Those lovely agents are also certain it's me. Let's not count out a woman yet." I slide my arm into the black button-down, a cold smirk on my face. "Or do, considering you are also inclined to believe it's me."

My voice holds nothing but the bitter remains of our last conversation. The distrust and lack of faith had left a sour taste in the back of my throat that had yet to go away.

"Thatcher—"

He pauses, and I let him.

It's the first time we've spoken since I came back and he'd given me a busted lip. Which might be the longest we've ever gone without vocal communication since we were children.

If he wants to be skeptical of me, so be it. I'm not going to beg him for his trust.

"When we were thirteen, I busted the windows out of every single one of Dorian's cars."

My lips twitch at the memory. It had been broad daylight, and I told him it was a terrible idea, that he would get caught, but he was hell-bent, riled up from the events prior that night and uncaring of the consequence.

"I recall being unable to step foot on the Caldwell property for at least six months after."

"Because you took the blame. You didn't ask me; you just copped to it and let my parents believe the worst about you."

"Yes, but everyone already did that, Alistair," I point out. "What were two more people on the list?"

"They were going to send me away if they found out it was me."

Yes, yes they were.

Throw him into some military or boarding school from hell and forget all about the son they'd created as spare parts for their heir.

"I'm not sure what this has to do with anything." I swallow, fumbling with the buttons on my shirt.

He sighs, probably just as uncomfortable with this conversation as I am.

I don't blame him, nor can I hold a grudge for the words that were exchanged between the two of us, not when I'm unsure of how I would have reacted in his place.

"Listen, I don't know what it is you do in your basement or why you fucking want to do everything alone." There is a pause of silence before he continues. "But I get it. I get you. Why you do it, these things you've always done. For Rook and Silas too. I get it."

I'm not sure when my motivations became so transparent to those around me, but it's starting to irritate me. I don't want to talk about why I do things or chose to protect him from his parents.

All it does is make my head hurt, fill it full of questions I'll never get answers to.

I do what I do, and that's the end of it.

"Is this your form of apology?" I tease, lightening the conversation. "It needs work."

"Not in this fucking lifetime." He laughs into the speaker.

There we go. That's much better.

"Did you and Rook find anything at terminal 13?"

I step into my slacks, changing the subject.

"Stephen wasn't there."

"Fantastic."

"But James Whittaker was."

My eyebrows pull together. "Coraline's father?"

I hear a door close wherever he is, and Briar's voice cracks through the speaker, muttering a hello.

He doesn't answer me, the line quiet. How nice of him to put me on mute while he makes out with his girlfriend. I glance down at my watch, biting the inside of my cheek.

Lyra should be back by now.

Alistair clears his throat. "We saw him meet at the port gate just after midnight, exchanging a set of keys for a hefty black duffle bag from two men. Rook snapped some pictures and is going to get Silas to walk him through how to run it through his computer to try and get some information on them."

Interesting.

"So James uses Coraline as his way in with Stephen. Prove he's loyal to the ring," I conclude.

"That's Rook's theory too."

I walk to my bed, flicking through the files I've been going through, all of the evidence we've collected and a few stolen documents from the police department, thanks to Rook.

Shifting through, I quickly find the photo that Sage had found in her father's belongings. The picture showing Frank Donahue, Greg West, Stephen, Conner, and James in the parlor room. We knew from Lyra that they had all been friends during their college days.

But did a couple of college parties and hard drugs bind the five of them enough to start a sex trafficking ring? How many men in this town are selling their own daughters to pay off some debts? The quick cash of human trafficking doesn't seem worth it, especially for someone like Whittaker.

I grab a sheet I'd printed from the internet, reading the contents. "Why is James involved? Elite is one of the most profitable petroleum engineering companies on the West Coast. It's unlikely he needs the money."

"Greed is a nasty fucking thing—there is never enough for people like that." Alistair's voice is bitter, hating the taste of his own family's wealth. "The Halo needs space to hide the girls coming and going, right? Elite's company campus spans three cities. That's a fuck ton of land."

Plenty of room to hide shipping containers full of missing girls without raising suspicion.

"So, Whittaker provides the safe house to hide the girls before they're sold overseas. Frank kept it quiet for the money, Greg was a pawn, and Stephen is pulling the strings." I press my fingers into my eyes. "And we have nothing solid to prove any of it."

"Bingo."

I run a frustrated hand through my damp hair. The world is moving outside without me while I remain stagnant in this room. The guys are working to get information on the Halo, and I've looked over files from the murders, but none of it is useful. None of it tells me who this Imitator character is.

My hunting is limited, and I feel like a caged animal in this room, useless and without purpose.

We keep gathering puzzle pieces that don't fit together, with no guidance on how to fix them. I knew getting involved in this was a bad idea from the start, that once we were in, it was over. We wouldn't stop until it was finished.

I throw the papers onto the made bed, straightening them carefully before picking up the book lying next to them.

I run my fingers along the cover, flipping it open to see Lyra's messy handwriting along the sides. I'd discovered that she enjoys the art of annotation and had quickly found myself borrowing copies of her books.

"I was in love, for the first time in my life. I knew it was hopeless, but that didn't matter to me. And it's not that I want to have you. All I want is to deserve you. Tell me what to do. Show me how to behave. I'll do anything you say."

I smirk at the note next to the underlined passage.

This is love.

And just below her own handwriting is my own, the red pen bright against the old pages.

No. It's unwarranted devotion. His desire to love her is only because of her unwillingness to love him. You can just say Sebastian Valmont from Cruel Intentions is your type, darling. No need to go through the text that inspired the movie to prove it.

This is the third book we've had a conversation in. Without her knowledge, of course, but something about it makes me feel closer to her mind without needing to be near her body, just existing between the pages of her favorite books, reading her thoughts as if she's right next to me, explaining word for word what it is she enjoys about each part.

"Thatcher, you still there?" Alistair's voice pulls me from the book.

I close it, laying it back on the bed before replying.

"Yeah, what were you saying?"

"I asked where Conner Godfrey is in all of this."

The sound of his name makes me recoil.

"In a casket." My grip on the phone tightens.

I hate the way he looks at Lyra. She's kind and too trusting sometimes; she doesn't see the way he stares. How he purposefully puts himself in her space. He may fool everyone else with his hip, cool teacher act, but I kill men as a hobby.

Everything you ever need to know about a man lives in his eyes, and he desperately wants Lyra Abbott, using her kindness against her, pulling her closer for far more than just friendship.

Anyone looking at her too long annoys me, but most of all, Conner.

Because she *smiles* at him.

That stupid smile.

It's blinding and annoyingly happy. Like a jar filled with those little firefly bugs that kids love to catch during the summer.

The one that lights up her face and illuminates any room she's standing in. It's impossible to miss. How the world doesn't notice it, notice her, is beyond me. Because once you do, it's all you see. She exists everywhere.

I've watched it grow over the years with her face but never dimming in its joy. Lyra likes to believe she is nothing but death and darkness, but inside her is a soul made to love people.

Her smile is a glimpse of her love. Of her affection. Her happiness towards others.

It's a smile she's never once given me.

"You have a problem with him?"

"I have a problem with anyone that close to the Sinclairs," I lie easily, rolling my tongue in front of my teeth.

There's a knock at my door.

That's something new. I suppose our night together has given her a little courage to approach me.

"Lyra stayed after to talk to him for a while today. I saw them hug just before I left. Ask her if she found out anything," Briar shouts from somewhere in the room.

"Sure." My jaw twitches, looking over my shoulder at the closed door, knowing she's waiting just outside. "Call me if you find anything else."

I know we all talked about her using her friendship as leverage to get information from Godfrey, but it doesn't mean I like it. I also don't like the idea of her staying alone with him for longer than twenty seconds.

Anger thrums through my veins. I told her what would happen if she let Godfrey touch what belonged to me. Just as I'd told her last night, even though I can't have her, I own her.

It's selfish and the worst kind of toxic, but I can't bring myself to care.

She's mine.

I toss my phone onto the bed and walk to the door. I hope she tries to protect him—it'll make the blending of his fingers in my morning smoothie that much more satisfying.

However, when I pull the door back and see her standing there, all my wrath drifts away like smoke in the wind, as if it was never there to begin with.

My icy facial expression defrosts.

I feel my eyebrows twitch, pulling together as I stare down at her frost-nipped cheeks. The below-freezing temperatures outside make her body shake in the warm house. Snow is still sprinkled throughout the curls of her ebony hair.

Winter's favorite rose.

Her lip is tucked between her teeth, and she carefully extends her arms, offering me the heavy rectangular box, all in complete silence as if she is waiting for my reaction before speaking.

"What is this?" The words shake in my mind but come out smoothly.

"A digital piano." She shifts her weight, trying to hold it up, but her weak arms are struggling, "I couldn't get a grand piano quick enough, and I wasn't sure how I'd get it into the house. So I thought this was the next best thing."

My stomach rolls, and there is a fluttering in my chest.

No one had been so outwardly *kind* to me.

I am the man made of nightmares. People pull their children tighter when I walk by. I'd never even held someone with warm intentions before Lyra.

I am not a man who deserves compassion.

Especially from her.

But here she stands, giving it to me regardless. It doesn't matter any of the horrible things I'd said or done to her—none of it had affected the way she looked at me, her skewed perception of what she believes I'm capable of being.

Her face falls at my silence. The excitement in her eyes dimmed just enough for me to notice.

"If you don't like it, I can send it back. I kept the receipt, so it's not a big deal. I just thought you'd like to have something to pass the time since you don't come out much."

My face heats as I lift my arm, rubbing the back of my neck, still staring at the box she's struggling to hold up. Her body slumps, readjusting her grip around the item.

I've never been in this situation before, and I know it's common courtesy to say thank you, but those two words don't feel like enough. I've been given gifts from my short list of family members but never from someone who owed me nothing.

Nothing I say will be enough to convey what's happening inside of me.

This *fizzling*.

There isn't any other way to describe it. It's the first time I'm experiencing anything like this. Like bubbles floating around my organs or digesting Pop Rocks.

I take the box from her, sitting it down against the wall in my room. When I turn back to her, she has already started to walk towards her room, taking my silence as an answer enough.

Instinctively, I reach my hand out, fingers wrapping around her cold wrist. She looks back at me as if I'd called her name, and she waits for words I don't know how to speak.

"I live in darkness," I blurt out, not able to catch my thoughts quick enough before they slip from my mouth. "Kindness doesn't live there. It's a box with no light. I know nothing of the world, and it doesn't know me. I don't know how to—"

I stop abruptly because she looks like she's about to laugh and everything I'm saying is stupid, her fingers resting over her mouth, which is curved in a humorous smile.

My mouth snaps closed, and I glare, only to hear her giggle in response.

My fingers release her, and I'm about to slam the door until it breaks loose from the hinges. But she reaches for me instead this time.

"Wait, wait. I'm not laughing at you," she breathes. "I just—I think I broke you."

Yeah, I think you broke me too.

Because nothing is working correctly. Nothing feels normal inside my body or my mind, and I hate the unfamiliar way I'm reacting. I want to go back to when I was angry about her hugging Conner Godfrey. I want to go back to when I could ignore her face in a crowd or the feeling of being this close didn't make me feral.

Back before I knew what her heart looks like when it beats for me.

I turn my head, meeting her green eyes with my own. A wave of uncertain ground stretches between the two of us. Neither one knows the correct way to handle it.

So I go for honesty.

She deserves that, at the very least.

I grab one of the curls that frame her face, spinning it slowly around my finger before tugging gently.

I'm trying, to no avail, to keep her at a distance so I don't have to admit that she scares me. A man who fears nothing is afraid of all she is. All she makes me want. All she makes me feel.

"Your gift," I state, that fluttering from earlier coming back, and I pause before I continue. *"You're sunlight."*

TEN
a dream within a dream.

Thatcher

"Mama! Mama!" I scream as I run down the long marble halls, slipping along the floor in my socks. "I did it"

My laughter bounces off the walls, and I can barely contain my excitement. Mama is going to be so happy when I tell her that I was finally able to play "Brahms' Lullaby" from start to finish.

Even the hard part in the middle that makes me stretch my fingers!

I love when she watches me play. Her and Baba, they listen for hours, even when it's not very good. But it doesn't matter because Mama always picks me up after I finish a song and spins me around.

"Schast'ye, my sweet, talented boy."

Everything I do is great in her eyes, no matter what I think, and Baba says that's what will make me great one day.

Taking the steps two at a time until I reach the top, I can hear her and Dad talking. Maybe tonight, he'll want to listen too.

I press my hands into the door, shoving it open with a smile. "Mama, come listen. I can do the entire song!"

But no one else is smiling.

The room feels sad and gray.

"Mama?"

She turns, her white hair spinning with the motion. Her face is all wet and red, a face I've never seen before. There are bags in both of her hands.

"Are we going on a trip?" I ask, confused as to why she's crying. She'd been so happy earlier.

She smiles at me, rushing towards me and dropping her bags. Her arms wrap me up in a hug, and everything feels a little better. It always feels better when she's around, like I'm safe no matter what happens.

"Thatcher," she whispers. "You and I are going away for a little while, just us, okay?"

I nod, my eyebrows pulled together. "Can we stop and get those gummy fish I like before we go?"

Her laughter tickles the side of my neck just before she pulls back, petting my hand and running her hands down my face gently, like she's afraid I'll disappear if she doesn't.

"Of course, rybka." She presses her lips to my forehead, "YA tak lyublyu tebya, moy milyy mal'chik. No matter what, okay? No matter what."

I giggle as she rubs her nose against mine. "Mama, I don't know that many words in Russian yet!"

The bathroom opens, the door slamming against the wall making me jump and step further into my mother's arms. Dad steps into the room. He's so tall, and he tells me all the time I'll be just like him one day.

"Hi, Dad," I say. "Mama and I are going on a trip!"

But he doesn't smile. He just stands there staring down at us, the way he always does.

"Oh?" he asks, looking at my mother and smiling.

"Henry—"

"Come here, Alexander."

His voice makes me move further into Mama's arms. It's cold and makes me feel like I'm in trouble. I shake my head, looking up at her because I don't want to go with him.

"We are leaving," Mama tells him, standing up so that I'm tucked behind her. "I won't bother you again. I won't speak of you."

I see Dad's feet moving towards us, and my heart starts to race. I can feel it banging against my chest, and my stomach feels sick. Curling my fingers into the material of her skirt, I cling to her, even when he reaches down and grabs my arm.

It's so tight.

"Dad, you're hurting me," I cry, trying to pull away from his grip, but he won't let me go.

"Henry!" Mama yells, grabbing at him so that he'll let me go.

But he doesn't. He just pulls me harder until he has me by his side, holding me there. I reach my other hand outward, jerking away. I don't want to go with him when he's upset.

He's so mean when he's angry.

Tears burn my eyes, and I can feel my cheeks turning wet.

"Mama, I'm scared."

"No," Dad says, looking down at me. His eyes are so dark they almost look black. "Look what you've done to him, Talia. You've made our son weak."

Mama cries harder. "Henry, please! Just let me take him. I'm begging you just let me have him, and you won't hear a whisper from us again."

My small body shakes, sobs making my bottom lip wobble.

I don't like this.

I don't want this.

"I won't let you ruin what I've created, Talia. He's my son, and you will not take him from me."

There are screams and yelling. I'm calling for my mother, over and over again. My voice hurts my throat, and the room feels like it's spinning. She runs for me, and I reach for her, but we never make it.

Dad shoves her backwards, and she fights against him. Fights to get to me until she can't anymore. He doesn't look like my father. He looks like a monster.

The ones Mama scares away before bed every night.

His big hands wrap around her throat and—

My first breath of air hurts my chest.

I gulp it down violently, sweat sticking to my brow as I sit up out of bed. My fingers are curled into the blanket, the whites of my knuckles caught by the moonlight.

My heart is slamming into my eardrums, drowning out the sounds of my heavy breathing. It's still dark outside, and the house is quiet. The sheets are pulled from the edge of the bed, and my head feels foggy.

I loathe this part of the night, the only part of my carefully sculpted routine I wish didn't exist.

It takes approximately five minutes for me to return to normal. For my breathing to level out and the fog to clear from my brain. Then, I can go back to sleep and fall into a dreamless slumber.

It's clockwork. It's been that way since I was young.

These dreams come to me a few times a week. Some of them are repeats; others are new. All of them figments of my unhinged imagination that I have absolutely no control over.

I roll my shoulders, rubbing my hands down my face in frustration and letting myself settle for five minutes until I'm able to get out of bed. My throat is dry, and I reach for the glass of water on my nightstand only to see it's not there. I look up at the digital piano set up against the wall, a smile pulling at the edge of my lips.

I push myself out of the bed, hearing the floor creak beneath my weight as I pull the door open. My head throbs, and I'm already planning to swallow a handful of painkillers to get it to stop.

But my walk to the kitchen is disturbed.

Just outside my room, lying across a small decorative love seat, is Lyra. The tiny couch is shoved against the banister in front of my door; the deep purple cushions make for great decoration, but I know for a fact it's uncomfortable.

She's curled around a pillow, her dainty arm dangling off the edge, with a thin blanket draped across her body. I smirk at her hair. It's chaotically thrown across the soft features of her face, curls galore sticking in every direction humanly possible.

The sound of my steps towards her must wake her up because I can see her blink herself awake, rubbing the back of her hand against her eye.

"Why are you sleeping out here?" I ask her sleepy state.

Still half-asleep and unguarded, she answers me.

"You have nightmares," she mutters groggily, taking her sweet time to sit up. "I sleep out here when they start, just in case you need anything when you wake up."

Lyra yawns, stretching her arms above her head. My sweater has ridden up her body, exposing her soft stomach and green underwear she's chosen to wear.

She's completely unfazed by her admission and the fact she's wearing my clothes.

My jaw is set painfully tight, the tips of my nails digging into my palms.

"I don't have nightmares."

My reply sounds unintelligent. Childish, even.

We'd had a civil moment yesterday. The piano had been a peace offering, an olive branch I accepted, and now she'd set it on fire.

"Okay." She shrugs, slowly standing up, looking even more of a mess standing in front of me now than she had been while sleeping.

How long has she been doing this?

"Then stop sleeping outside my goddamn door."

The curse word tastes foreign on my tongue. I don't need anything from her, especially after a trivial dream that has no effect on my life.

My anger must be the shot of energy she needs to fully wake up because she's much livelier, her arms crossed defensively in front of her chest.

"No," she declares. "I hear you. You shout and roll around for hours. I can hear you fighting whatever it is that haunts you at night."

I scoff, mimicking her stance. "Are you always so dramatic? Nothing haunts me at night. Besides you, of course. I can't seem to avoid you."

This conversation will be like talking to a brick wall because she's just as stubborn as she is dramatic. Once she believes something, there is nothing that will change it.

"Why do you do this? Every time you show any remote sign of being human, you shut it down." She chews the inside of her cheek. "There is nothing wrong with feeling, Thatcher. It doesn't make you any less perfect to have emotions."

I grind my molars so hard that I'm positive I've cracked several teeth.

"Scarlett," I mock, "here I thought you of all people would appreciate the beauty of things that were dead inside."

She is so set on seeing life inside of me.

As if I'm not filled with decay and reeking of rotting flesh.

She believes good still swims around in my bones and I'm able
to do things like feel emotion. It's all a delusion; I'm a figment of
her imagination. A dream of a boy who saved her that she made up
in order to bear her mother's death.

A dream can't just be a dream to her. No, to her, it's me fighting
demons. It's me being human.

How pathetic.

Anger flares in her reaction, her snippy mouth coming to play.

"As tempting as it might be to pin you up and store you in my
closet with the other toxic specimen, why don't you just try accepting that you're not dead."

Such a little stalker—she would enjoy keeping me forever in a
glass case.

"You make me fucking crazy." A heavy sigh shakes her shoulders. "Why are you still so set on hiding from me? Putting all these
walls between us. Have I not shown that you can trust me with yourself?"

I run a hand through my hair, a cold laugh vibrating my shoulders. "You give yourself far too much credit. I'm not hiding from
you."

"You are!" She raises her voice, taking a dangerous step towards
me. "Is it because you're trying to protect me from the Imitator? He
went after May, and now what? You're afraid—"

I meet her halfway, looking down my nose at her as my breath
fans across her face. Our feet are almost touching, and I can feel her
warmth radiating off her body in waves.

The intoxicating smell of cherries does nothing to calm my anger.

Tension consumes the space between our bodies. I can feel every ounce of her bitterness towards me, can see it in the way her eyes
crinkle in the corners as she glares up at me.

Unfearing. Unyielding.

"Do not"—I lift a singular finger, pointing it just in front of her nose—"insult me."

If she wants to be candid with her words, I won't be held responsible for how she walks away from this conversation.

"You've gotten far too comfortable, pet. Don't make me remind you of where we stand." I seethe, daring her to speak to me like that again.

A storm of unknown sensations boils in my veins. Where I'm normally cold, everything now burns. It itches in an unsufferable kind of way. Every word heats my skin to an unbearable temperature.

"Gods forbid you're scared of losing someone." She swats at my hand, hitting it out of her face, quiet fury rumbling beneath the surface of her skin. "Gods fucking forbid you actually give a shit about someone other than yourself!"

The urge to grab her by the shoulders and shake her until she closes her mouth is becoming far more appealing by the second.

"This would be far less disappointing for you if you'd just accept that I'm not the man you made up in your fragile imagination."

Her gaze turns molten, all of the fatigue from earlier forgotten. Wrath has woken her up, and it won't be leaving anytime soon.

"Why won't you let me in," she snaps, not a question but a demand.

My nostrils flare, trying to get oxygen to my brain so I don't do something we will both regret. I turn, ready to disappear into the four walls of my bedroom until she cools off, but she isn't having it.

"No." Her hands land against my shoulder, pushing me. "Tell me why you won't let me in."

Another shove with her small hands barely makes me budge. Her hair sways with the force, tears of pure rage pouring from her pretty green eyes.

My jaw pulses as I face her, feeling her palms dig into my chest.

"Why!" she exclaims. "What are you protecting me from, Thatcher? Just tell me!"

One last push and the dam inside of me falls.

It shatters, exploding into small pieces and leaving no chance for rebuilding.

"Me!" I yell, the sound echoing in my chest. I barely recognize my own voice. I grab the sides of her head, caging her between my palms as my fingers tangle into the hair at the back of her neck. "Me, you stubborn fucking girl. I'm protecting you from me."

She gasps, mouth falling open and eyes wide.

"I crave you," I exhale, the admission slicing my throat on its way out. "My body wants you every second of the day and twice as much at night. I want you in the most unhinged ways, ways that would scare you."

My forehead drops against hers, and my eyes close as her breath fans across my face. The exhaustion in my mind takes over, all of the ways she makes me weak coming to light in this dim hallway.

I make her crazy? What do you call this?

I'm falling apart, the hinges of my identity are broken, and I have no fucking idea of who I am anymore. I don't know how to be someone that cares about someone else. I don't know how to be anything but what my father made me.

"I was touch starved, and now you've fed me." I tighten my grip on her hair, our noses rubbing against one another. "Of course I'm fucking hungry for you."

The shock has worn off enough that I can feel her hands seeking my skin, fingers splayed across my cheeks as she holds me.

"Then take me. Have me, Thatcher. Let me give myself to you."

I bite down on my bottom lip, tilting my head slightly, my eyebrows furrowed in mental anguish.

"I can't," I groan. "I can't let you do that."

It's the only thing I want.

It keeps me up at night. The way I yearn for her haunts me.

Fuck, I want to own her in all the ways that I can, but I just—

"Why?"

It's so gentle, so Lyra, that I can barely take hearing another word from her mouth. I lift my head from hers, rubbing my thumb across her tearstained cheeks.

I look at her eyes, needing her to see this, needing her to hear what I'm saying so that she understands.

"I'm incapable of giving you what you want." My throat is raw. "A relationship? A man who loves you? I can never be that. You will always require more from me, and there is nothing more I can give. I'm uncaring and cold. Love doesn't live in my world. I'm a killer, darling. That's all I will ever be."

Vulnerability.

It makes me want to squirm out of my skin.

I've unlocked this place in my mind, and these words that have come out because of that feel like they've waited for eternities to be spoken out loud. Nothing will be the same after this; no matter how tragically we end, I will never be the same.

There will forever be a piece of me that is open, carved in the shape of her body.

"You don't need to protect me, not even from you." She holds me tighter, as if her touch will make the words soak into my skin. "I'll take what you can give me, don't you see that? I would rather have you like this than live without you. There is no one else out there for me. I was made for you."

Physical pain shreds through me. It hurts in a way I can never explain, in a way that I've give anything to forget.

I pull my hands back, wrapping them around her wrists to push her hands back towards her chest, away from my face.

"Please, Thatcher," she whispers, her lips glistening with tears. "Your sharp edges don't hurt me."

Taking a step back from her space feels like walking into the cold, further and further from the warmth that keeps us alive.

I walk to my room, pausing in the doorway.

I wish I could say that I don't believe in fate, but if it was real, I think I would've been made for her too.

"Do you know what thorns wish they could say to roses, darling phantom?" I glance over my shoulder, hurting myself more by looking at her.

The light from the kitchen downstairs twinkles onto the banister, dressing her in a dim orange glow. My sweater sleeves cover her tiny hands and drop just below her waist. She is all things chaotic and peculiar in a way that makes you want to believe in things like destiny.

Because no one is simply born this beautiful. This unbearably beautiful.

"That they deserve more," I begin. "You deserve more than I can ever give you. I'm incapable of holding your heart, of taking care of it. Stop giving it to me. Stop before I kill it for good."

This will be a night that lives in me till I take my very last breath. The look in her eyes will dwell in the depths of my mind as punishment for destroying her.

I step further into my room, grabbing the door and swinging it halfway closed.

"I don't want to leave you empty, Scarlett. Don't make me leave you empty."

ELEVEN
delivery man

Lyra

Hollow Heights is quiet, eerily so.

Usually, when students return from the Christmas break, it's buzzing with life. Friends have come back together, sharing stories and laughing about the size of their yachts or where they went skiing for the holiday.

But as I walk through the marble halls, I can hear my footsteps. There's a grim feeling cast across the grounds that has little to do with the snow. Fear had spread among the student body. Some hadn't bothered to return, their parents demanding their children continue their studies online until girls stopped going missing and showing back up in parts.

The school is in chaos mode, trying to reassure donors and concerned parents everything is being handled and that the campus is still safe for attendance.

But is it? Has Hollow Heights ever been safe for attendance?

This school, no matter how prestigious, is haunted by peril. It survived the rumors of ghosts, but it can no longer hide the growing list of deaths.

There's a meeting being held for each grade; the school wants to go over safety protocols moving forward until the killer is apprehended and taken into custody.

I tug my hood further up on my head, protecting myself from the freezing wind as I jog across the barren commons. My boots click against the ground as I make my way through the long sequence of columns, the space between them open and allowing snow to blow through.

The colonnades connecting the buildings of the Kennedy District are one of my favorite places to walk on campus. The sound of waves smashing against the coast roars just to my right, and if I had time, I would look out at the storming ocean. I love how it looks when winter comes. The sea is a raging obsidian color, and the jagged rocks below have a thin gleam of snow across the caps.

I'd told Briar when she'd first arrived about the ghost that haunts this hall, the one rumored to be the spirit of a girl who'd fallen in love with her English professor and jumped to her death with a broken heart.

During my freshman year, I used to walk through here around midnight just to see if I could hear her screams like they all say or if it was just one of those legends that upperclassmen use to freak out new students.

I'm busy thinking of ghosts, lost in my mind thinking about an obsession so deep you'd rather die than live without, when my body collides with another. The shock of the hit knocks the breath from my lungs in one big whoosh.

All of the items in my hands slam onto the floor, along with whatever the other person was carrying. Fallen pens rattle against the cold floor, and the last voice on planet Earth I want to hear snaps against my ears.

"Pay better fucking attention to where you're walking, freak show."

I roll my eyes, squatting down to grab my things so I can get away from this encounter as quickly as possible.

"You ran into me too, asshole," I mutter. "You know, it's common courtesy to say so—"

A square piece of starched white paper has popped up from the pages of their book. I wouldn't have noticed it, would have overlooked it if it hadn't been familiar to my eyes.

I snatch it up from the ground, my hands wobbling as I read the words across the paper repeatedly.

If they can't have you.
They will just take your friends.
Come out. Come out. Wherever you are.
X

These are the threats Thatcher was receiving just before May died.

The words are written in identical penmanship, down to the extra cross on the letter *T*. We'd all assumed the copycat killer had sent these as a game, a way to test Thatcher, to toy with him.

So, that would make the Imitator—

"Easton?"

I tighten my grip on the paper, crunching it in my hands as I slowly stand up. I meet his gaze with unbridled anger. He killed May. He'd been the one to frame Thatcher. Had been the reason I almost lost him.

My mouth waters for a taste of revenge.

Easton Sinclair is a top-tier douche, but a killer? I hadn't given him that credit.

Blond hair whips in the wind, pushing out of his face and exposing his blue eyes filled with contempt. It would seem the feeling between us is mutual. The idea of tossing him off the side of this building and watching him get impaled by sharp rocks is becoming more and more appealing.

But if he's responsible for this, I want to make his death a slow one.

A cut for every single person in my life he'd hurt.

"Get a job as a mailman, Sinclair?" I cross my arms in front of my chest, yanking at the puzzle pieces in my mind, trying to get them to fit. "Is cutting up women and scattering their body parts not keeping you busy enough?"

I've known Easton since elementary school. The sense of entitlement he wore had been fitted at a young age. Forever the golden boy, the apple of Ponderosa Springs' eye since before he understood what the word "reputation" meant.

Had the heart of a killer been living in the boy who'd cried in third grade when he skinned his knee? Existing beneath the surface while everything else had just been a well-crafted mask all this time?

His jaw twitches, and even now, as intimidating as he tries to be, I can't bring myself to believe he's capable of killing someone, let alone multiple. I can't see him being intelligent enough to pull something like this off, but what else could I think? When all the arrows point right at him?

What better way to throw us off the Halo's trail than frame one of us for murder? I suppose that plot was left up to his father, and everyone knows what dearest daddy wants, Easton gives.

"Unlike your boyfriend, jail isn't on my five-year plan," he snarks, grinning to show those porcelain-capped teeth.

We've been dancing around each other since the moment we witnessed the boys kill someone in the Ponderosa Springs forest. Easton knew what we did, and we knew he was interwoven in the Halo, but it was a matter of who could prove it first.

This has been the closest we've been to admitting our involvement, and something about it doesn't sit right.

"You still plan on running for office with that face?"

The scarred skin on his jaw ripples as he scowls. Mangled, stretched white skin to remind him every single morning what happens when you push Rook Van Doren a little too far.

Calmy, he scoops down, grabbing his things from the floor before readjusting the strap of his book bag. Easton still believes he's untouchable—why wouldn't he? When his father has fixed and handled every single part of his life since he was born. Of course he's unfazed.

"Careful where you step, Lyra." He hums in the back of his throat, winking at me. "You already know what happens when you get a little too close to me, don'tcha?"

Flashes of red flicker behind my eyes. The inability to breathe, smothered by gallons of pigs' blood. I swallow the memory, shoving it deep into the back of my mind.

"Did they tell you what I left behind for you?" I smile widely, thinking about the knives I'd driven into his pawn's eyes for touching me.

The gleam in his eyes flickers just enough for me to notice.

"If you wanted to frame someone," I accuse, "why not Rook? Get a little skin back that you'd lost. Did your daddy think it was too obvious?"

Whether it's him or not doesn't matter because he knows.

"Freak show, it's all hearsay. That note doesn't tell you anything. I mean—" He rubs his jaw, smirking. "—I've never even seen that paper before. You very well could've planted it. Anything to clear that psycho's name, yeah?"

I slit my eyes, glaring at the mention of Thatcher.

He's right—it's hearsay. I stand on uncertain ground, but one thing I'm certain of, Easton knows more than he's saying. He knows everything we need and is dangling it in front of me.

Easton steps forward to move past me, ready to walk away, but I grab his shoulder. My nails dig into the material of his shirt, and he slowly turns his gaze to where my hand is on his body.

I'm tempted to do something reckless, like make us the new gruesome story that haunts Kennedy Hall, forever engaged in the history of Hollow Heights. Students will spread it like wildfire, and it will live in infamy along the grounds.

They'll whisper about how much blood there was. People would argue whether I took his hands or feet first, and someone would get creative and say I frolicked through the snow-covered commons, painting the white ground in red while wearing his intestines as a necklace.

"If it's not you on a murder spree, hypothetically speaking—" I run my tongue across my teeth. "—why send notes to warn Thatcher? Why when you know it would help us?"

The very first one he'd got told him to leave Ponderosa Springs, which would have cleared his name before the killings started. It had been a warning, not a threat.

I know I should believe Easton is the Imitator, but something about it doesn't feel right. However, I do think he's writing those letters. I could be entirely wrong about all this—he could just be the delivery boy. He could be killing people, but I'm going with my gut and hoping I'm not fucking this up.

"Hypothetically or factual, I wouldn't do shit to help you." He jerks his arm from my grip with enough force to make me step back.

"Screw you, Sinclair. Sage was right about one thing—you're nothing but a puppet for your daddy's sick games. You're pathetic," I sneer. "You'll get what's coming to you, and I can't fucking wait."

"You and those deadbeats you follow around are going to get her killed." He points his finger, baring his teeth. I can feel the heat of his rage fanning across my face. "I promise you, Lyra Abbott, if that happens, there will be nothing to stop me from ripping you all to shreds."

I flinch, rearing back at his words.

"Her? Mary?" I ask, confused about what she has to do with this. "Don't worry, your bitch of a girlfriend isn't on the list of people to fuck over. She'll be perfectly fine to continue eating up Sage's leftovers."

"She was mine before Rook ever touched her." A twisted smile tugs at the edges of his lips. "I know all about her pipe dreams, from the way she moans in bed down to her favorite fucking ice cream flavor."

He was never talking about Mary.

He was talking about *Sage*.

"No amount of hate Van Doren has for me will change that. No matter how badly he wants it to."

My own anger surges at the audacity of him claiming he cares for my friend after everything he put her through. All the hell she endured, and he wants to pretend he cares?

No, men like Easton just get their pride hurt when their toys don't belong to them anymore.

I scoff. "You've got some fucking nerve, Sinclair. You want me to believe you did this to protect Sage? You're goddamn delusional! You sat by while her sister was murdered in cold blood and left her to rot in an institution, content to let everyone think she went crazy."

All emotion fades, his gaze turning cold.

"Believe what you want." He shrugs. "We all become what we need to in order to survive the families of Ponderosa Springs."

TWELVE
heart-shaped box

lyra

"We urge you to abide by the enforced curfew and make sure you're traveling in pairs. You're more likely to be targeted if you're alone." Odette Marshall stands in front of the rows of seats. "Do you have any questions?"

"Is the Imitator a psychopath?"

I outwardly groan, sinking further into my seat and tugging my beanie over my eyes as more hands shoot up in the audience.

"Yes," her partner, Gerrick Knight, answers. "A sadist. One who has no regard for human life and is void of feelings."

They are painting a picture, one that can depict over half of the population, yet there is only one image that is in everyone's mind right now.

Thatcher Pierson.

"This is so fucking stupid," Sage mumbles under her breath.

I nod in agreement.

While there are some here in hopes of learning how to stay safe, most, if not all, are sitting around like vultures, waiting for a crumb to feast on, patiently biding time until these federal agents admit Thatcher is their one and only suspect.

"Yes, you in the white blouse."

"So," she hums, "you're totally sure it's a man?"

"Yes, we've determined through our profile that the killer is a man," Odette continues, scanning the crowd with a watchful eye before pausing on me. "He will be incredibly manipulative, able to blend in and lure women with little struggle. He will be well-dressed, attractive, and highly intelligent. A true psychopath."

She holds my gaze, unmoving, as if she wants me to hear these words. For them to scare me.

I fight the urge to scream.

To stand up and shout until she understands that it can't be him. That most everything she said may be true, but the last part isn't.

Thatcher isn't a psychopath.

It's strange to think, and I can imagine it would turn a few heads if I said it out loud, but I know it's the truth. In lieu of his urges to kill and cold demeanor, he wasn't born a psychopath.

I believe he was conditioned by one.

Crafted, sculpted, and set by a man obsessed with his own legacy, so much that he wanted it to continue far after his arrest, his death even. Henry abused Thatcher into believing he was incapable of feeling and caring for others at a young age.

He was tormented and degraded anytime a spark of emotion showed. You can only handle so much before your brain does what it needs to survive. So Thatcher shut it off and started killing every good that came his way until one day, he convinced himself he didn't feel at all.

But beneath all of that, beneath the man, there is a boy who had dreams. Who felt and stood a chance if not for his father. I wish I could have seen him before the world turned him so cold.

He's still a killer and quite possibly is a malignant narcissist, but Thatcher isn't a psychopath. He's just a child who was raised to become one.

Last night, I saw it.

I saw what he looks like when he cares, when he allows himself to feel, and just how painful that is for him because he doesn't understand it. When you are raised by a wolf, all you know is bared teeth and feral hunger. Softness, kindness, emotion, it's all a foreign concept.

It's like waking up one morning and learning the sky has been green the whole time. Everyone else knew it, but you'd been left in the dark.

In my hallway, underneath all the anger, there was just a man so terrified of himself, of what he's capable of, that he'd rather deny me than hurt me. That's him putting someone other than himself first, putting *me* first.

Thatcher doesn't want to leave me empty, and I don't want to leave him lonely.

"Ladies, please watch out for one another." I blink, hearing Conner's voice echo across the room. "If anyone hears or sees anything concerning, please let me know, and I'll be happy to put you in connection with these detectives. My door is always open."

Conner smiles warmly before Odette and Gerrick give their closing remarks. Which takes another fifteen minutes before we are dismissed. I pull my backpack onto my shoulders.

"Alistair wants to meet up and talk about what happened with Easton," Briar says, staring down at her phone. "Do you guys have time before your next class?"

"Yeah, I've got an hour." I stand up from my seat.

"Lyra," Sage mutters beside me, brushing a few hairs behind her ear, "I'm not asking you to lie, so don't think I am, but can we please leave out any mention of what Easton said regarding me?"

My eyebrows pull together. "Why? What's wrong?"

"Nothing, nothing." She shakes her head. "I just—if Rook finds out, it's going to be impossible to walk him back from the edge. I can't handle losing him again."

"Sage, you won't lose him. He'd never leave you, even if you wanted him to."

There is no way Rook Van Doren leaves Sage Donahue. It's physically impossible in every universe.

"I will if he finds out. He won't let it go—it'll eat at him until he does something careless like kill him. I won't let him go to prison over Easton, over me. I can't."

I rub her shoulder, trying to soothe the fear in her voice.

"I'll keep you out of it, I promise."

She nods in thanks, putting an arm around my shoulder and pulling me into a short hug. Together, the three of us walk down to the front of the class, avoiding the group of girls talking to the detectives still in the room.

We are almost out the door when I feel fingers curling around my upper arm.

"Lyra."

I turn, looking at Conner. He readjusts his glasses, giving me a grin. The conversation of his warning me away from Thatcher had left a sour taste in my mouth, but he's still my friend.

He'd still been there during the summer, and I know deep down he was only trying to do what he thinks is right. I can't say if I was in his position that I would do any different.

I'm just a little more...apprehensive of him now. He's too close to Stephen, and while I don't want to believe he's involved, all signs point to him being right in the middle of this mess.

"What's up?" I ask, giving a closed-mouth smile.

"I wanted to see you in my office. Do you ladies mind if I steal her away for a second?"

Briar and Sage stare at him passively, nothing warm or welcoming on either of their faces, before they look at me.

I know that look. It's the *"Are you cool going with this fucking creep, or do we need to bail you out"* look.

"You guys go ahead. I'll meet you in the library after."

I know whatever Conner wants to talk about isn't as important as catching Rook and Alistair up to speed, but at the very least, I may be able to get more information out of him. Plus, we haven't talked in a while. It might be nice to catch up.

"Text us if you need anything," Briar reassures before glaring at Conner one more time and following Sage out of the room.

"Shall we go?" he offers, and I nod.

I follow him down the hall, the brief distance to his office. Godfrey swings the door wide, holding it open so that I can pass through.

My shoulder rubs his chest as I pass. It brings forth the memory of Thatcher reminding me of what would happen if Conner came close to me again. I make a mental note to keep the distance between us.

While I don't believe Thatch is an unfeeling psychopath, I know he wasn't bluffing. If he says something, he means it, and we need to avoid any unnecessary bloodshed.

When we are both inside, I take it upon myself to inspect the rows of books along the built-in shelves lining his walls. Most of them are academic studies, but there are a few gems nestled in the scholarly material.

Everything is a deep mahogany color, from the heavy wooden desk to the leather couch. A chess set is tucked efficiently against the two windows to my right, and a brown world globe rests just next to it. It's bold, rich, and puts on an accurate display of Conner's personality.

"Voltaire?" I trace my finger along the framed picture on the wall of the famous philosopher. "I pegged you as a Socrates kinda guy."

"Every man is guilty of all the good he did not do," he says from somewhere behind me. "My father read me Voltaire as a child."

I smirk, turning around. "Did he run out of Dr. Seuss?"

"Very funny, Miss Abbott." He grins, shaking his head a bit before leaning against his desk and crossing his arms in front of him. "Are you a philosophy lover?"

"I prefer poets, if I'm honest."

"I hope you're always honest with me." He waves me over. "Come, let's chat."

"If this is about my next project, I told you it's a secret. You'll just have to wait to see it when it's finished," I taunt, stepping around the desk so we're facing one another.

"I know you have genetics with Hayes shortly, so—"

My brows furrow together, alarmed and unable to keep my thoughts to myself.

"How do you know that?"

It's the new semester. My course load differs completely from what it was in the fall. Unless he'd specifically looked at it, he wouldn't know what I was taking.

He chuckles, placing his hands against the edge of the desk. "Lyra, how many times have you told me you dread learning signaling pathways?"

My teeth bite into the inside of my cheek as I nod.

He's probably right. With everything that's happened as of late, I'm not surprised by my paranoia. Especially considering Conner's choice of friends. But he's a professor at this college, and it wouldn't be odd for him to know what classes I take.

"I must have forgotten," I think out loud, grabbing onto the straps of my backpack.

"You seem stressed, Lyra. I know you run in the same social circle as Thatcher, and I heard about what happened with his grandmother. It was an awful thing, and with him being missing, that would take a toll on anyone."

Conner tilts his head, looking me up and down as if to check for injuries or bruises. "I guess I just want to make sure you're alright."

"I don't want to talk about that." My voice cracks like a whip in the relaxed air, an unwarranted reaction that comes out far harsher than I intended. A reflex of sorts with this topic of conversation. My shift in attitude must have come as a shock to Conner as well because the muscle in his jaw twitches.

I watch his grip on the desk tighten ever so slightly. My last intention is to offend him, but offending my friendship with Conner Godfrey is the least of my worries. I can't have him suspecting our intentions with Stephen, how close we are to finding something to nail him.

This could've ruined all the information we have gathered, all because I have no hold over my emotional recoil.

"I'm sorry." I twist the ring on my finger, letting out a shaky breath. "It's been a long few months. That wound is fresh—I know you're just worried about me. Forgive me?"

He stares blankly at me before blinking away the vacant expression on his face. The normal, relaxed smile returns.

"Already forgiven. Don't apologize for having emotions, Miss Abbott. It's a gift to feel as passionately about people as you do."

I give him an apologetic smile, hoping for all our sakes this wasn't a fuckup on my part.

"Now for the reason I drug you into my dungeon." Clasping his hands in front of him, he clears his throat. "The forensic entomology program at Dartmouth informed me you denied the application."

Fuck me.

I'd completely forgotten about that.

"Conner, I was meaning to talk to you about that." I bite down on my bottom lip, anxious for some reason. I don't want to let him down; he's a person I view as a mentor, and he believed in me enough to give me this opportunity. Of course I'm nervous telling him I rejected the offer.

"I'm beyond thankful for the opportunity. It's just bad timing, and I don't think it's the best fit for me right now. My friends…" I trail off, looking out the windows for a moment. "I can't leave them—I don't want to leave them. Not yet."

I don't want to leave Thatcher.

Not now, never.

But I keep that truth tucked away for myself.

To his credit, he keeps the same smile on his face. The same one he always sports, that lighthearted one that reminds me of the Conner I got to know over the summer.

"Your loyalty is one of the many things I admire about you. They are lucky, those friends of yours, to have someone like you."

"Thank you, and I'm sorry you stuck your neck out for me. I know it wasn't easy getting me an application."

"I would've done it for any of my students who showed your promise, Miss Abbott."

I peer at the picture of Voltaire on the wall, figuring since I'm in here, I might as well do some digging while I'm at it. A tiny piece of me still hopes he's innocent, not for any other reason than I believe he's a good person.

"Why Voltaire?" I ask, trying to gracefully shift the topic. "Seems like a lot for a kid to digest."

He looks at the painting with me before replying, "I grew up very poor. My mother was a seamstress, and my father worked multiple factory jobs while I was growing up. But he was incredibly intelligent. He didn't have the chance to attend college, but I suspect he would've thrived in an environment like this one. He'd believed knowledge was the only wealth a man needed. Told me all the time as a kid that we may be poor in materialism, but we will never be poor in wisdom."

I never knew he didn't come from a world of wealth. I'd always thought his money was how he and Stephen became friends. But it makes more sense that he grew up that way. I think it's what makes him so relatable to students. He just seems like a regular guy.

"Hence, philosophy for bedtime stories," I note, smiling a bit.

"And chemistry for breakfast, physics for lunch," he banters back, crossing his arms in front of his chest.

"What about your mother? Was she just as enthusiastic about school as your father?"

Something unreadable passes over his face, cold and stagnant, as if a gust of wind had just breezed past.

Sore subject, I'm assuming.

"She died when I was five." He tugs at the tie wrapped around his neck. "Why the sudden interest in my private life?"

Sadness washes over me.

"We haven't talked since before Christmas break. I missed you, I guess," I say sympathetically, even though what I want to say is *I'm trying to dig up your past to see if you connect to this rotten present.* "I'm sorry about your mom."

"Don't be. It was a long time ago."

"They'd be proud of you, I think. I mean, look at you now. College professor." I shrug, hoping that takes away some of the pain of remembrance. "Did you expect your friendship with Stephen to lead you here? Into the lives of the wealthy and entitled?"

"No, but I'm thankful for it. Stephen and I had similar yet very different upbringings. Our fathers were very hard on us. Which meant as men, we both wanted nothing more than to exceed every expectation they had."

"Daddy issues for bonding, how lovely," I tease. "So is academics how you and Stephen connected? Don't tell me you were both nerds."

"God no." He laughs, the light returning to his face, smiling as if recalling fond memories from college. "Stephen was awful in school, certified jock even in grad school. I was looking for an apartment on campus, and he needed a roommate. We knew little about each other, but a few months of living together tells you a lot about a person."

"Tell me about it," I mutter, thinking about how obsessively organized my coffee mug cabinet is now. I miss the clutter, but Thatcher needs to have everything straight. "Why do I get the feeling we would have been fast friends in college?"

Conner pushes himself off the desk, taking slow steps towards me, one hand in his pocket while the other rubs his five-o'clock shadow.

"Lyra," he murmurs. "We would've been much more than just that."

I feel my eyebrows pull together, my feet pulling me backwards from him, only for him to continue pressing forward. I can smell his teakwood cologne in thick waves. Too close—he's way too close.

"What—"

His teeth graze his lower lip, the back of his hand stroking my cheek, making me flinch. "You would have been my everything. I would have lived and died for you."

My heart echoes in my ears, thudding harder and harder by the second. I place my hands out onto his chest, pushing him away to create some space. But he's much stronger than I am.

"Conner, stop." The shake in my voice is evidence enough that I'm afraid. "Seriously."

He is no longer the man I admired, the teacher I looked up to. In thirty seconds, he's changed to a man I fear. Someone I want to get far away from.

"I could be so good for you, Lyra."

Then his mouth takes mine.

Forcefully, without my consent or desire.

My eyes widen, hands shoving harder against his chest, but he snakes an arm around my waist, gripping me tighter. His fingers slip into my hair and grab the strands. He jerks my head back, and I cry out in pain.

His tongue is cold and unwanted. His hands don't feel right, and my body feels invaded.

This can't be happening. This isn't happening.

With panic pumping adrenaline into my system, I sink my teeth into his tongue, biting hard until he grunts, detaching himself from me. Using his pain as a distraction, I shove him back, slipping away from his grip and putting several feet between us.

"What the fuck!" I shout, wiping my mouth with the back of my hand in disgust. My chest is heaving, and the room spins.

Tears burn my eyes, and my chest aches from the betrayal. My body aches from the violation. I spend my days digging through mud, covering myself in dirt, but right now, in this office, I've never felt so dirty.

I'd trusted him, given him my friendship. I fucking stood up for him and believed he was honest. For what? For him to pretend to be my friend so he could get into my pants?

"Oh my God, I feel sick." I push my hand into my stomach, battling the urge to upchuck my stomach contents.

There is a sound behind me, a sudden, unmistakable noise.

The click of the door opening.

I pray it's another student so I can slip right out without having to hear what he has to say for himself.

"Lyra, I'm so sorry." Conner holds his hand up, trickles of blood decorating his mouth. "Please understand, that was—"

I watch his eyes widen at whoever has walked into the room with us.

My breath catches in my throat.

And a voice, grim as liquid night, pervades the air.

"The worst mistake of your fucking life."

THIRTEEN
cat got your tongue?

lyra

The man I'm staring at is not the same one that stood in the hallway with me last night.

Last night, he had been tangible.

Someone I could run my fingers along, feel flesh and bone. I could sense his heartbeat, feel the pulse in his throat.

This one, the one currently in front of me? He makes gods kneel.

This is the charming nightmare Ponderosa Springs shunned. The man they fear. A cloak of heatless darkness, his intensity suffocates this office. Chills light up my arms, the winter air following him as he walks inside.

His black, fitted suit catches particles of sunlight that spill from the blinds. The shadowy material drains all the light, eating up all hope for anything other than violence.

I'm in such shock I can't even fathom how to ask all the questions I have. Why did he leave the cabin? Why is he here? How did he know where I was?

They race around in my head on a track, spinning and spinning.

But they all circle one blunt truth.

He'd come for me.

I am his, and he'd come for me.

Both versions of Thatcher belong wholly to me. The one who cares for me in a way he might never understand and the one who is a killer. A man who has no faith in any god and believes only cruelty can redeem sins.

"Thatcher—"

His head turns, and I find how dead his eyes are. There is zero recognition behind his gaze. I could be anyone standing in front of him right now. It knocks the breath out of me, the coldness.

"Did he touch you?"

The question startles me.

Not for me, not for Conner, but for the aftermath of Thatcher's actions.

Detectives are on campus. Conner Godfrey is a respected teacher. He's best friends with our primary target. This death would not go unpunished. And I can see in his eyes that he doesn't care.

I've witnessed what Thatcher looks like bloodthirsty. The way he changes, embraces the person his father created, and thrives. But this? I've never seen this. The regal elegance of a sadistic killer, one with no care of consequences and not an ounce of remorse for human life.

Can he be both?

Can he be a man that feels so much and also the one who feels nothing at all?

"Thatcher." Conner clears his throat. I observe him in my peripheral vision, the way he straightens a little. "There are quite a few people who have been looking for you. I don't think being here is smart for you."

Is Godfrey trying to protect Thatcher? Or rather, himself?

Thatcher is innocent of the copycat killings, but his entire life has been painted in blood. There isn't any person in Ponderosa Springs that doesn't believe every wicked rumor spoken about him.

They all fear him.

My throat narrows as I try to swallow. Thatch's gaze is intense. He watches me, waiting for my answer. Ever so slowly, as if he's gliding, he moves in my direction. Conner's voice may as well have been white noise.

"Do not make me repeat myself, Lyra," he says calmly, unbuttoning the front of his suit and sliding a hand into his pocket.

I hold Conner Godfrey's fate.

His heart is practically beating in my tiny hands, awaiting a blade. I'm judge and jury. Thatcher is the executioner at the gallows, waiting for my call. Whatever I say will decide life and death.

It's a power I've held before but never thought of until this very moment.

Regardless of the outcome of the disastrous fallout, I can't lie to him.

He knows I won't. I promised I wouldn't.

"Yes," I exhale, the word exiled from my lungs like black magic.

I can feel the threads of fate shredding. Thatcher closes in on me, blocking me in against the wall of books.

"Do you remember what I told you would happen if he came near you again, pet?" His fingers are icy when they touch me. Two fingers, stroking the side of my face.

The memory of us in the mausoleum unravels. The possessive, feral lust that had taken over his body. It was the first time he'd touched me intimately and when he'd given me the one and only warning of what would happen to Godfrey if he got too close.

This could ruin everything, would ruin Thatcher if someone finds out.

"Please," I beg, my eyes burning. "I'm not worth this."

His finger swipes across my cheek, catching the drop of water before it falls any further. My breath catches, and I can do nothing but watch as he presses his thumb into his mouth, cleaning my tears from his skin.

"Oh, darling," he purrs, swallowing my tears, "you're worth it. Bloodshed and all."

Thatcher

The grandfather clock chimes just as my hand slips into the

leather gloves. I squeeze my fist, feeling the material stretch over my skin.

Conner shifts clumsily in the chair I'd forced him into. His belt is looped around his arms and waist to keep him still, which was me being nice. Too much movement would make me sloppy.

"Careful," I advise. "Too much moving around and I'll nick an artery or cut off an appendage."

Grabbing the back of the chair, I turn him away from the desk so he can face the door. Let him see just how close sweet, sweet escape is. The seat groans against the hardwood floor, thudding once I'm finished moving it.

"This is ridiculous," he sneers, pushing against the restraint, "We were both caught up in a moment. Your jealousy is making you overreact!"

"Jealousy would require me to envy something you have, Conner." I toss my jacket on the couch nearby, circling in front of him. "You're here because you didn't keep your hands to yourself. You touched something that belongs to me."

Possessive rage is a nasty thing.

It festers.

It's an eternal wound struck with gangrene, turning your insides into a black, oozing infection. This wound had been rotting since I'd seen the way he looked at her at the start of the school year.

I catch the way his eyes hunt for Lyra, finding her tucked against the door. Arms curled around her waist, she stands in silence. It fuels that rage, his entitlement to her.

"Lyra, please explain to him. We're friends! You can't just let him do this."

My fingers grab his face, crushing his jaw painfully tight, forcing him to look up at me as I loom over him. The knife I'd pulled from my pocket sits sideways along his throat, grazing pieces of neck hair.

The gunmetal-gray blade has no shine. No glamour. It's matte, sharp, and made for gutting wild animals. Or, in this case, teachers with no respect for boundaries.

"If you want to leave with your eyes, I suggest you keep them off her."

Conner Godfrey doesn't have enough blood in his body to pay for this mistake. He'd faint or die before I got to the good part. If things were different, I would've waited.

I would have selected, hunted, and killed him. Added his name to the filing cabinet of sheet music on my desk. I would have taken my time, created a concerto that would leave a room silent, and his screams would sing along with every note.

"Thatcher." He gulps, the blade scratching his Adam's apple with mild strokes. Knowing Lyra will be of no help, he's turned to bargaining with me. "Let's just take a second here. We can talk about this."

I sink a little further into his neck, pricking at the first layer of skin. The hiss of pain he surrenders before collapsing back into the chair makes chills travel along my spine.

Oh, how I missed the sounds of screaming.

The way it rushes into my veins and pumps adrenaline straight into my obsidian heart. How it is ripped straight from the vocal cords, coaxed out by meticulous, excruciating torture.

I don't need music to relive this moment, not the way I had with the others.

No, I have something far better.

A witness.

One who would watch my every move, write it down in her brilliant mind, and keep it there as a permanent memory. And later, when I force my cock inside of her, I'm going to make her tell me everything she saw.

Every. Single. Detail.

Until she's coming, shouting my name to the memory of his suffering. It'll be her punishment for putting herself in this position, for being too trusting, being naive around men who have corrupt intentions.

"Do you think the board will view it that way?" My eyebrow lifts. "When they learn how inappropriately you behave with students? You believe they'll take pity on the man who holds no weight and ass-kissed his way here?"

If he thinks he can scare me by threatening to talk, he is sorely misguided. He'd risk everything going against me, wanted for murder or not. I hold more power in my left pinky than he does in his entire body.

He is nothing in comparison. Conner has no name or legacy, just pure luck he'd befriended Stephen Sinclair in college. He is simply a throwaway that no one would back.

My knife slices across the muscles in his throat, enough to make a narrow crimson cut appear beneath it. Fear pools in the depths of his eyes, and a twisted grin pulls at my lips.

Nothing checks a man's ego like a knife to the throat.

"You're going to kill me? Right here?" He grinds his teeth together. "You'll be caught before you even leave campus. These walls may be soundproof, but you won't be able to get rid of my body."

"How bold of you to assume there would be anything left." My tongue drags across the front of my teeth.

I'm consciously aware that I'm breaking one of my father's cherished rules, killing out of emotion. For the second time, I've drawn blood from a man for Lyra. The second time I've been pushed to this.

My father never had anyone worth killing for. He murdered with no purpose. Henry had never been driven out of his mind with madness. Had not been absorbed entirely by another person, that just the thought of anyone breathing near them was too much. Too close.

"Thatcher, please," he begs, jerking in the chair. "You are not your father. Don't be this man."

I pull the knife back from his skin, twirling it between my fingers, rotating the blade along my palm absent-mindedly.

"You're right, I'm not." I nod in agreement. "I'm much worse."

With a sigh of boredom, I stand up straight, turning to look at Lyra. Little Miss Death, quietly hiding in the corner. As if she could disappear from my eyes. Like she's not the only thing I see in a room.

"Darling phantom," I purr, flipping the knife in my palm. "Pick a finger."

Her eyebrows rush to her hairline.

"What?" she murmurs, panicked, eyes bouncing between Conner's shaky hand and my face.

"You're welcome to pick more than one."

She visibly swallows, shaking her head, those loose curls falling in front of her face. It throws a match on the gasoline-covered wrath inside of me. An inferno cracks through my icy exterior, and I no longer have the upper hand against my control.

Is she afraid for him? Does she *care* for him?

My chest burns at the question, molten heat searing my nerves.

"I can't—"

"Pick a finger, or I take the fucking hand, Lyra," I snap, my tone a feral growl.

"Wait, wait," Conner yells behind me, but I can't hear him over the roaring inside my head.

"Pinky!" Lyra shouts, clamping her hand over her mouth.

"Good girl," I praise, grabbing my bottom lip with my teeth. "But not nearly good enough."

With unbridled anger as my sole motivation, I look at Conner. He shakes his head, begging me not to. But I hear nothing as I grab at his mouth. My fingers shove behind his bottom teeth and jerk him forward so his back arches from the chair.

I rejoice in the way he tries to grapple.

With his jaw hinged open, I coil my fist around my knife, feeling the weight of it in my palm before making my move. My hand comes down in one fell swoop, striking the blade through the tender muscle of his tongue.

Stabbing is much easier than slicing. The human body is a difficult medium when you're carving through dense flesh, but stabbing? It's as easy as stabbing a fork through raw chicken.

Plush, slimy, easily cut.

Blood splatters onto my shirt, painting me with slashes of red. Conner screams, tears rolling down as I plunge through the floor of his mouth. I don't stop until the hilt of my knife meets his tongue. The slicing of flesh and the squelch of torn tissue echo in the room.

He rears back in agony when I release my grip on the handle, tilting his head back just enough that I can see the end of the blade protruding from under his chin. I smirk just as he chokes, spurting blood onto the front of his clothes. It flows from his lips, coating his chin in a glossy red. His neck is corded with crimson liquid, drowning the collar of his dress shirt.

That creature inside of me feasts on his pain, starved for it. It's been far too long since it fed. I pull my fingers from his mouth, shaking my hand and watching the blood splatter across the floor. Conner withers, then howls in the back of his throat.

The tongue is the only muscle in the entire human body that never stops moving. Which is normally a good thing, but for him? It's misery. Every time it twitches or tries to move, it's shredded.

More nerves sever, exposed to the open air. He feels every ounce of that pain, grumbling, strangling on words, unable to speak.

I tilt my head, flicking the top of the handle, making him cry out. "Cat got your tongue, Godfrey?"

I enjoy the sight of him suffering for a few more moments before I lean close to his ear. The metallic smell leaking from his body makes me shiver. I carefully undo the belt tying him to the chair so he can at the very least crawl to the door.

If the police grab me in the next ten minutes and throw me in prison, it will have been worth it to see Conner Godfrey poached and bleeding out. Stuck like a pig for acting like one.

"Let me make this clear. Don't ever touch her again. Don't breathe near her. Do not exist in the same space as her. Or I will rip your fucking head from your shoulders."

He blinks, watery eyes filled with panic. Slowly, he nods, trying to keep himself as still as possible.

"Good, very good." I pat the side of his cheek, standing up and walking towards the door.

"Oh, and Godfrey." I look over my shoulder. "Keep this between us. I would sincerely hate for you to lose your job right along with your tongue."

FOURTEEN
cravin

Thatcher

"**F**uck, Thatch!" Rook shouts through the speaker on my phone. "Fuck, bro. We are beyond fucked. So fucked. The most fucked you could ever be in your life."

"So we're only unfuckwithable when you do something thoughtless?" I lean against the shelf behind me, watching Lyra strike a match on the floor, lighting a singular candle inside the compact storage closet.

"Yes, because I'm the irrational one. Me. You're the anal control freak. This is not how—wait, did you just cuss?"

My eyes threaten to roll into the back of my head. Suddenly, I hear arguing in the background. I pull the phone from my ear as grunts and shouts echo through the speaker. Finally, Alistair's steady voice is on the other side of the line.

Alistair: 1

Rook: 0

"Can you stay out of sight until we can figure out how to get you off campus?"

I look around the ancient closet that has had no visitors in quite some time.

"Yes, but try to make it quick. This supply closet is disgusting."

"Sorry," Lyra mutters, standing up from the floor, the light glow of the candle highlighting the contours of her cheeks. "Next time you stab someone in broad daylight, I'll be sure to book a room at the freaking Four Seasons."

She'd been the one to find this room, concealed on the top floor of the Bursley District, inside an unused classroom that had once been a chemistry lab. I didn't bother asking her how she knew it was up here.

Probably another one of her secret hideaways.

"Just stay there. I'll call you soon. And Thatcher?" He lets out a heavy sigh. "Was he worth it?"

I look at the girl in front of me. Waves of ebony curls frame her delicate face. She tugs off the chunky black sweater she'd been wearing, leaving her in an unholy tight T-shirt and brown pleated skirt that hangs off her waist.

"No." I press my fingers on the bridge of my nose as my eyes close. "But she was."

The line goes dead, and silence is all that's left.

My adrenaline is crashing, plummeting with such speed that it makes my head ache. I want the lack of endorphins to cure my irrational behavior and wait for the feeling of regret.

But from the moment I shoved that knife into Conner's mouth to the second I left that office, I felt nothing.

No fear of spending my life inside a metal cage. No disappointment from getting caught. No anger at myself for letting my control slip.

I feel absolutely nothing.

I don't care.

He deserved what I did. It had only been a matter of time before Conner got what was coming to him.

"How'd you know I was in there? That I needed help?"

"I followed you from class. I thought you were in there far too long. I suppose I just have great timing."

"You shouldn't have done that." The floorboards creak beneath

Lyra's feet. "Why did you?"

I watch her take steps towards me, her small body stopping when her feet rest between my own. Lyra cranes her neck to look up at me, tucking herself into my body.

"Asking the question you already know the answer to?" I lift an eyebrow, peering down with curiosity. I want her against me, pressed into me so that I can erase every inch of Conner's touch from her body.

"I want to hear you say it." The smell of her brushes against my nose, and the softness of her hands brings heat to my skin as they rest against my abdomen. "I want you to hear it for yourself."

I lift my hand, cupping her cheek, rubbing my thumb across the bridge of her nose. It feels impractical to experience this. The way I was so hungry for violence seconds ago, and now...

Now I want to submerge myself in her softness.

I can't give her love, care for her in the way someone should, but I'm tired of not giving her me. Not when she's the only person capable of having me. The distance I'd created between us had been to protect her. But today, that distance is the reason she was alone with Conner.

"No one is allowed to touch you," I say honestly.

My chest tightens as her finger drags lower, rubbing against the material of my belt, fiddling with the clasp.

"Except you?"

A smirk pulls across my lips. "Except me."

I'm tired of fighting her. Fighting myself.

I'd never once indulged myself in something, never once allowed myself to give in to my wants.

Despite all the evil I've committed, how wicked I am, maybe I deserve to have one thing. This one good thing in all the bad.

Her.

"Darling phantom." I glance down at her nimble hands pulling my belt free, the purple nail polish on her nails contrasting against my black clothes. "What are you doing?"

The sound of my zipper being dragged down echoes.

"Thanking you for coming for me," she whispers. "For saving me, again."

I feel the world slow down. Everything outside the door in front of me no longer exists. It's just us in this storage closet. My teeth sink into my bottom lip as she drops to her knees.

Nothing has been as beautiful.

I tuck a few stray curls away from her face, cupping her chin, making her look into my eyes. Her breathing is uneven, and her nails dig into the sides of my waist, pulling at the waistband of my slacks.

My thumb brushes her plump bottom lip, aching to feel it wrapped around my dick. The air crackles, and my skin buzzes as she pulls my pants and briefs down, just enough to free my cock. It slaps against my stomach, and her breath fans across my shaft, making me suck in a breath.

"Do you know what I'm about to do, pet?" I ask, shoving my thumb through the seam of her lips. She sucks on it, and the sensation shoots straight to my cock. "I'm going to fuck the taste of him out of this needy mouth."

The light flickers across her hand as it roams upward, pushing my bloody shirt up and exposing my abs. It glows, showing the way they flex as she wraps a timid hand around the base of my length.

Her smooth fingers don't meet as they curl around me, a few inches of space between them, and I see the moment she realizes when her eyes widen. Lyra looks so sinfully innocent, unsure of herself, but the desire pooling in her eyes makes one thing very clear.

She wants me.

Wants to put her mouth on me, her tongue, her body.

My hips jerk at the thought, seeking the heat of her mouth.

"I've never—" She chews her bottom lip, her hand giving me an experimental squeeze.

Lyra could sit there, just as she is, not moving a single inch, and it would still be more than enough to send me over the edge. I'm not sure if that says more about me or her.

But I can tell she's nervous, and I know exactly what makes those nerves disappear. Reaching into my pocket, I quickly pull out the switchblade, clicking it open.

The sound makes my cock twitch, and she gasps.

"You never what? Let someone fuck your mouth?" I murmur, one hand coming down to stroke her hair out of her face. "That's what you're going to let me do, isn't it? Shove my cock into this sweet hole and use it up?"

Lyra nods eagerly, that pink tongue sliding across her lips, dying to taste me but unsure how to begin. I curl my hand around the sharp blade. The bite is quick, burns for only a second before blood rushes to the surface.

I look at the pool of crimson in my hand before returning my gaze to the floor.

"Open," I order.

Her mouth does just that, pink tongue sticking out, waiting for whatever I plan to do next. Pride swells in my stomach. How she trusts me this much with a knife, I'll never understand.

Setting the knife down, I bring my hand down, holding it just above her face before tilting it sideways. The stream of blood trickles from my palm, suspended in the air for only a moment before it drips into her mouth.

Filthy, pretty words make her melt her nerves away, and blood excites her so much that it's impossible for her to worry about anything else.

A complex, macabre fetish.

It's exhilarating to bleed for another person, willingly giving them the fluid that keeps you alive. It courses through the chambers of your heart, and to give another person access to that is potent.

Red dots coat her tongue, spilling over her lips and dripping down the curve of her chin. I'm painfully hard, watching her drink it down. The way she swallows, I'm so very jealous that I can't watch my blood pour down her throat, can't see the way it paints the inside of her with me.

This is my new favorite shade of red.

"Good girl," I praise, tilting my head a bit. "So pretty covered in my blood. Absolutely fucking divine. I'm going to use you up, feel your throat struggle to fit my cock, and watch as you choke on my come. And you're going to let me, yeah?"

Her response comes in the form of her tongue dragging along the vein that runs on the underside of my shaft, tracing it all the way to my engorged tip, which is leaking precome. It's a dream watching her lick at my throbbing head, painting me with my blood.

"Yeah, you are," I confirm, staring at the reddish-pink lines on my dick. "Because you're desperate for my come, aren't you, pet? I bet if I lift that skirt, I'll find you soaked for me. That pitiful, aching pussy is jealous of your mouth, isn't it?"

"Yes," she breathes, her knees falling further apart. One hand strokes me, more confident in herself, while the other flips her skirt up, showing the purple lace panties beneath, giving me a full view of how badly she craves me. How desperate that cunt of hers is. I hum my approval, chest heaving as my breathing becomes more irregular.

The unmistakable warmth of her bloody mouth enveloping the first few inches of my cock makes me weak. Her hollow cheeks, trying to narrow around me, give me a similar sensation to what it feels like when I sink into her tight pussy.

"Fuck me." The groan is ripped from the back of my throat, clawing its way out. I drop my head back against the shelf, knocking over several items behind me.

They clash and clank against the ground, but all I can think about is fucking her, burying myself inside of her for hours and hours, knowing I'd die if I left. I would live in her body.

Her movements are shaky, unsure of how far to go and what to do with her tongue. But I'm so overcome by lust I can't stop myself from shoving forward, sending my length into her waiting mouth with one thrust. I want all the way inside; I need my cock completely covered by her.

I expect her to gag or struggle, but the further I go, the more she takes. She makes a swallowing motion with her throat, and it makes my knees buckle.

No gag reflex?

Testing my theory, I press until the head of my cock touches the back of her throat, a few inches of my shaft still exposed, and instead of coming up for air, Lyra twists her hand around the part of my cock that doesn't fit.

"Shit," I hiss, looking at her lips spread open around me, diluted blood splattered across the bridge of her nose. "You want more? Does my pathetic, needy girl want more?"

Lyra nods, pulling back and swirling her tongue around my sensitive tip before sinking back down. I'm enveloped by her. The feel of her mouth, her smell, her hands. I'm standing above her, but she's got me like putty in her hands.

The frozen pieces of my exterior are melting on the floor. Thawing.

Drool mixed with blood streams out of the corner of her mouth, spit glistening along the length of my dick as she works me root to tip, bobbing her head in quick strokes.

The veins in my neck tighten. Both of my hands lace into her hair, the inky-colored strands corded around my pale skin. The bleeding cut in my hand mats against the hair. My grip is forceful as I jerk her closer, cramming myself into her mouth, forcing her lips to stretch around me.

Sweet, intoxicating mewls and moans come from her throat, adding light vibrations. My hips drive forward harder, filling the room with wet, lewd noises that I can hear just below the sound of my thudding heart.

"Open your throat for me. Let me ruin you."

Tears gather in the corner of her eyes, but she stays put, taking every inch in stride, the muscles of her tongue sliding around my head with every downstroke. She's completely at my mercy and willing to let me break her for my pleasure.

Those pink lips are swollen around my shaft, plump from all the slurping. I watch in awe as she pushes towards me every time I withdraw from her mouth as if she never wants me to leave.

"That's it. Such a good little pet," I grunt as the heaviness in my balls aches. "I'm going to fill your throat with my come, and you're not going to spill a single drop."

Her moans echo in my ears, begging for my seed, milking it out of me with her needy mouth. My orgasm coils in my gut; I'm so fucking close. I thrust until her nose kisses my waist, and I hold her there, hitting the back of her throat with the tip of my dick over and over.

The saliva and wet heat wrapping around me is almost too much. Groaning, I look down at my hands, the way they work her back and forth on my length, watching it disappear inside of her over and over again.

"Shit, I'm gonna come—" A moan takes my words before I finish. "Baby, fuck yes. I'm coming."

I plunge into her one last time, burying her nose against my lower stomach. My dick hits the back of her warm throat and twitches before I release. Lyra continues to suck, swallowing every drop that I force down, swirling her tongue, coaxing my cock as she drains me dry.

My vision is blurry, breathing erratic as I loosen my grip, petting her hair. When she removes her mouth, I fall back into the shelf, unable to stand up on my own.

When the light-headed feeling fades, I tuck myself back into my slacks before looking down at her on the floor, her flushed cheeks, tears staining her face, and mouth stained red. She drags her tongue across her lips, licking at the blood remaining there. I glimpse a few blood-soaked curls when she stands up.

Crimson-soaked and celestial beauty.

A gift wrapped in a quiet, forgotten package but within a brand of sunshine that exists only on days of mourning. Light that peers through storm clouds, daylight after a thousand years of darkness.

I never believed I had a soul, and now I think I understand why.

My hand grabs the back of her neck, pulling her into my chest. I feel her hands on my face as our lips meet in a clash of tongues and teeth. The salty, metallic taste on her lips has my cock twitching, spent but wanting her again.

Our mouths merge together, seamlessly made for one another. They move in sync as if far before our time, we'd done this before, met and spent lifetimes with our lips tangled.

My lack of a soul wasn't because of the evil that had infested my mother's womb or my father's corrupt DNA.

No, I didn't have one because it belonged to her.

I think when we were created, instead of splitting our spirits in half, they gave both of them to her in order to keep them safe. To remind me, when the time was right, that all I am is hers to carry.

Far before we stood in these bodies, someone had decided she would be the keeper of my soul, knowing I would have done far too much damage to it.

When I pull away, my forehead drops to hers, and I lean into her palms and kiss the tips of her fingers. My hand comes up, spinning the ring on her pointer finger with my own.

"I can't stay away from you, even when I know I should. It would be the only good thing I could do for you, Scarlett."

Lyra rubs her nose against mine, nibbling at my bottom lip before breathing.

"Don't be good. Don't stay away. Just be with me."

FIFTEEN
butterflies

Lyra

The cabin smells like garlic.

It's the first thing I notice when I walk through the door.

The second thing is that it's clean. Unnaturally clean.

My project is still taking up all the space in the living room, all of my supplies untouched, but everything else? Spotless.

I bite back a smile, trying to imagine Thatcher walking around my house cleaning. Gods knows what he found in this place along the way. I drag my finger across a shelf on the wall, the one that has jars of creatures soaked in formaldehyde, and when I lift my finger back up, there isn't a speck of dust to be found.

I didn't even know I owned a duster.

For the last two weeks, Thatcher and I have found a routine. I can still feel him keeping his distance emotionally, but he leaves the door to his room open during the day. The other night, I was up late working on my spider frame. He came down and sat on the love seat across from me to read.

We sat there in silence, just existing in each other's presence for hours.

His company is that of a shadow.

Quiet, subtle, but you know he's there.

My shoes thud against the wall as I kick them off, throwing my coat across the couch, before I make my way into the kitchen, where the smell of actual food, not the frozen meals I consume, is wafting from.

When I walk through the archway, I find Thatcher's back to me, a purple hand towel tossed over his shoulder, wearing a white button-down rolled to his elbows and his standard black slacks. Classical music plays from my speaker, and I watch in awe as he pulls the silver pan from my stove and flips the food in the air.

He turns, showing the side profile of his face. Pieces of his white hair fall in front of his forehead, just a few, and it's those pieces of hair that do me in every single time.

"You cook?" I question, moving to the fridge, trying to pretend I wasn't staring.

He peers at me over his shoulder, acknowledging my presence before pouring red wine into the pan, making steam erupt.

"I'm fantastic with anything that requires a knife."

I snag a bottle of water, smirking. "Should I be worried about where the meat in this dish came from, Hannibal?"

Thatcher rolls his eyes. "Human beings are disgusting. I don't touch them with my bare hands, and you think I'm going to eat their flesh? Some stalker you are. Do you even know me?"

My jaw drops. "You jerk!"

A smile pulls at the corners of his mouth, and a laugh bubbles up from my stomach. He's funny when he wants to be. Warm when he isn't busy convincing the world he's Jack Frost.

I adore this version of Thatch, the one only I get to see. I love it almost as much as the part that terrifies people.

He is both their nightmare and my daydream.

"Speaking of killing people." I lift myself up onto the wooden island in the center of the kitchen, scooting towards the middle before sitting cross-legged. "Conner Godfrey is officially on a leave of absence after his heroic run-in with the Ponderosa Springs Imitator. He still hasn't been able to identify the masked man responsible for the damage to his tongue."

"Tragic," he mutters.

"I know that Rook is sold already, but do you believe Easton is the copycat killer?"

Thatcher pulls a knife from the block, moving over to the counter, where he chops pieces of vegetables. "You don't?"

"I should. It's clear he's the one sending you notes, but I just don't know." I shrug, taking a drink of my water. "I've known Easton since elementary school. He's always been an asshole, but a murderer? No."

"There are many faces of a killer." His tone is indifferent. "It's almost never the creep in the corner. It's more likely to be the man in the center of the room. We're chameleons, able to blend in and copy emotions. If Easton is the Imitator, then he efficiently camouflages himself enough that even you don't believe it."

I know I shouldn't push him, that I should be thankful he's showing so much of himself, even if it's not nearly enough, but I've always been curious by nature. It's impossible to not want more from him.

How do you tell someone that you want to know everything? Every memory, every moment, every quirk and habit just so you can be closer. I'm jealous of all the seconds I don't share with him.

"Can I ask you a question?"

"You're going to regardless of how I answer."

"Probably." I pluck a piece of cucumber from the salad on the island. "How many people have you killed?"

The question rings into the warm air. I was hoping the casual delivery would distract him from the harsh question. Maybe he wouldn't even notice he was answering.

But he notices everything.

I'm met with only the sound of a sizzling pan and the thud of his knife against the wooden cutting board.

Chop, chop, chop.

When he stops, I expect some resistance. A snarky comment or outright lashing out for asking something so personal. But he simply plucks another carrot from the bunch and begins chopping again.

"Seven." He exhales. "Two every year since I was seventeen.

Minus this year, of course—someone stole my number eight."

My cheeks heat, and I'm thankful his back is to me. The picture of Michael left in the center of the circus ring with blades dug into the sockets of his eyes is something I won't forget soon.

"Seven," I repeat, trying to grasp that the man cooking dinner in front of me is the same one capable of murdering seven people. It should make me uncomfortable; it should scare me or freak me out, but I feel no different about him now that I know.

"How do you—" I wave my hands in front of me, trying to find the words. "—find them? I mean, do you have a type or just any man?"

Speaking these details out loud just reminds me how odd of a pair we make. How strange our dinner conversation is compared to others.

I'm not sure if he'll answer, if he'll share this part of himself. I don't even know if he's spoken about this to anyone else. But he surprises me. He continues talking as he works.

"My grandfather, Edmond, knew what my father turned me into. What I could do. They tried, both him and May, for a long time to love me back to normal. Give me a steady life in hopes it would change the inevitable, but there was too much damage done. Henry had shown me too much, trained me too well. So." He lets out a heavy breath, as if blowing the dust on an old record that hasn't been played in years.

"For my sixteenth birthday, my grandfather gave me a stack of files and a parting message. *Thou shall not kill, but if you must, kill those deserving of death.* All the people in the files were men who'd evaded the justice system. Other killers who preyed on the innocent, those who were weak. They each in some way weren't able to be caught, or the police couldn't convict them. They just kept showing up after Edmond died, always arriving on the first Tuesday of June and last Thursday of October. Left inside a PO box downtown that's billed to a fake name."

"You kill other killers?"

"Mm-hmm," he hums.

"And May never knew?"

His shoulders tense at the mention of her name, but he swiftly tosses the cut vegetables into the pan, shaking it to stir them.

"I think she suspected it but enjoyed a blissful ignorance. Edmond told me the only way to protect those around me was to keep them in the dark. He was the only one, besides you, who knew about this. To May, I would always be Thatcher, her grandson, never the man who killed people in the family estate basement."

She knew more than he'd like to think. Our conversation in the garden told me she knew, but I think she loved him. Maybe it had been denial, but May was more than aware of who her grandson was.

This—it makes sense. Why he's so secretive. He felt it was the only way to protect the guys, May, me, from what he is. The distance is to keep us safe from *him*.

"Wait." I furrow my eyebrows closely, fear spiking my pulse. "The basement? That's where you do it? Thatcher, the police raided the estate. Did you leave—"

"I'm not stupid, Lyra," he cuts me off, pulling some kind of bread from the oven and sitting it on the counter. "The basement is just that. A basement. I cleared any and all evidence of torture before they found May's body. Cleaned and left in impeccable condition."

Silence falls between us as he cooks, pulling plates from the cabinet. In this private moment, with the truth of him settling between us, I accept just how much I like him.

How much I love him. How I would shred the world with my teeth to have him. Would lie, steal, and cheat for his safety.

And yet, that still doesn't guarantee our happily ever after.

That fact alone cripples me. Knowing that you could care for someone this fucking much and it wouldn't be enough for the universe to let you live in that love.

My mother wasn't religious, I'm not religious, but if it meant keeping him forever, I'd pray.

The world has already shown me so much darkness, has given Thatcher more misery than one person should carry. I'd plead to whatever God I needed to for us to have a soft ending. A quiet one that requires nothing other than peace.

It is both a blessing and a curse knowing him.

It's more dangerous now. The stakes are raised after every layer

I peel back. The closer I get to him, the more I will have to lose at the end of this.

I stare at his back, the way he moves, and my heart sighs.

Please, I think, *let us have the ending we deserve. It doesn't even need to be happy. I just need it to have him.*

"I can hear how hard you're thinking," he says, sliding a plate of steaming food in front of me, icy blue eyes twinkling with amusement. "Care to share what's got you so perplexed?"

"I've never had a home-cooked meal before," I say abruptly, which may not be what I was thinking of, but it's not a lie. "It's a first for me."

Thatcher rests his hands on the edge of the island just in front of me, a smirk on his lips. "You can add it to the list of firsts I've stolen from you, then."

Warmth spreads across my stomach.

I try to ignore the blush on my cheek as I pick up the fork and stab a piece of chicken. "My mother was an awful cook. It's one of the things I distinctly remember about her. That and the smell of burnt popcorn."

Thatcher's food is exactly as I imagined it to be. Fucking delicious. I don't think there is anything he does poorly.

"Tell me about her." He leans on his elbows in front of me, the muscles in his shoulders flexing.

I swallow. "My mom?"

He nods, twirling pasta around his fork before looking up at me just as he takes a bite.

"Why?"

"You're not the only one intrigued by someone in this room, Lyra."

It's usually me interrogating him, forcing him to open up so I can learn all the things that make him up. I'm not used to being the one someone knows, and I think that's because I never wanted anyone to know me.

Not really.

I'm a ghost because I choose to be. It was always easier than sharing pieces of yourself.

"She was…" I trail off, trying to find all the words to describe my mother to someone who never knew how incredibly special she was. "There was never a dull moment. I know a lot of kids hate being homeschooled, but I loved spending time with her. She helped me catch ladybugs, took me to work with her and let me feed all the animals that freaked people out. I remember her being strict but still letting me eat dessert first."

The sudden hunger for something sweet makes my mouth water. Tears sting the corners of my eyes, knowing this is the first time in a long time I've spoken out loud about her.

"She never tried to make me into anything. There was no expectation of being anyone else. Whatever I became, she would have loved me for."

I feel a teardrop slip down my cheek, and I quickly wipe it away with my sleeve, smiling softly at Thatcher, who is watching with an expressionless gaze.

"I was obsessed with this butterfly dress when I was little. It was purple and had monarchs all over it. I wore it nonstop for months on end, and she washed it for me every night."

"You miss her," he says, carefully raising his thumb to dry my tears. It's so casual, like he does it all the time. The soft stroke of his skin against mine coaxes me into his touch.

"Very much." I lean into him, curling my fingers around his wrist. "I saved all of them for you, you know?"

He raises his eyebrow. "Butterfly dresses?"

"No." I huff out a laugh. "My firsts. I saved them for you."

Realization sparks in his eyes, and before I can say anything else, he moves the plates out of the way and grabs my hips, hauling me towards him. My knees are touching his chest, and he's looming over me.

"I think..." He trails off for a moment, as if to search for the right words. "I think I saved all my firsts for you too."

"You've never—I was your first?"

"I don't like touching other people, Lyra. You think fucking them would somehow be different?"

It feels overwhelming knowing I own these pieces of Thatcher. Pride swells in my chest.

Even like this, he's so much taller than me. I'm able to tuck myself into his body and feel surrounded. I knot my hands in the front of his shirt, holding him possessively.

"Knowing all these hands have done, what they will continue to do—" He squeezes me as if to remind me. "—you aren't afraid of them?"

I should be. It would be normal to be afraid.

"I can't change for you, Lyra. This thing between us won't change who I am."

I can feel his heartbeat beneath my hands. I can feel that he is just as much human as he's a killer. And humans, even this one who was designed for havoc, deserves love.

"No matter the cruelty your hands are capable of, they will always be the one place I feel safe. How could I fear fingers that were made to touch me?"

He watches me as if he's trying to decide if I'm lying or if I'm telling the truth. Whatever he determines has him lowering his mouth dangerously close to my own. A whisper of a kiss. So very close, but as fate would have it, my stomach lets out an animalistic growl.

I expect this to shatter the vulnerable mood passing between us, but it does the opposite.

It creates a memory. A core memory that I will never forget.

Thatcher laughs.

And it is not cold or sour.

No, it's rich and filled with passion.

Like ripples in a still pond after a stone has been thrown across it, it radiates outward, pulls at the edges of his eyes, and quickly becomes my favorite sound. I don't even realize it's made me smile until he pecks my forehead with his lips, the remnants of his laughter tickling my skin.

"Eat," he murmurs, "before your stomach eats itself."

SIXTEEN
danse macabre

lyra

This fitted gown was a much better idea three macarons ago.
But I wholeheartedly believe no dress is pretty enough to
pass up sweets. It was stunning when Briar fastened the last
button at the nape of my neck and would be just as beautiful with
my bloated stomach.

Red lights dust across the velvet material, the taut fabric practically sewn into my skin. Regardless of how tight, I hadn't been
able to say no to the long-sleeve gown, not when the color reminded
me so much of the blue-purple iridescence of the Pavon emperor
butterfly.

"I need a cigarette," Alistair groans, finally returning from his
parents' grasp. I watch him lean against a pillar, a drink pressed to
his lips.

I'd half expected him to show up wearing his leather jacket, but
he'd swapped it for a black dinner coat. Probably the same one most
of the guests here are sporting, but Alistair carries a different vibe.

No matter how badly his parents want to refine the notorious outcast son, he would always seep corruption. They needed an heir to take over all the land they own in Ponderosa Springs, someone to pass their legacy to now that the eldest Caldwell had fallen from grace.

But Alistair had owned the title of black sheep for far too long, and no amount of well-fitted suits would change his mind. He'd always be the spare. The shadow. Just to spite them.

"Not a fan of Valentine's Day?" I offer.

"Of course I am. Love it. Where else would I spend my Saturday, if not at another extravagant dance with Hollow Heights finest?" His voice drips sarcasm. "This just gives my father more opportunity to rub elbows with me in public."

The Saint Lover's Masquerade Ball is the school's way of being nice. A celebration of all we've overcome in such a short period. A time to rejoice in the bonds and relationships we'd made at Hollow Heights.

At least, I think that's what the flyer said.

"Have you tried telling him no? That you have zero interest in taking his place on the board or owning the town?"

"Every chance I get. I'm super polite about it too. I add a 'go to hell' after every conversation."

I stifle a laugh as my tongue licks the remnants of raspberry filling off my lips. Students mingle in every corner of the Salvatore Dining Hall. Golden hearts are sprinkled across the floor, red light reflecting off the murals painted across the ceiling, and cheesy music plays from the speakers.

"Where is Rook?" I ask, looking through the crowd of students on the dance floor, all wearing various masks. "We're supposed to be in recon mode, and my job is to provide you two with an alibi in case something sketchy goes down. How am I supposed to do that when I only have half of the twisted sisters?"

"You only came for the sweets." Alistair leers. "He's probably toking in the bathroom. God knows he's not getting through this night without smoking."

He tugs at his tie, pulling it loose around his neck. He pushes the silver mask up on his head, and I can see he's twenty seconds from lighting up a cigarette in the middle of this room.

"I meant to tell you this sooner." I chew the inside of my lip, looking at his side profile. "But I'm sorry for what I said at the funeral. It wasn't your fault what happened to me. You're only trying to protect B, I get it."

I'd been angry the day we laid May to rest. Rage was brewing, and I took it out on him. I wanted the world to mourn the way I was, and I was so blinded by my pain that I didn't see just how hurt Alistair already was by all of this.

He turns his gaze, looking at me carefully. "And you were protecting Thatcher. Never apologize to me for that."

I nod, an understanding passing between us that we would do whatever we needed to in order to keep the people we care about safe. Love is not always a pretty emotion. Sometimes, it turns you into a wrathful, vengeance-seeking creature. One that will shred anything that poses a threat.

"I haven't seen Easton tonight. You think he skipped it?"

"Probably. His father is here though—he wasted no time chatting up my mother. My money is on Godfrey showing up."

There's zero love lost between Alistair and Stephen Sinclair, regardless of his involvement in the Halo. The affair between Stephen and Elise Caldwell had done enough damage to that relationship over the years.

"Not if he's smart. It should take at least a month for an injury like that to heal." I press the glass of champagne to my lips, taking a sip.

"I wonder—" Alistair's smirk is all-knowing. "—what does one do to deserve a knife through the mouth, Lyra?"

A blush heats my cheeks. I raise an eyebrow at the question, shrugging as I hide behind the drink in my hand.

"I wouldn't know." The lie is cheap and obvious.

He laughs, deep in his chest, watching me with eyes that tell me he knows far more than I think.

"Thatcher will deny it." He crosses his arms in front of his chest. "But I've met no one as protective as him. There is no one else I'd want in my corner, even if he is a little testy."

This feels like an approval conversation, Alistair giving me a thumbs-up, the green light for pursuing a relationship with Thatcher. Although I don't need it, it still feels good. Being accepted was never something I was good at.

I'm just about to thank him when Briar and Sage enter through the front door, returning from their half of this surveillance plan. Briar's blue gown shimmers as she walks with all the glitter, waves of blonde hair cascading down her back.

When she spots us, she's quick to wrap her arms around Alistair's waist, resting her head against his chest while he curls his arm protectively over the small of her back.

"Is he bitching about Valentine's Day?" she teases. "Don't let him lie—he's secretly a romantic."

In a matter of seconds, Alistair turns from the brooding shadow in the corner to, well, still the brooding shadow, but with a smile at the corner of his mouth. They sorta melt into each other, the glow of her energy combining with all his darkness until they are a stunning shade of gunmetal gray.

"Find anything in Godfrey's office, little thief?" He looks down at her while she stretches her neck to meet his gaze.

"Fuck all," she grumbles, dropping her forehead to his chest with a thud. "He either had it cleaned out, or there was nothing to find to begin with."

"Is it sick I was praying we found a dead body?" Sage adds, an annoyed expression on her flawless face. She'd been Briar's lookout while she was snooping. "Literally anything other than another dead end?"

Obviously, our plan to find dirt on Conner was a waste of time. That's all any of this seems to be—a waste of time. I'm exhausted. Running circles, trying to find proof for something that doesn't seem to exist. It just feels like we're digging our own graves, deeper and deeper.

"You mind?" Sage motions to my barely drunk champagne.

"All yours." I offer her the glass as she gives me a sad smile before downing the sparkling beverage. She flips a piece of hair over her shoulder when she finishes.

I press a hand into my stomach, the swirling of sugar rushing to my head, and I suddenly regret eating all those sweets.

The girl found at Black Sands Cove was the last victim, so it's possible the Imitator is letting us catch our breath before continuing to wreak havoc.

"You all look depressing as fuck."

We all rotate, seeing Rook moving past a couple of students. His brown hair is untamed and curling at the collar of his suit. The red-horned mask he's wearing conceals most of his face, and I realize it's the same one as Alistair.

"No worries. I'm here to save the day." He grins, eyes hazy.

Rook wraps his arms around Sage's shoulders, pulling her into his body.

"Do not make a joke about your dick." She rolls her eyes, leaning into him further and kissing his arm softly. With her heels on, they are almost the same height. They fit so perfectly together, two puzzle pieces that click.

I'm jealous for a split second.

It's the last thing I should think about, especially right now, but I want what they have with Thatcher. I'm content with our private connection, and if that's the only way I can have him, I'll accept it.

I just can't help but want the public displays of affection. A claiming arm around my waist, a kiss on the forehead in front of people. Anything that shows our relationship isn't just a figment of my imagination.

"You'll get plenty of my dick later, baby." Rook kisses her cheek.

"Van Doren," Alistair interrupts, "do you have information that isn't horseshit or not?"

"Chill, Dad." He reaches into his pocket, pulling out his phone. "Thanks to Silas and his facial recognition software on his computer, I got some information on the men James met up with at the terminal. I just got their files back."

He tosses his phone to Alistair, and we take turns passing it around. When it reaches me, I struggle to keep my face blank so the surrounding people don't notice.

Name: Aaron O'Hara

Age: Thirty-three

Three counts of promotion of prostitution. Two counts of sexual assault. One count armed robbery.

*Was sentenced ten years at age twenty-two to **Attica Correctional Facility; Attica, NY.** Served eight due to overcrowding.*

In short, he's an ex-pimp or current who hasn't been busted again. I scroll past the mug shot taken years ago to the second name on the document.

Name: Declan O'Hara.

Age: Thirty-seven

Faced twenty-five years to life for organized crime charges. Accepted a plea deal for information regarding his involvement with drug and sex trafficking and ties to known organized crime members.

Was released from protective custody six years ago.

"There is no fucking way the Sinclairs are working with the mob," Sage whisper yells, looking around at everyone. "Is there?"

Alistair runs a frustrated hand down his face. "We need to get into Elite's company campus. If we find the shipping containers, it'll be enough leverage against James for him to rat out everyone involved."

The room spins a little.

How did Silas needing to avenge the murder of his girlfriend turn into this? Just how far down the rabbit hole had we fallen, and how do we expect to make it out?

"How the fuck do you plan—"

"Well, isn't this a lovely group?"

We all go radio silent.

The chatter of those around us is louder now that this stiff quiet has fallen. I wrap an arm around my stomach, the temperature falling a few degrees.

Stephen Sinclair stands at the edge of the circle we've created. His styled blond hair is in flawless condition, blue eyes cutting through each of us as he holds a calm, poised expression on his face.

"How is the new semester treating you?" he asks coolly, as if he's only the dean of Hollow Heights doing his due diligence and not a fucking snake in the grass.

Stephen has always been a pompous asshat. Easton gets it from him, honestly. They both walk around as if they own every place they step into. They believe they're above anyone and everyone.

"How's my mom?" Alistair retorts, never one to hide his distaste for anyone, no matter how to tricky the situation.

Stephen takes it in stride, grinning. "I was just talking to her. We were discussing your future as a member of the board. I hear you're thinking of accepting their offer after you graduate?"

I watch Alistair's jaw tick, Briar's hand squeezing his so tight that her knuckles turn white.

"Not likely." He speaks through gritted teeth.

"What a shame." Stephen frowns a bit. "It would have been nice to work together. But I suppose you have your own path to follow."

The air is so thick you could slice it with a knife. I can hear my heart beating in my ears.

He knows just how involved we are. He knows we're onto him.

"Well, I just wanted to stop by and say hello. Give my condolences and let you know I hope they find Thatcher soon. It's so odd not seeing him with you all." Stephen beams like it's a joke.

I will fucking kill him.

If he touches Thatcher, I will bury him my goddamn self, and I won't need any proof of his guilt to do it. My fingers tighten around the material of my dress, and I feel a warm hand curl around my wrist.

Looking down, I find Alistair's hand wrapped around my own, keeping me in place.

"Ladies." Stephen tips his head in our direction, making direct eye contact with me. "Try to be careful. I'd hate to see any of you hurt."

The night is ending. The music has turned softer, and couples have found their way onto the dance floor. A gentle tune that acts as a reminder that in the middle of chaos, we still have each other.

My anger had deflated after Stephen excused himself, disappearing to mingle with other socialites and board members. With him gone, I try to focus on anything but the Halo.

I smile behind my champagne glass as I watch Rook wrap Sage up in his arms, dancing more as one person than two separate people. They look so in love at this moment that I almost forgot the reason we came here.

Briar and Alistair left just after Stephen excused himself from the conversation, which means I'm trapped here because the two on the dance floor are my ride home.

Deciding to let them enjoy this moment, I slip through the throng of people and work my way up to the second level, looking down from the banister at all the people below.

I walk a little further, my heels clicking against the floor, before I see the two french doors to my right. Trying my luck for some fresh air, I press on the handle, finding it unlocked.

The frosty night air hits me immediately, and I'm thankful I went with a long-sleeve gown. However, it's not raining, which is a miracle, considering it's February in Oregon.

The ivy-wrapped terrace I step out onto overlooks the commons. It's lit up with expensive fairy lights, and I can see a few people leaving the ball to walk to the cars. It's just far away enough that I blend into the quiet of darkness, yet I can still hear the music from the party.

Below, I see a couple chasing one another in the snow. When the boy catches her, they spin, and their laughter tickles the back of my neck. I rest my elbow on the banister, overlooking two people very much in love.

Valentine's Day has always been my favorite holiday.

The chocolate and candy are only a small part.

I adore the celebration of love in all of its many forms. Big or small, between lovers or family members. It's more than just marriage proposals; it's about reflecting on the relationships you've developed.

I love being reminded that despite all the bad, there are so many people in my life that I cherish. As a kid, I was so jealous of all the students who got to address Valentines to classmates. It was the only part of being homeschooled that I hated.

Our definition of love has expanded far beyond the scope of just romantic. I've waited a long time to have the kind of connections worth celebrating, and maybe that's why I've loved Valentine's Day for so long.

For the hope of what I have today.

"Alone is a dangerous place to find yourself, Lyra."

My heels bend as I turn so quickly I nearly fall over. My fingers grab ahold of the banister, trying to find balance.

"What the hell are you doing here?" I whisper. "The whole point of you staying in the cabin is to actually stay there, Thatcher. You're going to be seen."

He steps from the veil of shadows further onto the platform. The glowing lights from the commons illuminate the sleek red box in his hands. The heart-shaped package makes my heart skip.

"Isn't that what the mask is for?" Thatcher points out.

It's the same as the other boys, a horned ghoul, except Thatcher's is matte black. It stretches across the contours of his face, leaving only his mouth exposed. I catch a glimpse of his slicked-back white hair just behind the horns.

It's hard to argue his point.

From a distance, it would be impossible to pick him out from any other masked student on campus. But if you get close enough, the chances of recognizing him increase.

Or maybe they don't.

Maybe it's just me that can distinguish his characteristics, even with a mask. He's etched so deep in my memory I would know him with my eyes closed, from the smell of his cologne to the way my body wakes up in his presence.

"Did something happen? What was so important that it couldn't wait till I got back to the house?"

Thatcher, for obvious reasons, had to stay out of our Valentine's Day operation, which he shared his distaste for multiple times. I know he's restless, and being confined to the walls of the cabin is slowly killing him.

But for my own sake, I wish he'd just stay put.

He walks forward, brushing my shoulder as he walks to the edge of the terrace, looking down below. The long lines of his body are squeezed within a tailored suit, an almost identical shade to my dress, which I know wasn't an accident.

Turning around so that his back is leaning on the banister, he wiggles the box in his hands.

"I'm an impatient gift-giver," he says simply, as if that's more than enough reason to show his face in public right now.

"I didn't know you made it a habit to give gifts." I wrap an arm around my waist as a chilly wind bursts through.

"I don't."

I can't see his eyes, and it's bothering me. The matte material shields me from the blue of his irises, and his mouth sits in a hard line.

"But." His chest expands as he releases a sigh, reaching the box towards me. "Valentine's Day is your favorite holiday. So, consider this a thank-you."

I bite my bottom lip, a smile breaking through as I take it from his hands. The smooth fabric across the box is warm beneath my fingertips. It looks expensive. Despite eating my weight in cakes and cookies, my stomach growls at the chance to eat chocolate.

"What do you have to thank me for?" I lift my eyebrow, dragging my fingers to the seam of the package, gently trying to open it.

"More than I'm capable of understanding."

When the top of the box comes off, my jaw nearly hits the ground. I'd thought he got me candy, maybe jewelry 'cause I know that's what most guys go for, and I would have been more than happy with anything he chose to get me.

But this? I never would've expected.

"Thatcher," I whisper, the wind catching the end of his name. "This is… Oh my God."

It's all I can come up with as I stare down at the sections where chocolate usually lies in these kinds of gifts, but all ten spaces are replaced with different species of spiders, all of them just as rare as the next. I'd written these down in my journal in hopes of ordering maybe one of them for my new display, but every one I'd documented sits in perfect taxidermy position right in front of me. All I would have to do is go home and strategically place them along the artificial web I'd built.

Tears sting the corners of my eyes, my hand resting just above my mouth, and I can feel the way my fingers shake.

"This is the nicest thing anyone has ever given me," I gush. "How did you get these? They are almost impossible to find."

With his hands shoved into his pockets, he shrugs as if it's no big deal. "Rook owed me a favor."

"Thank you." I carefully place the lid back on them, grinning. "How did you know Valentine's Day is my favorite holiday? Am I that transparent?"

Thatcher pushes off the railing, making quick work of the distance between us until he's pressed against me. I can smell his mint gum with every breath that fans across my face. He takes the box from my hands, setting it on the bench next to us.

The palm of his hand presses into my lower back, bringing us chest to chest, while the other trails the length of my arm. He leans towards the crook of my neck, and the side of his mask brushes my cheek, the plastic cooling down my blushed face.

"You're invisible to most, this enigmatic ghost. You are a mystery to the world, Lyra, and you've let me solve you." His words brush against my ear, making me shiver.

Carefully, more gentle than even he knew he was capable of, he cups my hand with his own. My arm instinctively curls around the back of his neck, and I can hear a familiar song drifting up from inside the Ballroom.

The world below buzzes with life, yet we move in our own bubble up here. Untouchable, trapped in a magnetic force field that refuses to break.

I've waited all my life for this. For him.

For him to see me not as the girl who hid in the closet or the ghost he demanded I become but as a woman capable of standing at his side. A person who would weather storm after storm if it meant we came out of it together.

His equal.

"Have I ever told you that I hate when you wear your hair up?"

I pull back, my eyebrows lifting to my hairline. "Sage specifically said this kind of dress was made for updos. How else was I supposed to show off the back?"

His fingers work their way up my spine, touching the buttons along the way until he meets the nape of my neck. I feel him searching for all the pins holding my curls up, pulling them out one by one.

"No dress is worth hiding these away."

The sound of metal clicking against the floor beneath us rings in my ears. He makes quick work of taking my hair down, pulling all the pins out and letting them fall to the ground without a care.

I feel the weight of it against my shoulders when he finishes. My outgrown bangs are dangerously close to covering up my eyes, and I know for a fact I look like I just stuck my finger in an electric socket.

But I savor the way he massages my scalp, how he wraps the dark strands around his fingers, brushing the curls with his large hands. If things were different, he could be a pianist with those fingers. They were made to play music.

When he is satisfied with the mess on my head, he returns his hand to my back.

"What are we doing?" I whisper as we sway in tune to the melody of the music, his hands on my body guiding us.

"It would be a shame for you to look this beautiful and not have someone ask you to dance."

"We've danced before, Thatch."

"And just as I told you then, that was a distraction," he corrects, stiffening his grip on my hand before pushing me outward.

I squeak as my body spins, his arm raised high in order to keep me twirling. My dress lifts, fabric whirling in the star-soaked night. I don't notice the smile on my lips until it makes the edge of my eyes crinkle.

When he pulls me back into his chest, I land ungracefully, my palm laid flat just above his heart.

"This," he breathes across my lips, "is dancing, darling phantom."

If I could live in one moment forever, it would be this one. This is a night you look back on if you're lucky enough to make it to eighty. You long for it and wonder what you'd do to be young again.

I want to exist with him like this forever. Just me and him.

The nightmare of Ponderosa Springs and his darling phantom.

"When this is over, what will you do?" I think out loud, wondering about what the future will look like for the both of us.

His smirk is wide. "Try to avoid prison for the rest of my life."

I laugh, just as he spins me again, the world moving in only colors and blurs.

"And me?" I ask breathlessly when he catches me in his arms. "What will I do?"

"You'll be just as you are right now," he begins, tucking a piece of hair behind my ear. "Haunting me. Existing for me."

Those three words dance on my tongue.

They are right there, begging to be said out loud. My heart jumps and skips in my chest, screaming over and over.

You love him! You love him! Say you love him!

This could've stayed only an obsession, but it had bloomed into something lovely and dark. A rosebush with twice as many thorns, but still breathtaking. I'd thought I loved him before, knew I could be the only one to do it, but this, this is love.

The kind I'd read about since I was a child. People wish on stars for this kind of love. The one where two people who were always meant to be clash and finally accept that the universe does put people in your life for a reason.

I want to say it, but I don't.

Only because they aren't enough right now.

They are not enough to capture this moment. Will never be enough to explain the way my heart beats with a different rhythm for him. They are simply just not enough, and he deserves more.

So I swallow it and replace them with something else.

"I have a gift for you too."

177

SEVENTEEN
my bloody valentine

Thatcher

My mouth is watering.

The idea of devouring Lyra whole while she wears that pretty little dress becomes more and more tempting now that we are hidden away from prying eyes.

I wasn't sure when I'd become such an addict, so uncharacteristically strung-out on the taste of cherries and the sound of her voice, but I'm here now. Wholly, utterly obsessed with my little stalker.

I'd known letting her into my world would cause irrevocable damage. When you live your life in black and white, it's impossible to not be tainted by someone who exists in full color.

But I don't think I could have predicted this.

This hunger, yearning for experiences I'd never thought of before. I'd always been content knowing Lyra was mine, this secret voyeur who belonged to me in the shadows of the night.

I never expected that I'd want to be hers though. That I wanted to belong to her just as much as she belonged to me. If this copycat killer wasn't intent on ruining my life, I would've already made it more than clear that we were it for each other.

My hand is interlocked with hers as she pulls me through the cabin. I would've followed her just about anywhere in that dress. With her back to me, I admire the arch in the small of her back, the plump curve of her ass, and how that dress leaves little to the imagination of what she looks like naked.

If it makes me weak to crave her, then let me be weak.

Being strong means nothing if I can't have her.

"Promise me you won't freak out." Her voice shakes as we wind down the hallway to the door at the end.

It's the only one in the house that stays locked. The one room she forbade me from entering. Although I was curious and slightly annoyed with her keeping it from me, I hadn't pushed the issue.

"I've seen a heart beating inside someone's chest cavity." I raise an eyebrow. "There isn't much left to freak me out, darling."

When she reaches the door, I watch in admiration as she rises onto her tippy-toes and grabs the key from the top of the frame. With wobbly fingers, she stuffs the key into the lock until it clicks into place.

I can feel her erratic heartbeat. Whatever lies beyond this door is not something she's shared with anyone else. For two seconds, I think that I'm about to find a slew of dead bodies in here.

"I'm scared," she whispers, twisting the doorknob but not moving to open it.

I step until my chest presses into her back, my mouth declining so that it rests just next to her ear. I'm captivated by the way she immediately falls into me, completely trusting me to catch her.

"Nothing about you could ever scare me, Lyra Abbott," I mutter. "All your darkness is my own. We're the same."

I don't need to see her face to know she's smiling. I can feel it in the way her shoulders relax. The door creaks loudly as it opens, the shrieking sound echoing through the halls.

Lyra takes a breath before walking across the threshold, and I watch as darkness engulfs her body. I follow her blindly, the door shutting behind us until we become fully submerged in the dark.

A dull flick echoes before the walls are plunged into an ominous red hue. Pits of darkness contour along nooks and tables. It takes my eyes several seconds to adjust, but when they do, I find myself looking at, well, me.

I'm occupying every inch of this room, my presence tangible in the stillness.

Hundreds of photos of me in various stages of life strung up along threads that are bannered from wall to wall. Developed photographs are plastered against the walls, more dispersed on the floor.

I reach up, plucking one of them from the clothespin that kept it fastened to the thread. I'm walking out of a downtown coffee shop, my head down and sunglasses shielding my eyes.

There is one of me inside the art museum, another of me jogging, several of me with the guys in various places. I notice a few of them are of me in the high school pool after hours. They span years back, and I'd be surprised if there were no less than five hundred pictures altogether.

It's a shrine of my existence, all documented through Lyra's artistic eye. I was the only person in every photograph she'd watched and devoted time to. My ego purrs beneath my skin, and I don't care if it's strange to admit that this is attractive.

I like that she's infatuated with me, that she only has eyes for me—haunts, exists, breathes just for me.

She is my obsessed angel, and I am her possessive god.

"What is it you see?" I break the silence as my fingers flutter across the rows of pictures. "When you look at these, at me."

Lyra is pressed against the wall, her feet clicking together as she tries to shrink from embarrassment, not fully understanding how thrilling it is to know I've always been the only one on her mind.

No one else stood a chance.

She is solely captivated by me, and I refuse to let her stop.

"A boy who was turned into a weapon before he knew what it meant," she hums, pulling a photo down of me when I was maybe fifteen. "I never understood how they called you a monster when you were always so beautiful. This was how I kept you close when I couldn't be near you."

I don't think I'll ever understand Lyra's perception of me. How she so easily saw past all the terror I inflicted to see the man I could be for her. Or maybe she never had a different impression. Maybe she had accepted me for the wicked man I was and wanted me, regardless.

Looking at Lyra feels a lot like looking into a mirror.

I flick the picture in my hand to the ground, walking towards her small figure. The hard red light contours the edges of her face, but she feels just as soft when I cup her cheek with my large hand.

"Do you know why I wanted to kill you, Lyra?" I ask, dragging my tongue across my bottom lip.

"Because you hated how I followed you around?" she offers, unsure of her answer.

I huff out a laugh, tracing the seam of her lips with my thumb. The plush skin is smooth against my finger. I try to remember a time when I wanted her dead because of how much I hated what she represented.

How could I have ever wanted her anything but alive and mine?

"My father told me when I was young that if I ever felt, I had to kill it. That was how I remained perfect." My other hand snakes around her waist, hauling her from the wall and into my body. "I wanted to kill what you stood for, what you did to me."

Lyra licks at my thumb. The velvet sensation of her tongue almost makes me groan. I remember the way it felt wrapped around my cock, rubbing against my shaft, making me come.

I draw my grip from her face to her neck, enclosing my fingers around her throat. My nose brushes against hers, and I can feel every single pant expelled from her lungs.

"Every single time I saw you, I'd stare at this pretty little throat and think about the bruises I'd wanted to leave just so everyone would know who owned you. I wanted to hold you so tightly your ribs cracked. When you spoke to anyone else, I was half tempted to rip them apart. I wanted to ruin you, end you, just because I knew I could never fucking have you."

She lifts her face, pushing towards my touch instead of pulling away from it, craving more. Her hardened nipples brush across my chest through the tight material of her dress, and I'm very close to checking if she's naked beneath it.

"You had me then; you just never realized it. You can have me

182

now." Lyra's sneaky fingers pull at the buttons of my shirt, undoing it casually. "Forever, if you want."

I squeeze her neck, making her gasp.

I smirk. "Do you know what I want, darling phantom?"

"What?"

I lean my head down so that my lips are a breath away from hers. I can savor being this close. Her heartbeat flutters against my fingertips, matching my own, and I'm not so sure we don't share a heart.

"I don't want to be perfect if it means I have to live without you."

Our mouths clash, a mixture of tongue and teeth as we chase the taste of one another, intent on filling our bodies up with each other. Slipping my tongue between her lips, I feel her fight against me until she eventually loses and I'm free to explore the inside of her mouth.

I'd lost my jacket earlier, but now her hands make quick work of my shirt, stripping it off my shoulders with rash movements. She glances down at her fingers as they tug it open and reveal my lean torso.

I let her stare, watch as her eyes trace the hard lines of my body.

My shirt falls to the floor, and I'm quick to even the score. My fingers weave through the folds and ripples in her dress, searching for any ounce of bare skin I can press my palms to. I grab at her hips, hiking the material up to her waist.

"Hold this up," I command. "Show me how obsessed your pussy is for me."

She takes her dress from me, keeping it just above her hips and showing me the thin scrap of material she calls underwear. I groan in the back of my throat at the dark spot at the center of the cotton.

Unable to help myself, I press two fingers against her cloth-covered slit, feeling her wetness seep through onto my skin. It's warm, sticky, and all Lyra. She whimpers when I graze her clit, jerking her hips towards me.

"Whiny, greedy thing," I pant through wet, swollen lips. "Your cunt is selfish. All it craves is me, isn't it? My fingers, my tongue, my cock?"

"I need you so badly." She pivots against my hand, following the slow circles I'm spinning against her core. "I ache for you everywhere."

My cock twitches behind my slacks, pressing painfully into my zipper, begging to sink inside of her to aid the ache she feels. I bite down on her bottom lip, sucking it into my mouth, rubbing it with my tongue before releasing her.

"You want me to fuck you, Lyra?" I slip my hand beneath her panties, greeted by her liquid center. The evidence of her arousal coats my palm as I cup her greedily.

"Please." She wraps an arm around my neck, her wet lips finding my neck. "I want you inside me."

I groan, tilting my head back to give her ample access to my skin. Lyra bites, nibbles, and sucks at my throat, moving towards my collarbone, no doubt leaving red welts as she goes.

Marking me. Claiming me.

"Earn it." I tangle my spare hand in the roots of her curls, jerking her suction-cup lips away from my neck so that she can look at me. "Grab the knife in my pocket. Make yourself bleed for me while I make you come."

Her eyes are bleary, glazed with desire, as if she'd injected some kind of lewd drug into her system and she's all blitzed out now. I drag a finger down her slit, teasing her entrance with my middle finger.

Lyra's hand moves until she's dipping into my pocket, her small fingers wrapping around the switchblade. When she pulls it out, holding it between us, I slide inside of her.

She cries out in pleasure, arching into me, her teeth holding her bottom lip captive as her warm inner walls clamp around my finger. God, she's beyond tight. It should be illegal for one human to feel this good.

Tapping into what control I have left when it comes to Little Miss Death, I remain still as I wait for her next move. I want her to show me how badly she craves me, what she's willing to do in order to have me.

"Go on, pet," I purr, swiping my thumb across the sensitive nub between her thighs. "Bleed for me."

Unafraid, fueled by lust, she flicks the blade open. Holding it in her right hand, making direct eye contact with me, she slides it across her left palm, refusing to break my gaze as she splits her skin.

A pool of crimson gathers in her hand, and my finger pushes deeper into her. I leisurely finger her tight hole, pushing in and out of her with torturously slow strokes.

She lifts her hand up, offering it up to my mouth. Desire stiffens in my gut, my cock pulsing as I bring my mouth to her palm. Drinking down her blood, I taste the metallic liquid that fills my mouth before it slides down my throat.

It spills down my chin, warm as it drips onto my chest.

My thumb continues to move in circles, eliciting a loud whimper from the back of Lyra's throat. Her pussy leaks onto my hand, making it much easier to add another finger, forcing her walls to stretch around me.

I swirl my tongue along the grooves in her palm before pulling my mouth away. Her eyes widen, and she pushes the knife back into my pocket just before she presses her lips to mine. Her nails dig into the tops of my shoulders, and I moan into her mouth.

We devour each other in a messy, chaotic way that is anything but soft. It's all-consuming, uncaring of technique, just desperate attempts to touch and kiss every single inch of open skin.

The speed of my hand increases, reaching that hidden spot that sends her over the edge. It only takes a few more sloppy thrusts before she's creaming all over my fingers, narrowing around me, and moaning so loud I feel the vibrations on my tongue.

I pull away from her, staring down at her red lips, my forehead dropping to rest against hers. "Good fucking girl."

She pants, lungs heaving as her body trembles with the aftershock of her orgasm. I prefer her messy like this, with lust infused in her features, panting and wanton, desperate for the release only I can give her.

Lyra's hand moves, the tip of her finger drawing across my skin. When I glance down, I find her painting hearts with the blood that drips from her veins.

Tiny bloody hearts.

They connect and leak down my chest, drying in messy strokes. She's covering me in them. Marking my skin with the proof of her obsession.

And I let her because I'm tipsy.

Blood drunk on a girl intent on loving me until it kills her.

Until the grave. That's what we are, have always been. The kind of connection that began in death and would last far beyond it.

Such a very grim, morbid declaration of love.

So very Lyra.

"A part of me will always be inside you," she insists, pressing a kiss to my skin right in the center of my sternum.

My mind screams, *You've been inside me far before this moment, darling.*

But my mouth stays shut, closed and denying access to those thoughts being spoken out loud.

Instead, I choose to kiss her again because I don't know how to explain what's happening inside of me right now. We become a lustful dance of clumsy kisses as I walk her backwards to one of the tables. Our bodies collide with the edge, knocking over bottles and pens.

I remove my mouth from hers, spinning her around so that I can force her onto the flat surface, facedown, cheek pushed against a slew of pictures of me. The dress she chose tonight is striking, hugs her in all the places it should, and is flattering from every angle, so it's unfortunate that I have to ruin it.

My greedy fingers grabs at the hem of the neckline, ripping the material apart until I hear the satisfying clicking of buttons pouring across the floor. I expose the miles of smooth, pale skin across her back.

"I liked that one," she mutters, glancing at me over her shoulder.

I'm quick to drop a kiss to the center of her spine, looking up at her with a hooded gaze. "I'll buy you a million more."

Whatever she wants, she will have it.

I'd give her the world if she asked me for it.

Together, we tug and jerk at the dress until it's discarded across the room, flung haphazardly behind me. I'm left to appreciate the sight of her bent over the table, miles of milky skin, soft muscles, flaws, and perfections all on display.

Just her in a pair of panties, waiting for me to take her any way

I want.

I run a finger down the length of her spine, grinning at the chill bumps that I leave behind. The sound of my belt coming undone makes her breath hitch, and I watch as she squirms with excitement. Her ass backs up, wiggling against the front of my slacks, rubbing up and down along my length, which is pleading for me to fuck her.

I let her play, tease herself as she grinds herself into my cock. I bring my hand down onto her ass, the pale skin turning bright pink. She jolts, a soft whimper tumbling from her lips.

"I've never seen anything so fucking pretty." My voice is heavy with desire as I yank her panties down her legs, letting them shackle her ankles. "You bent over, pussy dripping, begging for me to fuck you raw."

I shove my pants down just far enough to release my cock, the thick, angry tip dripping precome onto the contours of her ass. There isn't a force on this planet that could pull me away from her right now.

"Thatcher," she moans, broken and pleading, like she'll die if I don't fuck her this second.

Wrapping my fingers around the base of my cock, I stroke myself while watching her juices stream down the insides of her thighs, that tight cunt crying for me, begging for me.

I torture myself for a little longer, bringing the tip of my dick to her slit. Dragging it up and down, I cover myself in her arousal, the glistening pink of her pussy pulling me in.

Leaning my body over hers, pressing my chest to her back, I wrap my fingers around the front of her throat. I snap at her earlobe, my hot tongue flicking at the sensitive skin there.

"Needy, cock-obsessed little whore," I growl. My cock is forced onto the warmth of her body, making my hips jerk. "Tell me how bad you want it."

Lyra withers against me, her hands stretched in front of her as she claws at the table. "Please, I need you," she begs. "Please, *angel.*"

I sink my teeth into the junction of her neck and shoulder at her sweet voice calling me such a virtuous name. A name I have no right to own, but I swallow it down, eating it like I haven't touched food in days.

Standing up, tired of playing with her and tormenting myself, I line my cock up with her entrance, feeling the heat of her walls the moment I squeeze into her. I slide in inch by inch until I feel myself bottom out, both of us groaning in tandem at the relief. The pressure of my fingers digging into her hip bones is enough to leave welts.

Everything is heightened, every nerve ending lit on fire. My head falls back, relishing in the feeling of her hot, slick walls hugging and contorting around me. It was like she was made for me.

Overrun by lust, I grab the knife from my slacks and trace the ridge of her spine while her pussy throbs around my length. I hold the tip of the blade just between her shoulder blades.

It's primal, the way I dig the sharp edge into her flesh, carving the letter *T* into the softness of her back. She screams, pushing her ass into me as blood seeps from the mark.

"It hurts." She moans around the words.

"You can take it, baby. You're doing so good for me, pretty thing."

There is a carnal possessiveness that awakens in me at the sight of her bleeding in the shape of my initial. She's been branded, claimed.

She's mine. All fucking mine.

"So big," she grumbles, holding the side of her face against the table. "So full."

I grin in sadistic pleasure, wanting her to be so full of me she won't be able to walk without feeling me inside of her. Drawing out all the way, I give no warning before slamming back home.

The potency of my thrust has her breath catching, a ragged groan slipping past her teeth. But she sits still like the good girl she is, staying put, just as she should.

"Is it too much, pet? Are you too full?" I coo, patronizing her as my hips pull back before driving back into her cunt.

She shakes her head. "No, no. I can take more."

Each thrust is rougher than the last, the sound of skin slapping and heady moans growing. I look down, watching my slippery shaft impale her pussy, seeing the way she grips me like she never wants to let go.

It sets my blood on fire, and I release her hip bone, snaking my hand up her back until I get a fistful of her hair. Her body arches as I jerk her upward until my chest is flush against hers.

The sweat coating our bodies mingles together, and my warm breath is in her ear.

"You were made for my cock." I slam into her again, feeling the ripple of her ass against my stomach. "This sweet, tight pussy was made to take every single inch."

With my lips pressed to the dip underneath her jaw, I can feel how erratic her pulse is. Lyra is so close; I can feel her tell. The way her tight channel quivers, clamping down like a vise. My free hand goes to her front, two fingers finding her clit.

The table bangs loudly against the wall as I rub her bud in rhythm with my grueling plunge. It fuels her cries of bliss, her hips crashing back into mine, meeting every single drive.

I'm incessant, barely staggering, as my head buzzes with ecstasy. I can feel my balls tighten, my orgasm cresting up my spine.

"Drown my cock," I groan. "Come for me, baby."

Lyra quakes as she comes, trembling and falling over the cliff. Her body spills over my shaft, soaking me. She stiffens around me, refusing to let me pull out of her tight little body. I have no choice but to spill inside of her.

My cock twitches, a jagged groan ripping from my chest, and empties ropes and ropes of my come deep inside of her. I keep thrusting inside her, pushing my seed as far as it will go, pouring so much that I can feel it leak out of her cunt, seeping around me.

Everything feels foggy, a haze of release washing over me as my forehead drops to her shoulder. My legs shake as I pull out of her, feeling her rotate beneath me so that she can catch my drooping body.

Her face buries against the crook of my neck, nuzzling into me. I hum as her hot breath brushes against my damp skin. Our chests are pressed together, both of our breathing trying to level out.

"Your heart is racing," she whispers, placing a hand over my chest as if to steady the thrumming in my chest.

I laugh, pieces of my damp hair falling in front of my face.

"No one told you? I don't have one."

She smiles, bright and blinding. All Lyra and all mine.

Her lips kiss the hickeys on my neck, and she preens beneath me, so proud of her claim on me, admiring the dried bloody hearts still staining my skin.

My chest aches uncomfortably when she speaks again.

"You can take mine."

EIGHTEEN
fate

unknown

He loves her.

I saw it in his eyes tonight when he thought no one was watching them.

I can't blame my sweet Lyra. It's not her fault that she is being deceived by him. I've waited too long, and now she believes Thatcher is her one true love.

She doesn't understand. She just doesn't see it yet.

But she will.

Soon, she will see how we were always meant to be together. That there isn't a more perfect match. Thatcher was merely my placeholder until the stars aligned for us.

When she finally understands, she will be apologetic. She will feel so very guilty for making me watch the two of them together. Lyra will make up for every second she was in his arms and not mine.

Because she will see that we were made for one another.

There is no one better for her than me.

History will not repeat itself this time. I will not lose her to another Pierson.

Not this time. They do not win this time.

This time, I get the girl.

NINETEEN
the mourning of a rose

thatcher

Mourning is a difficult thing.

It's a stain that never goes away. The sting of loss fades, but you're still left with this laceration that doesn't scar. It just continues to weep, and you accept that.

There comes a time when you've lost so many people that all you are now is one massive wound. All you can do is bleed for the ones you've lost and hope you don't die of blood loss.

May Pierson deserved a better life than she had.

She deserved a better son, a better grandson. She was far too lovely of a woman to go through her life with such little affection. May deserved a family who hugged, laughed, and spent evenings with her in the garden.

I was warmer to her than I'd been to anyone else, and yet our relationship was still cold.

When I woke up this morning, Lyra was draped across my chest, her body attached to mine like a spider monkey, hips straddling mine and legs tucked at my sides.

We must've fallen asleep in the living room after she demanded to work on her project now that she had the spiders to fill it. The couch was ridiculously uncomfortable, but when my eyes had adjusted to the morning light, I withstood the pain for a few moments. A few prolonged instances where I admired her while she slept.

Lyra is not a sweet sleeper. She does not look angelic or peaceful. Instead, she looks more like a wild animal.

Bushels of hair sweeping in every direction, so fluffy and curled that it's almost hard to see her face. She sleeps with her mouth open, and there isn't an alarm clock in the world loud enough to wake her.

But she'd been beautiful.

In a chaotic, feral way.

That same unfamiliar ache ricocheted in my chest, which had been more than enough to get me moving. It made me panic.

I'd carefully detached her from my body, tucking a pillow beneath her head and a blanket over her legs before disappearing from the cabin.

My plan was to go for a run through the woods around Lyra's home, but I'd just kept running until I found myself here, at the gates of my family cemetery, out of breath and covered in an obscene amount of sweat.

I'm not sure why I'm here or what possessed me to run this far in the early morning hours, but if I had to guess?

Maybe because I knew the only person who could explain what was happening to me would be May. I might've been able to tell her about this sudden onset of what feels like the worst case of heartburn I've ever experienced, and she'd have an answer for how to treat it.

The wet ground makes a horrible squelching sound as I walk through the graves of my ancestors. Everyone with the Pierson last name, dating back to the man who'd founded this town, was buried here.

I weave through until I find the newest tombstone. A tall angel statue sits atop the grave's base, and I can't help but smirk thinking about how much she would've hated this gaudy thing.

When I was fourteen, my ninth grade English teacher publicly ridiculed Silas in front of an entire class of students. He'd gone over the misconceptions in his paper out loud and essentially told him it did not matter how much money his father had, it would not change the fact he had schizophrenia and would never amount to anything because of it.

I left a dead deer on her front porch, guts strewn across the entry steps and a simple painted message in the animal's blood on the door.

You're next.

I'd been more than delighted when she put in her resignation the very next morning.

That idea, or at least the seed of the idea, had come from May.

Now, she didn't specifically tell me to leave a cut-up animal on the lady's doorstep, but she had identified what was wrong with me the moment I came home from school that day.

My friend had been wrong, and it was okay for me to be angry, she'd said.

It was the first time anyone had recognized an emotion in me and let me know it was okay to feel it.

Squatting down, I run my hand across the tombstone. A rose lies perfectly still on the grave marker. The grass beneath my feet is finally growing. The earth takes no time for remembrance; it simply continues as if our grief does not exist.

I don't believe in speaking out loud to those that have passed. Wherever they go, I don't think they can hear us, and if they can, what good would my words do?

However, just this once.

This one time, for May, I will do what I should have done while she was alive.

"I wish you'd ask me to play something that tells you how I've been." I trace the grooves of her name in the stone. "I'd play 'Clair de lune' 'cause I know it was your favorite, and I would hope it would tell you that I miss you."

Death is an unavoidable fate. But if anyone deserved more time, maybe even immortality, it would've been May.

"I'll find who did this to you, May. I was not the perfect grandson, but this? This I can promise you."

I grieve for her, just as I had grieved for Rosemary. I'm angry that two people who warranted a better ending never got it. It makes

199

no sense to me that people like me could still breathe and people like Rosie and May would never feel their own heart beat again.

Scooping up the flower from its place, I roll the thornless rose between my fingers. Whoever had left this behind must have done so only a few hours ago. Bringing the petals to my nose, I can smell the freshness of the flower, as if it had only been plucked from the bush hours ago.

The floral, sweet aroma burns my nose. The scent plucks at my memory, swirling thoughts around that were buried long ago. My stomach lurches, and suddenly, I drift from my grandmother's tombstone and enter a memory I'd locked away.

"Roses each have their own unique smell." His voice is like charcoal. "Just as every woman carries a specific fragrance. Even in death, that deserves to be recognized."

My fingers are raw, the palms of my hand burned from too much exposure to chemicals. I can see new blisters forming where calluses would eventually grow once they healed. I'd used too much bleach tonight, but I had no other choice.

There had been far too much blood for just one jug.

My father's gloved hand reaches inside the bucket just to his left before he spreads the contents across the top layer of freshly laid soil. Homemade fertilizer for the brand-new rosebush in the estate gardens.

"This will bloom into a rich apricot color and pale towards the edges," he tells me, as if I care what color the flower will turn. "And the smell..."

Henry trails off, lifting his head to the sky as if to take a deep breath, recalling a scent from long ago.

"Will smell just like tea." He presses his hands into the soil. "It's the first thing I notice about a woman. How she smells, how to pair it with the perfect rose."

I look down at the white tag in my small hands. "Lidia" is scrawled in messy script across the material. I'd seen many tags just like this, but the name was always different.

Jennifer.

Yolanda.

Nina.

Dawn.

All women he'd turned into his new favorite flower. Women I'd seen hang from the rafters of the garden shed.

I knew nothing about them. Not their favorite color or if they had children. If they were scared of the dark like I was or cut the crust of their sandwiches. They were strangers to me in life and in death.

But I know what their blood looks like. What it feels like in my hands, how it burns my nose, and the smell alone is what wakes me up every night with cold sweats. How is it possible to know the inside of someone's body so intimately but still know nothing other than their name?

I swallow the lump in my throat, waiting for him to finish. When he's done, he extends his hand, the inside of his gloves stained pink. Walking forward, I place the name tag in his hand and watch as he tethers it to a small stick poking from the ground.

Henry stands up, dusting his hands and turning to look down at me. The wind blows, brushing my hair in front of my face, and when he reaches to push it out of my eyes, I step back, avoiding his touch.

"These roses are my design." He looks out into the garden. "But you will be my legacy. My perfect creation, Alexander. Do you remember my very first rule?"

I look down at the ground of freshly laid soil, the last resting place of a woman named Lidia. Her family will never know what happened to her in that shed. They will never know the details of the cleanup or that my father turned her into homemade fertilizer for his rose garden.

They can never give her a proper burial because besides the limb he leaves for the town to find, no one will ever find the rest of her body.

"Never speak about what lies beneath the roses."

The flower falls from my hand, tumbling onto the wet earth, and I have the sudden urge to vomit. I press my hand into my stomach, bending a knee. I count to three. I take deep breaths. I count to ten. I take deep breaths. I count to twenty-five. I take deep breaths.

But the unshakable nausea persists. Memory after memory slams into the front of my mind with an unrelenting demand to be remembered. A dam had shattered; the box I kept it all in had exploded, and now I'm left with moments I never wanted to recall.

The wind howls, trees groaning with the force. A thunderstorm is on the horizon. The blue sky is turning a sickly gray, the crackle of lightning illuminating clouds in the distance.

I thought when they lugged Henry Pierson away to prison, that was the last of his game. He had no more control over me the moment they slammed the bars of his cell shut.

I was free of him. Of his rules.

Of course he'd dig his claws into me from prison. Find a way to invade my life from a distance. The narcissist needs to know he still affects me, needs to remind me who made me the man I am today. I am his marvelous achievement, his pet, the prodigy. He can't just leave me unscathed.

Henry demands control, and he'd lost it once he went to prison.

This is his way of amending that power.

He refuses to rot without making sure I know that if not for him? I wouldn't exist.

Roses.

The Imitator's only distinct pattern difference from my father's is the roses he leaves with the body parts.

The only person who knows what Henry Pierson did with the bodies of those women is me. The police never found them, never made him crack enough to reveal it.

It was just him and I.

Our final little secret.

I'd only kept it as leverage so that if something like this were to happen? I would threaten to expose where each woman was left to decompose. His burial, those bodies? It was his last thing he had over the police. Once he lost it, it would be over for him.

I'd been so blind. The answer had been staring at me this entire time, right in plain sight. The Imitator was playing games with all of us, but the flower? That wasn't his doing.

My father knows exactly who the copycat killer is.

The body parts, the notes left in the skin, those were for the police. Those were for the boys.

The roses? Henry told him to leave those for me.

He knew I'd figure it out.

And now he has left me no choice.

It's the last option I have if I want the people around me to make it out alive.

It's time to pay daddy dearest a visit.

TWENTY
execution

Thatcher

Thatcher:

> I know how to find our copycat killer.

Alistair:

> What did you find?

Rook:

> Me too. Sinclair Manor.

Thatcher:

> Sorry, Van Doren. It's not Easton.

Rook:

I mean this, from the bottom of my heart, fuck right off.

Alistair:

Do you have proof?

Thatcher:

No. But I can get it.

Alistair:

What do you need?

Thatcher:

A distraction.

Alistair:

What kind exactly?

Thatcher:

The kind that can get me in and out of prison undetected.

Rook:

Ohhhh hell fucking yes.

Alistair:

Rook do not even think about it.

Rook removed Alistair from group chat.

Rook:

Now that Dad's gone.

Let's fucking torch this place.

TWENTY-ONE
midnights and crimson

Lyra

"The only way to get rid of temptation is to yield to it."

*Did this help motivate you in your pursuit of me?
Or is it highlighted only because you think it sounds
important?—T.*

I smirk as I sink further into the tub, my neck resting on the edge as water wets the hair at the back of my head. Unruly pieces of hair have fallen down from the messy bun, but I don't have the energy to wash it today.

Instead, I pull the cap off my pen with my teeth, writing just below Thatcher's neat script.

*You flatter yourself far too much. Not every quote I
like ties into you.—L*

Thatcher's reannotation of some of my favorite books is quickly becoming one of my favorite ways to pass the time. The constant back-and-forth along empty spaces of book pages, his snippy little remarks beneath my own private thoughts, or his own highlighted lines.

When he'd finish reading a book I'd already annotated, he'd slip it beneath my door, like a secret message, and when I was done defending all my favorite quotes or my reasoning, I'd place it on his nightstand.

*"The world is changed because you are made of ivory and gold.
The curves of your lips rewrite history."*

"To be seen as ivory and gold"

—that's what I'd written on the page years ago in this copy of The Picture of Dorian Gray.

The world is changed because you are made of midnights and crimson. The curves of your lips rewrite my purpose.—T.

My toes wiggle beneath the water, the smell of my cherry blossom bubble bath wafting into my nose. I blame the aromatic scent on the reason my eyes sting with tears.

It feels like we're strangers who'd picked up the same novel, unalike and unknowing of each other's faces but connected so deeply through these little notes we'd written between the lines. I'd found out so many new things about him, things he probably never noticed he was sharing.

The kind of thoughts I never would have known by simply watching him. Knowing Thatcher at this depth is unlike anything I'd ever experienced, and I never wanted to stop living it.

"I want to make Romeo jealous. I want the dead lovers of the world to hear our laughter and grow sad. I want a breath of our passion to stir dust into consciousness, to wake their ashes into pain."

I'd left little hearts around the quote.

This is a novel about a narcissist whose self-obsession killed him. And this is what you underline? You're an incurable romantic, darling. How did I become your fixation?—T.

I snort unattractively. It would have been much easier to fall in love with literally anyone else. But I don't want easy. I've never wanted easy.

I want a love that's worth the fight. Consumption, unhealthy entanglement. The kind where you can't really tell where one person ends and the other begins. I want love that hurts because it's real.

I'd always known Thatcher would be the only person who'd give that to me.

Careful, this annotation battle feels very romantic. I might be turning you, angel.—L

"Do you ever sleep?"

I jump a little, looking at the door to see Thatcher there. His mussed, messy hair tells me he just woke up, and I've never seen anything more adorable.

"Were you born a nocturnal creature?" A yawn takes over his body before he runs a hand down his face. "Should I worry about you sprouting wings and turning into a bat?"

I look over from my bath, tilting the book over my mouth to hide my smile.

His shoulder is pressed into the doorframe, arms crossed in front of his bare chest. Thatcher is only wearing a pair of tight black boxers, the material stretched across his strong thighs. My eyes practically lick the contours of his abs.

My heart soars at the pretty, purplish-red bruises that decorate his collarbone and chest. I feel a little guilty for tainting someone so perfect, but I love that they show the world he's mine.

The sleepy look on his face seems so vulnerable.

My nipples harden beneath the warm water, stomach tingling with desire.

I'm insatiable.

Before he touched me, I wouldn't have considered myself a sexual person. I mean, I'd never been kissed before Thatch. But now that I know what he feels like, how he makes me feel, I'll never be able to get enough.

"Did you have a nightmare?" I ask, closing the book after putting the pen between the pages to keep my place. I sit up a little further, the cold air brushing across the top of my breasts as I reach forward to sit the book on the lid of the toilet.

"They're just dreams, Lyra." He rolls his eyes, once again denying how little he sleeps because of the night terrors that plague his dreams.

Turning my body, I place my arms on the edge of the tub and rest my chin along them, watching as he walks further into the bathroom, scooping the book from the seat and flipping through the pages.

"Will you tell me about them?"

"My dreams?"

"Yeah."

"Why?"

I sigh, rolling my eyes. He can be so difficult sometimes. Everything in his mind has some twisted ulterior motive. As if the idea of someone just wanting to be kind isn't plausible.

"Because I care about you, Thatcher." I let my head fall to the side of my arm, leaning against the edge of the tub. "I want to know these things about you. I want to know about your dreams. Why you left yesterday morning like someone had set you on fire and came back drenched in sweat. I know this is hard for you to understand, but you don't have to deal with everything alone anymore."

He thumbs through the pages of The Picture of Dorian Gray, the tattered copy cracked at the spine and pages tinted. I let him sit in his silence, allowing him to choose how he wants to respond.

If he doesn't want to tell me yet, I'll understand. I won't push him to give me more than he's ready to give. You can't demand a lion turn into a zebra. I can't demand a boy who knows nothing of love to navigate a relationship flawlessly as a man.

When he remains silent, I reach my hand out, tracing my mother's ring on his pinkie finger with gentle strokes.

"I'm going to see my father."

The admission makes my head rear back, and I flinch at how those words attack my defenses. The water swishes around me at the sudden movement.

"What?" I choke on the words as they fall out. "Why?"

I hadn't been expecting that. I'd thought he would say something about his dreams. Not this.

How long had it been since Thatcher had laid eyes on his father? Spoken to him? Replied to a letter he'd sent? The very last image he had of the man was being shoved into the back of a police car.

"Not by choice," he corrects pointedly, as if that is going to reassure me. "I went to May's grave yesterday morning. I realized something there—Henry knows who the Imitator is. If I had to guess, he involved himself just to get close to me again. Regardless, he might be our only option in ending this entire thing."

My heart sinks to my feet.

Fear rushes through me, and my fight or flight seems to kick in. I won't let him do this.

He can't do this.

"Okay." I nod. "So send Alistair or Rook."

"The only person he will talk to is me." He turns so that he's completely facing me in the bath. "He did this to get my attention; sending them would be pointless. I know my father."

Panic rises into my throat, the sudden urge to vomit or scream hitting me like a barreling wave. Tears sting the corners of my eyes as I recall the look in Henry's eyes the night he killed my mother.

How brutal they looked. Cold, unforgiving, they weren't even human. Thatcher's had never, ever looked like that. Not once. They've been harsh, sharp, cold even, but nothing compared to the raw lack of empathy that night.

"I'll go, then."

Thatcher's eyes turn into slits, his jaw tightening, the muscle in his cheek twitching. His voice is so dark it makes a chill echo across my skin. "Over my dead body."

The water around me is steaming, but I feel so very cold. Tears slip from my eyes, the back of my throat constricting. I have so much I want to say, yet the only thing that comes out is "You can't go."

Seeing the distress on my face, he leans forward, eyebrows pinched together as he loops his pointer finger around a loose curl, tugging on it softly.

"He's not going to kill me," he assures me. "You're giving him far too much credit, darling phantom. I'll be fine."

"I'm not worried about that." I chew my bottom lip, my head shaking forcefully. The ache throughout my chest is so tangible, this emotional pain causing such a visceral physical reaction.

"Then why are you so adamant I don't go?"

"I just—" I pause, not sure how to say this, feeling a little crazy. "I just got you. Finally, after all these years, I have you. I've peeled layer after layer. And now I've made it inside here."

I lean up onto my knees, exposing the upper half of my torso to the chilly air. My nipples harden immediately, but I ignore my nudeness. Instead, I poke at his chest, just above his heart.

"I'm in here now, and I'm scared of who you'll be when you come out of there, Thatcher."

Henry had done irrevocable damage to Thatch. Unforgivable, awful things. The man made his child feel like he had no emotions, killed his youth, and turned him into a killing machine.

The closer Thatcher gets to me, the further away he drifts from Henry's authority. What will he be after facing his father after all these years?

His hand falls to cup my cheek, rubbing at the tears streaking across my cheek. I push into his touch, shutting my eyes as my body shakes with panic.

I can't let him do this. We can't go through this.

"Henry Pierson does not control who I am anymore," he replies, his tone adamant, as if he's trying to make himself believe it.

I'm not sure who needs more convincing, me or himself.

"Who I am, who I become, that has nothing to do with him anymore."

"He is the reason I lost everything. I will not lose you to him."

A nasty streak of anger zips through me. I have never hated anyone the way I hate Henry Pierson. It would be a joy to watch him die. My hand curls around Thatch's wrist, tightening around him until my nails begin to dig into the weak skin at his pulse.

"I swear, Thatcher, if he is the reason I lose you, I will kill him. Do you understand that?" I urge, pleading with him to comprehend what I'm capable of doing if something happens to him. "I will, do you hear me? I will—"

His movements stall my words.

He stands, lifting his leg and stepping into the water with me. Long, lean arms encircle my waist as he sits himself in the bath, and a staggering sense of safety takes over. The water sloshes out on the sides, but we ignore it as he hauls me into his lap, arranging us so I'm straddling his waist and his back is resting comfortably against the edge of the tub.

"Easy, Little Miss Death." He drops his forehead to mine, his fingers rubbing circles into my lower back. "Knives away. I'm not going anywhere. I'm right here."

My fingers curl into the hair at the nape of his neck, tugging at the strands. Our breath mingles together as I inhale every exhale of his, wanting to only breathe the air he provides.

"Don't do this to me, please," I beg.

My body thrums, and I press my weight into his lap, craving the closeness that comes from him being inside of me. I want beneath his fucking skin at all times. I need him to get lost in me right now, forget all about going to see his scum father and never think of it again.

"I'm doing this for you, Lyra," he mutters, hands sliding down until he's grabbing my ass with both hands. "If we want to make it out of this, I don't have another choice."

I can't seem to stop the tears from flowing down my face. Maybe it's a cry I've needed to let out for a while now. But my sorrow does not tamp down my want for him. My breasts push into his broad chest, bare skin against bare skin.

He's going to go regardless of my pleas. There is nothing that will change his mind once he decides something. He's far too stubborn for his own fucking good.

"If you forget who you are in there," I whisper, swirling my hips against the bulge in his boxers, "remember what it feels like to be with me."

The left side of his mouth tilts up. "How could I ever forget?"

My lips steal any words we had left. It's not feverish or rushed; it's a tender kiss, one that says I want to memorize every groove of your mouth, I want to protect these fragile pieces of you that are too sharp for others to carry, but I have gloves now, and you can't cut me. Even if they sliced my palms, it would be okay.

For him, I'd bleed. For him, it's worth it.

I taste the salt of my own tears as I lick at the seam of his lips, plunging into his mouth and tasting him. My hips grind along his hardening length, and I moan as his thick shaft brushes against the bundle of nerves between my thighs.

Our hands roam, bodies dancing in a waltz of need. His lips move to the corner of my mouth, across my jaw, and down my throat. I feel his hands cup the underside of my breasts, pushing them up as his tongue sweeps across my nipples.

Thatcher's hot, wet mouth sucks gently on the bud while I roll my hips into his. He takes his time on each breast, massaging them with the tips of his fingers and biting down on the sensitive flesh before licking away the sting of pain.

I want to keep him far away from his father, protect him from the hurt, away from the harrowing influence Henry still has over him. I crave it, even if it is unrealistic, and I let that need fuel my lust.

My blood burns, simmering in my lower stomach. I let my fingers sink into the water, jerking the band of his boxers down until I can wrap my hand around his throbbing cock.

He groans into my skin, squeezing me tighter. I bite down on the hickeys already present, swirling my tongue as my thumb rubs across the tip of his sensitive head.

Together, we shove his boxers down enough to expose him fully, my body shifting to hover just above his waist.

"Ride me," Thatcher demands. "Let me feel you take every inch of me inside that obsessed pussy."

His words crack against my skin like a whip, making the dull ache in my core intensify to an almost painful point. Reaching beneath me, I curl my hand around the base of his shaft, stroking him a few times before dragging the head of his cock through my slippery folds.

I shiver when he catches against my entrance, the slow teasing killing both of us. Finally putting us both out of our misery, I let my weight fall, sinking onto his length and taking him all the way to the hilt in one go.

The undeniable fullness of him makes me whimper. I can feel him everywhere, all the way to my toes. My stomach tightens at the completeness. I savor the feeling of this for just a few moments longer, clenching tight around him before setting a slow pace.

Thatcher's fingers grip my hips, guiding me up and down his shaft. The water laps over the tub's edge, spilling onto the floor, swaying around us as he thrusts upward into my body.

"So fucking sweet," he groans, tilting his head back and exposing the threads of veins cording his neck. "So tight."

I lean into him, my hands resting on his shoulders to keep my balance. When he looks back at me, our faces touch, lips just inches apart but not moving to kiss one another. I rock my hips, working his cock in and out of me as we breathe each other in, exchanging moans and gasps.

"Such a pretty little thing. Such a good girl for me, darling."

This feels different from the other times.

With Thatcher, it's urgent, desperate, brutal, us chasing the high that comes from each other's bodies, but this? It feels sorta bittersweet. We cling to one another, afraid of losing the warmth. We're quiet groans and pounding hearts.

"You feel so fucking good," I murmur, lacing my fingers into his hair. "I never want to stop."

I ride him quicker, and he meets my thrusts from beneath, rutting into me. My breasts bounce in tandem with my riding. His lips ghost across my cheek, my eyelashes fluttering against his forehead.

"Then don't."

Biting down on my lower lip, my thighs burning, I continue our pace until my orgasm creeps up on me like a secret. It's not an explosion like last time—no, this is a soft wave that crests over me, sending me into bliss just as hard.

I feel it everywhere, the coil in my stomach snapping as my inner walls clamp down on him. I whimper against his skin, eyes shut tight as my body stiffens in pleasure. Thatcher presses my hips down harder, pumping into me with sloppy thrusts.

His thighs smack against my ass as he fucks me through my climax, coaxing wave after wave of pleasure, drowning me in warmth. My clit rubs against his toned stomach as he plunges into me, the overstimulation almost too much to handle.

"Come for me again," he groans, breathless.

I circle my arms around his neck, burying my face into the crook of his neck as I shake my head.

217

"I don't think I can," I whisper, the buzzing against my clit intensifying.

He wraps an arm around my waist, forcing me to stay put as he heaves into me. The slapping of wet skin echoes in the bathroom, his heart beating against my own as my nails dig into his back.

"Be a good girl, baby. Give me one more," he coos, hitting that spot deep inside of me. "I wanna feel your pretty cunt tighten around me. Milk my come from me."

I let out a choked sob of bliss into his shoulder as he fucks me harder, stimulating my clit in the process. It's all so much, too much, that I have no choice but to fall over the edge again.

"That's it," he bites into my shoulder. "You feel my cock begging your pussy to come? You're so very sweet for me, pet. Such a pretty girl coming all over me."

It's an electric current that buzzes through me, my pussy tensing and releasing several times as I come again. Thatcher practically growls in my ear, my name an exasperated sigh on his lips, thrusting into me one more time before spilling into me. I've never been more thankful for birth control in my life.

I lean back so that I can look at him, so focused on the aftershock of my orgasm that what I see almost takes my breath away. His eyebrows are furrowed, and his tempting lips open slightly as he lets himself get lost in pleasure. He is none of the things the world paints him as in this moment. He isn't a monster or a killer—he looks angelic, trapped in euphoria.

Our bodies come down together, regulating our breathing as we sink into exhaustion with one another. I slump against his chest, and he makes no move to pull out of me.

We just exist with each other like this.

Before I can think better of it, I speak.

"I think I knew you in a past life. Do you think that's crazy?"

My fingertips trace the lines of his collarbone.

"No." I can hear the smile in his voice. "But me wanting to know you in every life after this one might be."

TWENTY-TWO
a mild distraction

rook

"Where have you been?"

"Hell."

Alistair stares at me, unamused as per usual.

No amount of Briar's pussy is going to make this dude any less a pain in my ass.

Carrying in the last two cans of gasoline, I look around at the empty lobby of the historic building. Town hall has been here since the founding of Ponderosa Springs. It's the perfect victim, remote enough that it won't spread to another building, but it also sits atop a small hill that looks over the town. One of the very first buildings, the Van Doren family had built it with their bare hands.

We are a legacy of judges and lawyers. This is our heritage inside these walls.

It feels poetic that I'm the one about to burn it down.

"Are we sure your dad is going to hold up his end of this?" he asks, picking up a can of lighter fluid from my pile of flammable liquid that sits on the floor in front of us.

"If he wants to keep his job, he will." I bite down on the match between my teeth. "I doubt they'll let him take the judge's seat if everyone finds out about the years of abuse."

It had been a very long time since I asked my father for anything. I suppose this doesn't even count, considering it's blackmail. But we need to get Thatcher inside Rimond Penitentiary, and unfortunately, the only person I know with those kinds of connections is Theodore Van Doren, Ponderosa Springs' most notorious district attorney.

We needed an in, so I got us one.

"He's not thrilled to be helping us, and Thatcher was prickly as fuck about having to work with Theo, all things considered."

Alistair's shoulders tighten, and I watch him bristle.

"You didn't tell him why we're doing this, did you?"

What exactly does a guy gotta do to get some trust around here?

"I'm not fucking stupid, jackass. All my father knows is that Thatcher needed to get a visit with Henry. He doesn't even know about this"—I wiggle the jug in his face for emphasis—"part of the plan."

I obviously had to share that Thatcher was alive and I knew where he was located. Which my father could easily turn over to the police, but they don't know him like I do.

He sees himself as righteous; he only does immoral acts in the name of his God. If I tainted that image he's painted for himself, he'd waste away into fucking nothing. Which is tempting, regardless of if he keeps quiet or not, but I've been working on forgiveness.

Whoosah and all that shit.

"And if he says fuck his reputation and turns Thatch in? Or doesn't follow through? Then what, Rook?" Alistair crosses his arms in front of his chest, pushing me. "Involving Theo was a bad fucking idea. I told you that."

I grind my teeth together, annoyed at his bitching. I am not in the mood to fight with him. We have shit to do, and us throwing punches isn't on the list. It would be much easier if I didn't get why he was so anxious.

We refuse to lose another friend, a brother in every sense of the word besides blood.

"Then we kill him," I say explicitly.

He thinks I'm above killing the man who beat the shit out of me for years? Who birthed this desire to hurt? Skewed my vision until I genuinely believed the scars I wore were payment for all my sins?

"I'm doing everything I can to end this. We had to take the risk, Alistair. For Silas, for Rosie. I want Sage safe, and she won't ever be until this is over."

As long as Stephen and Easton Sinclair are alive and free, Sage will struggle. Sleepless nights, bad dreams, no eating. I watch her day in and day out, the way she slips on a strong, pretty mask for the world.

But I see her when we're alone and how the fire burning within her is shivering to embers, withering away by the second, and it's fucking killing me. Her eyes are sad, and they don't burn as bright. At night? She clings to me like it's the last time she'll ever touch me, every single night.

Sage is so skeptical of the future it's eating her present alive.

There isn't a thing in the world I wouldn't risk for her, including myself. I would blaze through hell to get back to her if they tried to take her. I want to get her out of this toxic place, push her to chase her dreams and breathe all the lives they stole back into her.

I want everything for Sage Donahue because she deserves it. I'd grab the world with my bare hands, burnt and bloody, for her.

"We have twenty minutes to torch this place," I remind him. "I need you to place the gas cans around the room, but don't fucking open them until I come back."

"What are you going to do?"

"I'm going to work my way from the back, burning as I go. So be prepared to run."

I move towards the hallway, the smell of gasoline making my blood heat. My fingers twitch at my sides, knowing in a few short minutes, this entire building will be up in flames. There won't be a single resident in town that wouldn't see this blaze. This is my arena. Fire is my weapon, and I am more than ready to wield it.

Alistair grabs my shoulder, keeping me in place.

"Don't catch yourself on fire." His face is stone, but the voice is all stern and dad-like. Always looking out for me, even when I hate it.

A wicked smile grows on my face, the matches in my pocket practically singing.

"Lighten up, Caldwell. This is the fun part."

alistair

I'd made Briar a promise months ago. One that I'm regretting as the smell of fire builds and I finish placing all the closed cans of lighter fluid and gasoline around the lobby.

I swore to little thief that I'd make it out of this.

In the moment, listening to her talk about our future and what she thinks it will look like when we leave this place, it had been easy to promise I'd live to see it. So fucking easy, just like everything else is when I'm with her.

I want to be the man who keeps his word, but I knew what I'd do if worse came to worse.

I wouldn't flinch to sacrifice myself if it meant she made it out unscathed, alive. Briar, she's strong, she'd survive my death, she'd move on eventually and find the happiness she's earned.

If anything happened to her though? I would not say the same for me.

I'd always been comfortable in the darkness; I'd been born in it. But now? I don't know how to live in a world without the light she gives.

My fingers flex. Not being in control of my fate irritates the shit out of me.

I glance at my phone, checking our time, watching it dwindle by. I'm pissed that this was our only option, seeking help from Rook's piece-of-shit father. The only good thing that could come from Theo Van Doren opening his mouth would be that I finally get to crack his neck beneath my shoe.

Looking down the hallway, I see gray smoke billowing beneath the closed doors. It climbs the walls, blazing vines that work their way to the ceiling. Sweat gleams across my forehead as the temperature of the building rises. My lungs are burning for fresh air.

I'm two seconds from going to find the pyro when he kicks

through the doors of the town council meeting room, a puff of smoke following him through, a roaring fire just behind him.

With his hoodie up and the black fabric mask covering his face from the nose down, he blends in with the smoke as if they're the same thing.

"We gotta go." He walks to the corners of the lobby, unscrewing the caps on the closed gas cans I placed around the room.

"You think?" I mutter sarcastically, looking at how low the visibility is.

We move towards the exit, knowing we have about five minutes before every available police officer and firefighter is busting inside of this shithole. My hand grabs the doorknob, twisting it in my fingers.

"Don't!" Rook shouts from behind me, tossing a cap at the back of my head. "It's like you're trying to fucking kill me. When we open that, the air is going to light this place like a motherfucker. Let me finish this, then we can open it together."

My molars grind together, jaw tightening. If he blows me up, I swear to fuck... When he's done, he jogs to the door, taking a deep breath and giving me the go-ahead to open the door.

"Meet you at the Styx?"

I nod. "At the Styx."

I shove the door open, and I feel him take off in a dead sprint.

"Go, go, go..." he mutters, sprinting off the front steps of the building and heading towards the plush front lawn, where a small fountain sits.

Sensing his urgency, I follow suit, running after him. When my feet hit the grass, the rattling of the explosion behind me forces me to the ground. The waves of heat pouring from behind me make me cringe.

I'd seen a lot of his fires before, but they'd never been like this.

The sound of glass shattering and wood splintering echoes. I rotate, my ears ringing loudly, seeing the town hall wrapped in a hue of orange and red. Vengeful flames lick the sides of the building, consuming the roof.

It's one giant middle finger to the people of this rotting town.

"You think that's a big enough distraction?" Rook smirks as he

225

watches on the ground next to me, lying flat and inhaling the fresh air.

As if they heard his voice, the sound of police sirens whines in the distance, and the urgency to get the fuck out of here returns. Getting ready to stand up, prepared to get to the car and get away as quick as possible, I hear a voice.

The reason we'd started this. Why we stayed in Ponderosa Springs. It's the voice that never asked us to go through with this, but we refused to let him do it alone.

His revenge had become ours. His pain was something we shared.

The fourth and final member of Ponderosa Springs' bastard founding sons.

"I leave and you let Rook take the lead?" His voice is smoke, quiet, lingering. "You've lost your edge, Caldwell."

Welcome home, Silas.

TWENTY-THREE
the creator

Thatcher

Chains rattle just outside the thick metal door.

My fingers run along the built-in shelf just above a small bunker-style bed, all the books listed in alphabetical order. The bed beneath holds a mattress that is dated, worn, stained a horrid color of yellow, but perfectly made. Newspaper clippings are pasted along the dingy white walls, and there is a metal toilet carrying God knows what diseases in the corner.

It smells of mold and musty clothes. Clean, but it still carries a certain stench. A familiar one.

If I reached my arms out, I'd only need a few more inches to touch both walls of this room. This is the hole my father had been left to perish in. No contact with the outside world, no sunlight.

Just a six-by-nine concrete block.

The groan of the door being pulled open brings my attention to those entering inside. *I am in control*, I tell myself again. There is nothing he will do or say that will break my poised appearance.

I am in control.

Henry Pierson has always been a conventionally attractive man. A man you might see out at the grocery store with bright blue eyes so clear it might cause you to take a second look. The fit dad with well-styled blond hair across the street who smiles as you jog by. Maybe even the blind date your friend set you up with who dresses nice and carries an air of approachable confidence.

Likable, digestible, average.

Prison air and time have not been kind to him, not that I expected it to be.

"You have twenty minutes," the guard behind him reminds me before shoving the inmate into the cell and shutting the door, effectively locking us in here with one another.

Silence crackles in the air like dry lightning, ready to strike at any second. The hairs on the back of my neck stand up in warning as I take in the man standing in front of me.

With all the time spent in here, it looks like he's found time to keep up his physique. Still tall and lean, just as I remember. The mangy beard, however, is new. Wrinkles around his nose and mouth have aged him, or maybe it's the solitary confinement.

But his eyes.

They haven't changed a bit.

"Hello, Henry."

He tracks me, the changes over the last several years since he saw me painted in the blue-and-red hue of police lights. I'd been a child, standing at the front of the house, watching him being taken away.

"Alexander!" His voice is silk, a snake waiting in the grass. I used to tremble when he spoke. "Look at you!"

He clasps his hands together in front of him, shaking his head as if he's so overjoyed to see me, so overwhelmed by parental admiration.

I realize I stand a few inches taller than him now. He no longer looms over me like he did when I was a kid. This was the man that held power over me growing up? The one who controlled my every move?

"You look strong," he says, nodding his head with approval, a smile on his face. "I did quite well, didn't I?"

It's not unlike him to take credit, the grandiose sense of importance that entitles him to everyone's success regardless of his involvement. Narcissistic tendencies die hard.

I decide to ignore the comment entirely, not giving him the attention he seeks.

"Forgive me if I don't repay the sentiment," I hum in the back of my throat, rubbing my thumb and forefinger together. "Orange doesn't suit you."

Henry laughs, a cackle. It's a whip against raw, wet skin.

It's in his nature to remain calm, steadily unaffected, because he cares little about the sentiments of other people. An aloofness that made him scary, made people fear him.

That laugh used to seep through the walls of the shed while he *worked.* I listened to it in tandem with bloodcurdling screams for hours, waiting for him to finish so that I could clean up his mess.

Always cleaning up his messes.

"Have you finally come to apologize for leaving me to rot in here?" he asks, rubbing his wrists where the cuffs keep him shackled. "It's been how many years since I last saw my son?"

Not long enough.

"I wasn't aware I was the reason you were thrown in prison." I cock my head to the side. "Had I been murdering all those women that whole time?"

The thing about Henry is he loves to play games with your mind, gaslight and manipulate until all you believe are the words that come from his mouth. He's smart that way, but all psychopaths have a weakness.

His is his ego.

"Don't treat me like I'm stupid, son. You left that rat of a girl alive, a witness. Now this"—he shakes the chains keeping him locked in as if I can't see them—"is what I've been reduced to. I'm owed an apology from you, at the very least."

My molars grind together, and I bite down on the hot streak of anger that wants to lash out of my mouth. Of course he'd blame his downfall on me. As if he hadn't killed Phoebe Abbott out of pattern, in a fit of panic because she was going to tell the police all about what she'd seen him doing in that shed.

No, of course he'd never admit he panicked. Not Henry Pierson. This man is perfect, unaffected—he would never be his own downfall.

"I didn't come here to talk about the past with you," I say instead, my tone level.

He smiles, grim and without showing his teeth, before he takes a seat in the small wooden chair in the corner. The orange jumpsuit swishes as he moves.

"Of course not," he chides, waving me off. "Why don't we talk about what you've been up to? Have you started in the family business yet?"

Killed anyone recently?

I straighten my cufflinks, grinning. Of course he wants to know. Talk shop, fuel his fantasies with grim retellings of all I've done without him. But I won't give him that satisfaction. Let him wither away with his memories.

"You have a copycat." I lick the front of my teeth.

Crossing his ankle over his knee, he rests his hands on top of his thighs. A smirk is etched on his features, and I try not to shiver. We look so alike sometimes, with so many similar habits.

He is so painfully normal like this with his mask on.

"How flattering," he coos, clapping his hands together, eyes curious. "Leaving limbs and all?"

I nod, feeding his curiosity enough to grab his attention. "Notes carved into the skin, and no full bodies recovered."

He hums, rolling his lips together. "I love the attention to detail."

"There is one thing different though." I observe him, the way he reacts to my next words. "He leaves roses with the body parts."

As if he senses my suspicion, he schools his facial features, giving me a bland response.

"All serial killers have a calling card, even those inspired by me."

"The roses were left for me, a gift from you." I run my fingers along the spines of his books, plucking one from the shelf. "Who is he, Henry?"

"You think I know?" I don't need to look at him to know he's got the perfect image of confusion mapped across his face. "How could I? I haven't had visitors in years. It could just be your subconscious missing your father."

I drag my fingers through the pages, looking up from the book to find him poised, smirking, proud of himself for getting me here. He thinks he's got me in this cat-and-mouse game, trapped me in, and he's ready to toy with me.

Except he's forgetting that he doesn't know how I work.

Henry has shown me all his cards from the moment I was born. I know how he operates, the way his brain works, his next move, how to read him. He's shown me everything, and I learned.

No one knows the abuser like the abused.

But he is forgetting that he showed me everything he knows. I know everything about how he works, how he operates. He knows nothing about me, only what he thinks he made me into.

"Huh." I furrow my eyebrows, snapping the book closed. "That's a shame. I thought…" A little chuckle leaves my lips. "Well, I guess it doesn't matter what I thought."

I set the book down, moving towards the cell door to knock and let the guard know I'm ready to leave, when he shifts abruptly, holding his hands up.

"Wait, what did you think?"

"Well, his work is…" I lick my bottom lip, making a show of it. "Excellent. I didn't know anyone other than you that was capable of something so…elusive. I thought you had to be helping him, but I suppose even the greatest can be recreated."

I shrug, lifting my hand to the door.

The best way to attack a narcissist is to stroke their ego. He needed a platform to brag about his work, to own what he'd done. Forcing it out of him would do no good for me here.

"Nothing can beat the original. He is, at the end of the day, only a copycat." His voice is sharper, the void in his eyes becoming more evident.

The fog of humanity is clearing on his features, and I can see the arrival of the man who raised me creeping to the surface. His charm is fizzling away, and the mask of empathy drops.

"Oh, I don't know about that. You should see what they say about him in the papers. They can't stop raving about it. He's practically rewriting history, a prolific killer so renowned they won't even remember the man he was imitating."

The chains securing him rattle as he stands, his chest brushing against my shoulder, our bodies close enough that I can feel the heat pushing off him in waves.

"They will always remember me." His eyes turn dark, jaw set tight, not in anger but disrespect.

There he is.

The Butcher of the Spring.

"Time has passed," I say nonchalantly. "They know you'll never get out of here. What damage could you possibly do? They aren't afraid of you anymore."

Manic laughter bubbles from his mouth, hysterically high-pitched, that drips venom. My spine stiffens, fingernails digging into the palms of my hand.

All those women that died to that sound.

Their flesh strung up on meat hooks. Racked and bleeding like animals.

My mother, my sweet, kind mother.

You are in control, I repeat to myself. Inhaling through my nose, I tighten my jaw. *You are in control. He does not own you. He did not make you.*

"The only reason this copycat exists"—he tosses his hands in the air—"is because of me! It's my memory that scares them, not him!"

The smell of his breath makes my throat constrict, the urge to vomit curling in my stomach. I didn't want to be here, had not want-ed to come here. Anger licks along my spine, quietly brewing.

I should never have come here.

"You gave your approval to an impotent man who wasn't cre-ative enough to come up with his own design?" I lick my teeth, grin-ning out of spite. I look down my nose at him because I want him to know that I see him as beneath me. Dust billows around my oxfords. "Prison has made you weak, Father."

His breath fans across my face, and the smell of him has the room starting to spin.

Bleach scorching my fingers, the smell of blistered flesh.

Human corpses being slashed by metal, ground into bits.

His breath in my ear. "Not a drop of blood on this floor, Alexander. Not a drop."

We're two spiders spun in silk. If I was going to die in his web, he'd die with me. I have him where I want him, but I'm losing my grip. My chest burns, and my brain aches as memory after memory liberates itself.

Chains snap inside of me, the cages I'd placed my childhood self inside bending open.

He stares at me, watching. The edges of his mouth contort into the picture of a predator. I slit my eyes, refusing to be his prey.

"Well played, son. Very well played." He nods his head, running a hand down his chin, making the shackles click together. "Did you do all of that for the sweet little Abbott girl?"

This concrete room is not big enough for the amount of rage that burns my veins. I could drown him with it. In a matter of seconds, he went from the center of my trauma to a target. He morphs into all those men I'd hunted down. Nameless faces that shrieked beneath the weight of my blade.

He has absolutely no clue what suffering is, but he's about to find out.

"The Abbott women have a nasty habit of seeking things that are bad for them. Does she taste as sweet as Phoebe did?" He grins wickedly. The yellow tint on his teeth makes me sick.

I grab the front of his jumpsuit, fingers coiling in the material. Fury and adrenaline pump me with strength I didn't know I had. I pick him up from the floor by his shirt, hurling him into the wall behind him.

He grunts as I hold him there, looking at me like he's never seen me before. As if he doesn't recognize the man in front of him, and I can't disagree. I can't even recognize myself.

"Who are you working with, Henry. The Halo? Sinclair?" I hiss, needing to watch him hurt.

"It's poetic, Thatcher. A generational curse. Do you plan to repeat our history?"

I pull him, the fabric stretching, the sound of tearing echoing before I slam him back into the wall with a harrowing thud. His spine

235

connects with the concrete, and I pray it snaps in two.

"I'm done playing games with you." My voice is cracked, a twisted growl scratching my throat.

I'm met with emotionless eyes.

"There it is," he breathes. "My beautiful, perfect monster. This is your birthright, Alexander. You can't run from it. You and I are the same."

"We are *nothing* alike."

"Careful, son. It looks like you've given her the power to end you." He scoffs. "Lyra Abbott cannot fix what you were born to become. She will run from it like they all do. No one will ever be able to love what I have created in you."

It wouldn't matter to me if Lyra could love me or not.

I would take her obsession. I would take it and feed it every day of our lives.

And if she is the reason for my downfall? So be it.

I'd let her do it. Hand her the knife myself and let her finish this legacy. The Pierson line could die with me.

It could only ever be her that gave me my ending, because it had been me that gave Lyra her beginning.

"I made you perfect, and look what you've let her turn you into."

I tug him forward, sending him right back into the solid barrier in front of me. Bones rattle, and he winces in pain. Again, again, and again. All I see is red as I sling his body into the concrete until his shirt is in tatters, shredded in my fingers.

His body slinks onto the floor, coughing as blood splatters onto his chapped lips. He heaves for a breath, groaning as he looks up at me.

"You ruined me!" I scream, my voice rattling the walls. Spit sprays across his face. I press my hand into my chest. "You took a healthy, normal child and turned me into this."

"Dig, Alexander."

His fingers wring the life from my mother's eyes.

"If you feel, you kill it, son. Kill it."

Sweat gathers at the collar of my suit, my large frame looming over the person who torments my dreams, who took away all hope of a regular life and forced me into becoming a monster.

"You were born this way. I only nurtured what was already there. I tried to make you into something great. It's not my fault you failed." He wipes the blood on his mouth with the back of his hand.

I squat down so I'm at eye level with him.

"Do you know how I repay you for all that nurturing you did, Dad? All your rules? All the cleaning?" I grab his face in my hand, squeezing his jaw between my fingers. "I kill men who are just like you. Sad. Pathetic. Weak-minded scum. I outsmart them, overpower them, I butcher them. Every single time I watch the light drain from their eyes, it's always you on the table. When I skin them, remove their organs, it is always you dying at my hand."

The reality of my words drowns me. Acceptance rattles in my stomach, and something inside me shatters open. It's like I've been staring at a mirror my entire life and see only a dark, ominous figure staring back.

No facial features, just a picture of a bleak, shadowy presence.

I finally can see myself in the reflection.

"You did not train a protégé. You created your demise."

I stare down at him for a moment. This feeble man. Hair thinning, aged, creeping closer and closer to his final day, where they will end his reign with a lethal injection.

Coming here, I wasn't afraid of him regaining control. He has no power because I refuse to give it to him. I'm better, stronger than he could have ever imagined.

I feared coming because of what it would make me remember.

All the skeletons of my past are coming back to life, breaking free of their unmarked graves and crawling to the forefront of my mind, and I'm not sure how I'll deal with the aftermath of this.

I turn from him, spitting on the ground of his cell as I walk to the door and knock on the thick metal.

"Alexander," he coughs, but I don't give him the satisfaction of turning around. I simply pause. "I may have done a few bad things, but I never hurt you. That must count for something."

This is not remorse.

It is a game.

A chameleon turning colors in order to evade death. He knows the bonds that tied us together have collapsed, that I'm walking away and will never return. This is his final opportunity to lure me back in.

The guard's keys jingle just outside. Our time together has run out, the sands of time finally drained. I hear his voice once more just before the door to his coffin shuts again, and I leave him to rot.

One last gift from the Butcher of the Spring.

It might very well be my favorite.

"Conner Godfrey."

TWENTY-FOUR
natural born predator

lyra

"Finished!" I shout, shooting up from my sitting position. My thin-stripe T-shirt rises to just above my belly button, a cold draft breezing across my exposed skin.

The smile on my face falls a little when my only company is the sound of Edwyn Collins playing through my speakers. I have no one here to celebrate with me, which only makes me think about *why* I'm the only person in my home right now.

Working on the spider design was supposed to act as my distraction.

I look down at the ornate black Victorian frame, my fingers tracing the swirling pattern. Behind the glass is my artificial purple web that took far too long to make. The entire time, I just kept thinking about how talented spiders have to be to weave them so effortlessly.

Several spiders are situated on top of the web, sideways, upside down, right side up. They're sprinkled around so the final project looks complete and full. I wonder if Thatcher would let me hang it up in his room since he was the one to purchase most of the specimens inside this glass frame.

Probably not.

He could buy them, but as for staring at them every night? Doubtful. I still hadn't convinced him to feed Alvi, who, mind you, is the sweetest snake on the planet. It was slow progress trying to convince him that all my creatures and insects weren't that bad.

My phone buzzes on the table, reminding me that I need to update it, and the time flashes at the top of the screen.

Almost midnight.

It's been hours since he left, and my worry has only escalated the longer I've sat here. I want him to walk through the door, whole and alive. But I'm terrified of the version that will darken my doorstep.

Sweets. I want sweets. The only logical response to this stress is to fill up on as much sugar before going into a diabetic coma.

I pad through the living room and into the kitchen, my bare feet tapping against the hardwood floor as I shimmy my way to the pantry. A grocery trip has moved up on my list of things to do very soon because my shelves are practically empty.

I scan through the boxes of oatmeal that I've never touched—I think I only bought them because I told myself I'd start eating healthier, which lasted approximately two days.

"Bingo," I whisper to myself.

I stand on my tippy-toes, stretching for the Queen Anne cordial cherries on the top cupboard. The container grazes my fingertips, and I reach a little taller, extending my body as far as it can go.

Almost…almost…

THUD. THUD. THUD. THUD. THUD.

A scream erupts from my lips. My heart leaps into the back of my throat, the uneasy rhythm making the fine hairs on the back of my neck raise. I press a hand onto my chest, willing my heart to slow down.

I face the opening of the pantry, ears on high alert. My fingers curl around the frame, peering into the living room and at my front door.

Music continues to play as I stare at the door, waiting, blinking, hoping the sound is only a figment of my overactive imagination.

The song comes to an end, trickling off the speakers before there is a brief pause of silence.

I count how many times my chest rises and falls just before the thumping returns.

THUD. THUD. THUD. THUD. THUD.

My body jerks. The force of the pounds on my door makes it rattle, shaking the wood as whoever waits outside demands entrance. I wet my dry lips, legs a little wobbly as I jog to the kitchen counter, grabbing a large chef's knife from the block.

The blade shines in the dim light, and I clutch it tightly in my fist. I take my time walking to the living room, listening for footsteps outside or voices, but I'm only met with stillness.

Another song plays, and I curse myself for turning it up so loud.

I can hear my pulse in my ears as I wrap my hand around the doorknob. Taking a few steady, deep breaths and lifting the knife, I ready myself to attack as soon as it opens.

The harsh air whips into my home the second I swing the door wide.

There is nothing but perfect darkness outside. Fallen leaves whirl into small tornadoes in my front yard from the breeze, and I quickly flick on the porch light. It hums to life, casting a small glow, but I still don't see anyone.

My brain tells me it was just the wind. But my gut says the wind doesn't have hands strong enough to pound on a front door like that.

Taking a step through the frame, my bare feet hit the damp porch. It's a chilly Oregon night, and my jeans and T-shirt are doing a shit job of keeping the cold out. Lowering the knife in my hand just a bit, I look left and right, seeing only the porch swing and a small table.

Everything is in its place. Nothing has been disturbed.

"Hello?" I call to the dark.

The forest surrounding my property stares back at me, trees groaning from the force of the wind, a gust of it brushing my hair in front of my face.

Yes, Lyra, good move. The psycho killer is definitely going to reply. Gods, you act like you've never seen a single horror movie cliché. Not a fucking one.

Giving one more scope of the porch and my front yard, I step back inside into the heat and lock the door behind me. It clicks into place, and I release a breath, dropping my forehead to the wood.

"Stupid," I mumble to myself, lifting my head from the door and dropping it back down. "It was probably just a raccoon, a large one. A rabid raccoon!"

I laugh as I turn around. When my eyes rise up, the air in my lungs plummets and evaporates until I'm not sure how to breathe. Because it was not an animal creeping onto the porch.

"Conner?" I hesitate, trying to swallow as I stare at the man in my living room.

Conner Godfrey stands above the coffee table, looking down at my finished project. A gun rests at his side, and for a brief second, I think to myself, *This is how I die.*

"You finished it," he says quietly, smiling. "It's beautiful."

I walk forward, the knife still fisted in my grip. A bullet travels much faster than I can throw this at him. That's if I even hit my target.

"What are you doing here?"

"I came here for you." He winces slightly as he finishes his sentence, the soreness of his mouth and tongue probably making it difficult for him to speak.

The last time I saw him, he was skewered with Thatcher's blade, and I left him there to bleed. The last time we were together, he'd tried to shove his tongue down my throat.

"You shouldn't be here, Conner," I say calmly, not wanting to irritate the man with a more powerful weapon than me. "You need to leave."

His eyes are glassy when he looks at me, lifting his head but also lifting the gun. He points the barrel in my direction, tilting his head.

"Have a seat, Lyra." He motions towards the couch in front of him. "There is something I want you to see."

I bite down so hard on the inside of my lip that I can taste blood on my tongue. My pulse presses uncomfortably against my temples. Thatcher will be home soon, right? He has to be home soon.

All I need to do is stall until he shows up.

I cross into the living room, moving cautiously as his gun tracks my movements until I'm sitting on the couch like he requested.

"Put that on the table. You don't need to protect yourself from me, Miss Abbott." The smile on his face makes me sick. "I would never hurt you. Unless you make me."

A tragic case of déjà vu washes over me.

Henry hadn't *wanted* to hurt my mother. Her actions, her turning on him, had resulted in her death. That's what he told her.

I try not to think often about how my mother fell for a man like Henry Pierson. What had occurred between the two of them that made her love him. Although Thatcher shares traits with him, he's never been like his father in my eyes. I have always seen the remains of empathy and humanity beneath his cold exterior.

I think I now understood how easy it was for her to fall into his trap. She thought she knew him, trusted him, but it had only been the mask he'd wanted her to see.

I'd done that with Conner.

While our relationship hadn't been romantic, I'd trusted him as a friend. Thought he was kind, gentle, and wanted the best for me. An innocent, harmless man who wouldn't hurt a soul.

That mask had all been a lie.

One great, twisted lie.

Am I forever going to be cursed with bad judgment? Is it a hereditary thing to trust blindly? To forgo all the bad and only see the good in someone?

"I've waited so long for this moment."

My eyes zero in on the way his hand reaches out, trying to brush a curl out of my face, but I flinch, jerking away from him and towards the back of the couch.

"Put the knife on the table, Lyra," he demands, pointing the gun at my chest. "I won't ask again."

His expression sours. I no longer recognize this person standing in front of me. Conner had always been this normal, everyday kind of guy. Casual clothes, neat appearance, inviting brown eyes.

This person? Dressed in black, hair tousled as if he's run his fingers through it one too many times, eyes beady and tainted—I don't know him. They feel like two separate people.

I do as he asks, hoping wherever Thatcher is that it's close. The knife clicks against the table, and my hands fall back to my lap. The muscle in his jaw twitches as he pulls his hand back, reaching behind him to pull something from his back pocket.

"This would be much easier if I was able to talk more, but I brought something for you to read so that you can understand, to make you see what I do."

He tosses a brown leather journal onto the table, small with several pages, something you can keep on you at any second of the day.

"Conner, what do you want from me? Why are you here? Is this about Stephen—is he making you do this?"

I have no doubt he's here of his own free will, but maybe I can pacify him for a little while longer by playing his game, pretending to care. I'm sure he's here to get back at Thatcher, using me to do so.

His ego has been bruised, and this is his retaliation.

"I want you to read this," he repeats, wincing as he says the words. "Once you do, everything will make sense."

"Why can't you—"

"Read it!" His voice makes me jump, and the coffee table shakes beneath his fist as he slams the gun into the book and shoves it closer to me with the barrel.

"Okay, okay." I try to swallow the lump in my throat, but with every move of the gun, my heart stalls. My hands shake as I lift the leather-bound journal into my hands.

I open it on a random page, planning to skim the words written just to appease him, but after the first few sentences, I find myself actually reading.

Entry #20
I knew from the moment I saw Lyra Abbott arrive at Hollow Heights University she was my second chance at love. All grown up and beautiful. Phoebe was not grateful. She did not appreciate me. She'd chosen Henry even after I'd told her what he'd done, after I'd shown her what he was capable of. She still wanted him. Loved him. And it killed her. Lyra will be different. She will be mine.

Entry #37
She is a vision, spun in beauty and obscurity. I ache to touch her.

I listened to her talk for hours today in the lab. School is starting back soon, and I know I will miss our private moments together. Will she miss them too?

Entry #41
The music box was perfect. I knew from the second I saw it in the shop, she would love it. Her lovely voice whispering thank you into the darkness had almost been enough for me to reveal myself. It's a shame our secret moment in the Library Tower was ruined by her friends. They are getting closer and closer to the Halo, which means I'll have to deal with Stephen's bad mood for a while longer. Seeing her is worth it, though.

He'd been the ghost in the Library Tower, had heard everything the girls and I talked about that day and reported it back to his master like a lost fucking dog.

I flip the pages, digging, searching for the words I know are coming. There is a boiling inside of me, burning, and I can feel it heating my blood.

He isn't here for revenge on Thatcher for wounding him.

He is here for me.

Entry #45
Stephen is still having a problem understanding my fascination with Lyra, but I don't question his desire to keep Coraline Whittaker in his basement even though we were supposed to sell her a year ago. I think he knows now the only way I'll start mimicking that ego-obsessed roach, Henry, is if I can have Lyra at the end of all this. And Stephen needs me, knows I'm the only one capable of doing it. Maybe what he struggles with the most is that I no longer crave the money and power we discussed ages ago. All I want is her.

Entry #50
She is not my mother. She is not the kind of woman who throws her body around or torments those who love her. She is not like the filthy, disgusting women who infest this world with their manipulation. I know that. I know that my gentle girl is simply...distracted. But it is,

*however, discouraging, knowing that she is with him. Runs to him.
I'll make him suffer for touching her.*

Entry #58
*I can't wait to leave this place behind. Stephen's constant raging
about taking back the town that righteously belonged to his family
is growing tiring. It's the same story as when we met in college.
However, I cannot judge his motivations. Not when he has always
known what I am, what I do behind closed doors since we met years
ago. I can keep killing these girls for his gain if it means I have his
protection on the back end. As long as I can be with her in the end. I
wonder where Miss Abbott would like to go? I'll take her anywhere.*

Entry #62
*I will slay that stupid little fucking prick. I've been killing longer
than he's been alive and he thinks he's scary waving his knife around?
Stabbing me in the mouth? He has no fucking clue the pain I can put
him through. Only a few more weeks. Just a few more weeks and I'm
going to slit his throat while she watches. She will see that I'm the
only man for her. She will apologize for disrespecting me.*

I stop reading, having seen enough.

Conner Godfrey is the Imitator.

It's his hands that were responsible for all those dead girls turning up. Innocent girls who had done nothing to deserve the fate they
were given.

An eerie calm settles into the marrow of my bones. The rotting
of my soul had begun, and I can feel the infestation of darkness
swarming inside of me like a horde of flies.

It isn't anger or sadness that I feel. No, it's utter desolation. The
world had left me barren, and I want to fill the gaps it left in me with
so much vengeance I alone could fuel a thousand wars.

I set the book down on the table, staring at him but not really
seeing him. It could be the adrenaline that absorbs my fear of the
gun he is still holding, but in this moment, getting shot doesn't bother me.

Nothing does.

"You killed May."

It's not a question, just an impassive statement said with a steady tone and mild temperament. I had once again been left to show the world how cold my gentle heart could become.

"I had no choice." He shifts, walking around the table in a rush. Squatting down in front of me, one warm hand cupping my cheek, he stares up at me with eyes filled with twisted adoration. "Don't you see? I did all of this for us so that we could be together. You and I, we are the same. You are unafraid of the darkness—you embrace it. We were meant to be, Lyra."

"You knew my mother."

"I tried to protect her from Henry, I did. I tried to love her, Lyra."

I blink coldly. "You're the reason the police are hunting Thatcher."

The motivation to pacify him until help arrived had drained from me. I no longer need or want help. I am perfectly content exactly where I sit.

His grip tightens a fraction, lips pressing into a thin line at the mention of Thatch.

"Don't talk about him. We can worry about him later." He sighs. "I want to talk about us. This is the start of our forever, sweet girl. I have waited my entire life for you, the one who understands me. Sees me."

There is a crack in me. A shattering.

I'm not sure if he can hear it or the chains rattling, dragging against my rib cage. That slender creature is creeping from the depths of my soul, mouth watering, teeth snapping.

I've become nothing but an oblivion. There is no beginning or end. I am simply a living, decaying corpse. Lifting my eyes, I stare into the brown irises in front of me.

They widen slightly as I move.

I lick my canine teeth. My revenge sits on a platter just in front of me, and I spare not a second longer to dig my teeth into the ripe flesh of retribution.

Suddenly, the world spins and turns until I leave it painted in a beautiful shade of vermillion.

TWENTY-FIVE
aftermath

Thatcher

"I guarantee Lyra has food, unlike you losers," Rook declares, slinging the back door to my car open before I've even put it in park. "Next time you want a distraction, ask Alistair for it."

"Get the fuck over it, you child," Alistair groans, tired of Rook's complaining. "We can't help everything was closed on the way here."

Rook takes off, walking towards the cabin, Alistair close behind him as he slides out of the passenger seat.

"Miss the quiet yet?" I ask the person in my back seat, who still hasn't made a move for the door.

"I never minded the noise," he says lowly. "As long as it's not in my head."

Silas Hawthorne looks...good. Skin lively, eyes a little less dead, body strong.

I've known him for years, seen him alter and grow. I've witnessed many versions of him, but this is the best he's looked in years. Healthy. The excruciating image of him the days after we found Rosemary's body had been burned into the back of my eyelids for months.

It's nice to know that he could come back from it, no matter how much of him he had to leave behind in order to do it.

"Are you alright?" I find myself inquiring. "I know you'll say yes in front of Rook regardless of how you actually are, so I thought I should ask."

He takes a second, staring out the windshield. I've always found that my conversations with Silas have been long ones due to the prolonged moments of quiet that exist in them.

We're very different, him and I.

I will say unkind, false things to distract people in order to avoid questions I don't want to answer, but him? He's brutally honest. I've never heard him lie. He takes his time, making sure that when he speaks, it's exactly what he means.

There is no reading between the lines or mistaken words. If he says it, it's what he means. End of story.

I've always been jealous of that.

"I'm taking it day by day. The medication is great, but I have bad moments. I'm glad to be home, seeing my family, but I still feel like a burden some days. There is a constant ebb; I'm just figuring out how to ride it out."

I nod. "So today, then. How are you today?"

"Today is good." He gives me a tiny smirk, just enough for me to see.

I think I'm one of the few people he does that to.

A man of few words always.

When we were younger, it was his house I visited the most. I craved the silence he provided me. We didn't need to talk; we just sorta existed in each other's company, aware of the demons that haunted us but not speaking about it.

I'd missed Silas's brand of quiet. It's always been my favorite.

"When Rosemary…" He pauses. "When Rosemary died, I never thanked you. You let me hate you so I had a place for all the hate to go."

"I'm not sure what you mean," I say blankly, turning off my car.

"Rook, he mothered me more than my mother. Which, for a time, I needed. Alistair let me be angry, showed me a way to let out the hurt. I also needed that." He looks up at me in the rearview mirror. "But you, you made me move. You forced me to push forward, even when I hated you for it. Thank you for caring about me more than I cared for myself."

I swallow roughly, giving him a curt nod in the mirror before grabbing the door handle and pushing it open.

"Well." I step outside of the car. "You blacked out prison security cameras for me. Let's call it even."

"De—"

"Thatcher!"

The sound of Rook's scream makes my blood run cold. Dread twists in my gut as he bursts through the front door, his face ashen, void of laughter and color. He doesn't look like himself.

Lyra.

I sprint the rest of the way to the porch, furrowing my eyebrows as I reach him, staring down at his grim expression.

"Where is she?" I demand, rib cage heaving as it tries to gather oxygen.

He lifts his hand, motioning through the door.

"She's—there is so much—she—I, I—" He can't finish the sentence. Whatever is at the end of it, he isn't able to communicate.

My throat constricts. I leave him on the front steps, barreling through the door and into the cabin. I am attacked immediately by a familiar smell.

There is a quality to blood that no one tells you about. It's simply an experience you must go through to understand it. The older wet blood becomes, the sweeter it smells. Ripe, fruity, almost like pomegranates left out in the sun to blister for too long.

It's all I can smell.

Sweet, sticky blood.

There is a strain in my chest. The muscles of my heart stretch, tearing. This sinking feeling in my stomach of knowing but not wanting to accept the truth.

She'd begged me this morning not to leave. Told me over and over again that she had a terrible feeling in her gut about me going, but it hadn't been for me. It was for her. I told her it would be fine. That everything would be okay. We would figure it out, and I'd come back to her.

She begged me to stay, and I left her here.

My strides take me past the living room, a broken coffee table greeting me. The spider enclosure is shattered on the ground. Moving towards the kitchen, I find Alistair standing just outside of it.

"Thatch—" he starts, but I don't stay to listen to him finish.

I move past him. It's there that I find what had turned Rook pale.

Lyra's kitchen used to be a space I'd describe as comforting. A warm room filled with knickknacks and mismatched cutlery.

Tonight, it's a Jackson Pollock.

The walls are coated in messy strokes of red, the feathered splatter of arterial spray. It stains the cabinets, lingers in the cracks on the floor. Blood leaves no wall untouched, every counter drowned. It drips from the vent hood above the stove into a stagnant, dark puddle.

When I step forward, the ground beneath me makes a sticky squelch noise like water being pressed from a wet sponge. The stench of death and rotten fruit clings to the air as I try to take in the scene in front of me.

I've seen carnage. This isn't that. There's gory, and then there's this.

Every swing forward, every time the knife penetrated flesh, was personal. An emotionally charged crime scene that oozed hostility and overpowering resentment. There wasn't a murder.

It was an annihilation.

There is a male body resting on the wooden island in the center of the kitchen. I can only tell it's male due to the height and build. I don't know who he was—might as well have been a stranger—but I doubt any of his closest loved ones could identify him in this state.

His legs dangle off the edge. Barely any material of pants remains. The muscles of the thighs are ribbons, strips of disconnected flesh, as if a wild animal had clawed through the tissue to gnaw at the bone beneath.

Shredded hands, mauled and split from aggressive slicing, lie next to his side, barely hanging on to the arm. The torso is a constellation of gashes from short, narrow whacks to harrowing carved lacerations. He'd been cut so many times in the gut that pieces of yellow fat were left flayed open, oozing.

This body had become a pincushion. Stabbed, cut, and sliced no less than two hundred times, if not more. Do you know how difficult it is to stab someone that many times? How physically exhausting it is?

A dozen murder weapons are scattered across the kitchen. The object responsible for this person's indistinguishable face is sitting in the sink. A meat tenderizer had been slung into this man's skull enough times that it had lost its shape, a concave mixture of blood, tissue, and bone congealed together like soup.

The pure, raw rage in this room was palpable.

"It's Godfrey," Rook announces from behind me somewhere.

"The Imitator doesn't kill men." I look at the ceiling, watching clumps drop onto the floor, before turning to look at him and Alistair in the doorway.

"No." He shakes his head, grimacing at the scene before pointing at the body. "That's Conner Godfrey, or what's left of him. I found his car parked in the backyard."

I glance back at the distorted body, and suddenly, this makes much more sense. The rage, the emotion, the disregard for human life. Conner had come for her, and I hadn't been here.

I can only assume she found out about him and what he'd done.

Of course she would slay her own monsters. My girl is a knife; brutal, unforgiving, beautiful.

Lyra is an emotional killer, attacking when provoked with no remorse afterwards. She is a trip-wire assailant, fragile and deadly in the way bombs are. Once you pull the clip, there is no stopping her.

It makes her dangerous. Far more than I have ever been.

"Where the hell is Lyra?" Alistair grunts. "Did she run?"

I look around the kitchen, spinning in a circle until I spot the closed door to the pantry. Now that I have an image of what occurred tonight, I don't need to question where Lyra is.

"Can you three get rid of the body?" I roll my sleeves up to my elbows, walking towards the pantry.

"Yeah," Silas answers me, and I nod in silent thanks.

I have a decent idea of what I'll find on the other side of this door, but I still don't think I'm prepared for it. The single lightbulb illuminating the tiny cupboard is enough to show me what sits on the floor.

My darling phantom.

Lyra rests against the shelves, her arms dangling by her sides weakly, legs outstretched, and face depleted of energy. Her curls are matted against her head from the blood. It still looks wet on her clothes, but I spot a few dried stains on her face and arms.

She looks so...pure, delicate, this tender, caring little thing. How is it possible for such a feral beast to lurk beneath the surface of a body so unsuspecting?

I hate the world for what it had done to her.

Fate had gifted Lyra with a bleeding heart. A beautiful, tortured, bleeding heart that feels everything a little too much. The world had abused it until it became a weapon, forcing her to become this version of death reincarnate to cope with feeling too much. The look in her eyes is ghastly.

But a little carnage never scared me. Nothing about Lyra Abbott would ever make me fear her.

She doesn't move when I come inside, crouching down so that she can see my eyes. There is no expression, no recognition in her void gaze. Just total unfeeling, lost in her own mind. Trapped inside the forgotten place inside of her.

The closet.

The place where she shuts the world out.

But she'd promised me, swore that I'd never be locked out. She would always keep me inside, no matter how badly she needed to disappear. I run my tongue across the front of my teeth, cautiously reaching out a hand.

"Lyra, baby," I purr, voice soft like honey. "Look at me."

My fingers graze her cheek, and it's like flipping on a light switch. She blinks, her bleary eyes moving until they find my own. I let her stare, let her see that I'm here and this is real.

"There she is," I praise, a small smile tugging at the edge of my lips. "Welcome back to the land of the living, darling." My hand tucks into the crook of her neck, letting her fall into it. "Let's get you cleaned up."

She's dead weight in my grip when my other arm scoops beneath her, picking up her body until I'm cradling her against my chest. I let myself be something she can lean against, a feeling she can trust. Her rigid, stiff body drops into me. If it wasn't for her eyes, I'd think she was dead.

I shield her from the scene in the kitchen, walking through the rest of the house, counting the slight rise and fall of her chest. We quietly make our way up the steps, winding down the hallway and into her bathroom.

I'd promised myself a long time ago that I was finished cleaning up other people's messes.

Yet, I stand in her bathroom for hours and bathe her. I scrub her body with strokes so gentle I barely recognize my own hands. The *T* I'd carved into her skin is red, in the early stages of healing, and she wears it like a dream. I wash her hair until the water runs clear. I dry her off and dress her, all in total silence, until I realize…

I was done cleaning up after everyone except Lyra.

She is the exception in every capacity.

Everything I knew myself to be does not apply to who I am with her.

Lyra can barely sit up in the bed as I brush her hair, and when I finish, she collapses onto the sheets, burying her face into the pillow as exhaustion finally overtakes her mind.

Her worries about me forgetting who I am with her are void. Not when I know that I'll always come back to her. That the me I was always meant to become is who I am with her.

We are two halves of a broken hole. Two mangled people trying to find solace in all the darkness we'd been given. For years, I wished I'd never met her. That the night we met could be erased and forgotten.

But now, all that matters is the girl inside the closet and the woman who came out of it alive. I wish I could've done more to save her mother, if only so I could thank her.

For creating the only person on Earth I can't bear to live without.

I wish I would've stopped my father, if only so I could tell Phoebe Abbott that her daughter would never be alone again. That no matter what end we meet, she will always have me.

In life and in death.

"Do-Don't—" she mutters in her slumber.

I look down at her, relinquishing everything I am to the tiny, murderous woman in this bed.

Painfully, wholly hers.

And even though I don't know what she wants to say, I still reply, "I won't."

The fire sizzles in the night, burning high and cracking as it chars what remains of Conner Godfrey.

Leaving Lyra to rest was for the best, and even though I'm just outside, I hate the idea of her waking up and me not being there. However, there was a ridiculous amount of cleanup that had to be done.

No one can ever accuse her of being gentle again.

We'd dragged the body outside and worked together on trying to clean the house. The bad news is I have to tell Lyra that her moment of blackout rage is going to result in us redoing her entire kitchen.

The good news is I have a feeling we'll be leaving her cabin in the woods and moving to the estate soon.

"The Halo has been around since Stephen's great-fucking-grand-father," Alistair shouts from my left, standing next to the open flame, flipping through the pages of Godfrey's left-behind journal. "The Sinclairs started it to, and I quote, '*exact revenge on the daughters and sisters of the founding families.*' They built their fortune from this shit."

I've been up for nearly twenty-seven hours, and I've yet to feel tired once. Until now, as my adrenaline plummets and the weight of today settles into reality.

Another body to bury, another secret to carry.

"All those innocent girls because of jealousy? Sounds like bitch is a trait all Sinclairs are born with," Rook grumbles from the lawn chair directly across me, the burning wood separating us.

A blunt dangles from his lips, his hoodie pulled down over his eyes. The fatigue is tangible—we all feel it. Maybe because it's been so long since we've felt like we could actually rest.

"This has everything. James Whittaker's involvement, Frank, Greg, their plans from college. Motive. I mean, Godfrey was a sick fuck, but this?" Alistair wiggles the book in his hands. "Is gold."

The fire roars in response, embers flying into the wind.

"Enough to bury Stephen?" I ask, staring into the flame.

"And then some."

We settle in the reality, that this, our revenge, may finally be—

"It's over," Silas speaks from my right, hands buried in his pockets. "This feels like it's finally over."

"Pending Odette Marshall believes a word we say," I say, unable to help my skeptic ways. Nothing good ever remains, not in this group.

"Thatch," Rook calls, releasing a puff of smoke. "For twenty minutes, I want to pretend it's over, okay? Even if it's not, even if it's just twenty minutes of me thinking about all the ways I'm going to fuck my girlfriend in peace and take her far, far away from here. So please, just…shut up."

I snort in time with Alistair's chuckle. I have a feeling that the two of us were heading in the same direction, but just this once, we will abide by Rook's wishes.

We are at the end. Two inches from the finish line.

And each of us submerges into silence, trying to prepare ourselves for what that might mean for the future.

We process the two years of pain.

We accept the fact Stephen Sinclair and the Halo will not dominate our thoughts every second of the day. We deal with the harsh reality that the ghosts we've built will stay with us for a lifetime, but the blood will eventually wash from our hands.

We are transported to a place that mirrors this moment in time.

When we were freshly graduated and the world was immense. The possibilities of what we were to become were boundless, and we each were ready to move forward from this town and the black streak they'd given us.

Rosie's death had put us on pause, and tonight, in this moment, we'd press Play again.

But now, we are different. Changed.

We will never be those people again, who we once were.

Our goals and dreams have been altered, swayed by influences we never expected. We live in a present that we never would've imagined for ourselves two years ago.

Alistair can never go back to the vengeful, resentful guy he was before. Not when Briar is there to constantly remind him of all the things in this world he can be, and none of them are angry. Rook was damaged before, and this year had healed him in ways he never would've gotten the chance to. He would have run from his pain. And now, because of Sage, he's able to face it.

And me, well, I hadn't been entirely sure what I was going to do after graduation. I knew I wanted to study medicine somewhere far away from Ponderosa Springs. Only because I refused to accept who I was.

Now? I don't really care where I end up. As long as darling phantom is there with me. I want to spend lifetimes beside her, and I've wasted too much of our time already.

"Thank you." Silas speaks over the fire, looking at each of us for a prolonged moment before continuing. "For staying. Putting your lives on hold and on the line."

"Always." Rook's response is immediate.

"No thanks needed." Alistair, always so humble.

For a long time, I have denied what each of them means to me. Revolted against the idea of *needing* anyone other than myself. Content in freezing myself from the world if it meant I didn't have to get close. I cut, sliced, and killed those who tried to get in with the shrapnel my father left embedded in my skin.

But I knew, maybe even from the moment we met each other all those years ago, I knew.

DNA did not make me a killer.

And it doesn't determine who my family is.

"Who else would have protected you three if I didn't hang around?" I lift an eyebrow, shocking them. I'm not exactly known for responding warmly in these types of situations.

"I just know Rosemary is so fucking pissed she missed out on Thatcher becoming a decent human being," Alistair snarks, crossing his arms in front of his chest, his white T-shirt splotched with blood.

"I'm still stuck on the human part," Rook adds.

"Imagine how May feels knowing you're always going to be a tool," I bark.

It's the first time we've all been together to really mourn both of them, sitting in each other's grief and recognizing what they both meant to each of us.

It's quiet for only a moment.

"Would you stab me if I said Lyra freaks me out?"

"No." A sigh leaves me as I look at Rook. "But she might."

We had seen each other through days so dark it felt like the sun never existed. Our bonds had been forged from hellfire and bloody knuckles. We don't love each other or care in a way the world would ever understand.

We'd found each other as children, each of us stained with a mark we never wanted, and together, we learned how to own them.

Four bastard sons who found comfort in each other's chaos.

I watch the sunrise peek over the horizon, tipping above the evergreen pine trees, stabbing through the fog with milky orange rays of light. The cold air I inhale almost feels new.

"To the Styx?" I offer.

"To the Styx," they echo.

TWENTY-SIX

so, this is love?

Lyra

The room is dark when I wake up.

My head throbs as my eyes adjust to the darkness. It takes me several minutes to detach myself from the sheets, sitting up and feeling the thin veil of sweat on my body from sleeping.

I feel gross, and my mouth is dry.

How long had I been asleep for?

The days and nights seem to blend as I stand up on shaky knees. I'm so weak, still so tired even though I'd just woken up. Almost as if I'd rested too long. I take my time going to the bathroom, keeping the lights off as I clean myself up.

The steam from the shower clears some of the fog from my mind, and I feel fresh, better than how I did when my eyes first pried themselves open. I finish brushing my teeth and pad back into my room with a little more energy. I slip on a pair of underwear and run my hands along the options of shirts.

After tugging one of Thatcher's white button-down shirts off the hanger and slipping it over my shoulders, I take my time to fasten the front before burying my nose into the sleeves.

I inhale, once, twice, and on the third time, when I open my eyes, I look down at my hands, and on the tip of my pointer finger is a deep red stain. As if I'd pricked my finger or dipped it into paint.

There's a switch in my brain that snaps into place, like someone had flicked the electricity on in my brain. Turning, I dash out of my bedroom and to the one next to mine.

The very last thing I remember was reading Godfrey's journal. Everything after that is blank. There is a thick, black wall inside my mind. I'm standing right in front of it, banging my fist against the hard stone, but it doesn't budge. Whatever is beyond it wants me to stay out.

Carefully, I open Thatcher's door, hoping that he's in there. How did it go with his dad? Is he okay? Did he even make it back home to me? What happened to Conner?

My heart beats faster with every single question. My hazy memory is the sole reason for my panic.

However, when I find Thatch asleep soundly in his own bed, it soothes me enough to take a breath. Moonlight hits his naked torso with harsh streaks, beaming through the blinds and reflecting off his pale skin.

His white hair tumbles in front of his forehead, brushing against his eyelashes, and I'm tempted to touch those messy strands. I wonder if he'd notice?

I'm already walking quietly to the edge of his bed, creeping onto the mattress in slow motion, gentle so he doesn't feel it shift beneath my weight. The silk sheets he insisted on melt against my touch.

I crawl until I'm propped up next to him, my hand holding my head up as my elbow digs into the plush pillow. I'm far enough away that we aren't touching but close enough that my fingers are able to walk along the toned plane of his chest.

When he's sleeping like this, he looks just like the boy I met all those years ago, just with harder features. I savor this moment because who knows who he'll be when he wakes up? Who knows what kind of damage Henry did to him in that prison or what twisted, sick fantasy he planted into his head?

I know May told me his father had crushed all the soft things about him long ago. But I don't think that's true. I think he just became an expert at hiding it.

He is soft.

In ways you wouldn't expect.

He's soft in the mornings, just before he's had his coffee and his gaze is still sleepy. That's when he picks out which mugs we're drinking from that day, and somehow, he always makes sure they go together. Soft when he cooks us dinner, and even more so when he's annotating my books.

He couldn't be anything but that.

Not when the only thing he's ever loved is the sound black and white keys make.

There is nothing else he could possibly be.

Not when the word *piano* in Italian translates to mean *soft*.

He jerks beneath my touch, and I'm quick to pull back from him, holding my breath as he turns his head, eyes squinting tight. The peaceful slumber he was enjoying disappears, and I can see the physical shift in his face.

Nightmare.

He's having a nightmare.

I know that you need to let people wake up organically from night terrors; I've heard about it for years—I know that. But for some reason, my first instinct is to reach out and touch the side of his face. It's a knee-jerk reaction to try to soothe whatever pain he's facing in his mind.

That was a mistake. My mistake, not his.

That's why I can't blame him for the way he wakes up. His eyes fly open, bleary and glazed over, still trapped in the dream. I can't blame him for the way he flips his body, smothering me beneath him. I can't even blame him when I feel the knife pressed against my neck.

He hovers above me, a dangerous look on his features, and I can tell he isn't fully aware of his actions. My pulse spikes, and I widen my eyes as the knife digs into the curves of my throat.

"Thatch, it's me. It's only a dream," I breathe, trying to reach up and touch him, but his knees are pressed against my wrists. "Angel, look at me. It's me, it's Lyra."

I think he might actually kill me for a solid two minutes until the fog of his dream fades away and his mind catches up with his body. The pressure of the blade softens, and he blinks.

"Lyra?" he croaks, speaking around gravel in his throat.

Sadness washes over his features. I've never seen such a candid emotion flash across his face before. As if the horror in his dream had dropped his shield completely.

"I'm sorry," he whispers, rolling his body off mine. "I'm so sorry."

I watch as he pushes himself to the edge of the bed, burying his head into his hands, his shoulders tensed up. My heart aches for him, knowing I can't take away whatever it is that is hurting him.

Taking a chance, I crawl across the bed, sitting on my knees behind him and wrapping my arms around his waist. I rest my chin on his shoulder, nudging his head with my own.

"It's okay. It was just a dream," I reassure him, knowing the last time we had this conversation, he was adamant he didn't have them.

"They're my memories."

"What?"

"My nightmares. They're my childhood memories," he admits, his chest moving as he sighs. "I think I repressed them, and the only way I could recall them was when I slept. That's why I didn't want to go see Henry. I knew I'd remember it."

I listen to him talk about visiting his father. How he remembered all those women and all the ways he was forced to clean up after. My chest burns as he talks about watching his mother die, having to help Henry bury her afterwards.

I listen to every horrible, awful thing he was put through, and I break for him. The little boy who had never deserved the terror he'd witnessed. No one should be forced to become a monster to survive.

"I killed Conner, didn't I?"

It's the only option that makes sense. Thatcher had been at the prison, and I know Godfrey showed up at the cabin. I didn't create that in my imagination. Had I become a monster in order to survive too?

"Yes, Little Miss Death. You did." He leans back into me, turning his head so that the bridge of his nose rubs against my cheek.

"Do you remember it?"

I shake my head. "No. It's all foggy. I don't know how I ended up in my bed or how long I slept. It fades to black after I found him in the living room."

"Sometimes, I think, we go through certain things so horrendous that our brain does its best to protect us from reliving it." His lips brush my skin. "Do you want me to tell you what I saw?"

"Yes." I dip my head into the crook of his neck. "But not tonight."

I lay a kiss on his shoulder, tightening my grip and inhaling the smell of him. Tonight, I just want to be with him. I don't want to think or worry about what will happen when we leave this room.

In here, he's mine, and I'm his.

The end.

In here, we get our happily ever after.

"Can I ask you a question, Lyra?"

I nod, pulling back so that he can turn his body to face me. My eyebrows furrow, concerned. Thatcher is always sure of himself; he doesn't ask questions. He just does.

But I can tell whatever he wants to say is making him uncomfortable.

"I—" He stops, his throat working as he finds the words. "I feel things sometimes, I think. They're these physical reactions to certain situations, but I can never identify them."

He'd been conditioned so long he can't even tell what his emotions are. Thatcher lived most of his life killing and shutting out feelings—of course he doesn't know what they feel like.

"Okay, so tell me what they feel like to you."

A deep V creases his forehead. "What do you mean?"

I bite down on the inside of my cheek to keep from smiling. It's a little funny that the know-it-all is so lost.

"When you woke up from your dream and realized it was me beneath you. What did it feel like?"

He grabs one of my curls, twirling his finger around the strand and tugging slightly.

"It felt wet. Slippery, like raindrops on clothed skin," he answers candidly.

"Sadness, sorrow, despair," I tell him, trying to think about what they feel like for me. "It varies depending on how hard the rain is. Give me another one."

"Fizzling. Bubbles floating around in my stomach. I felt it when you gave me the digital piano. It's a constant popping."

I smile, wide and bright. "Happiness."

We do this, back and forth, for a while. Him explaining what each of these feelings is and me trying to identify them. We talk for hours, shifting around the bed multiple times. At one point, his head is in my lap, and then later, I'm resting against the wall while he rubs my feet.

We glide and float, filling the gaps of our relationship. All of those little things no one thinks about but end up being the most important. If I could, I'd stay here forever with him, just like this.

At some point, he finds himself on top of me, his large body spreading my legs open, head resting against my chest as I massage his scalp. It's a slow progression, how our hands start roaming and bodies become alive until his hands hold my cheeks, cradling me in his grasp before he kisses me. I fall into the way his mouth moves with mine. I push up into him, chasing the taste of him. He groans against my lips, pulling back just enough to mutter a few words.

His hands slip beneath my shirt—well, his technically—and I feel his palms expand across my ribs, traveling upward. Our tongues are desperate lovers, caressing, rolling, dancing. I moan as he settles between my legs, the smooth material of his boxers rubbing against my inner thighs.

My hands tug on his shoulders, pulling him further against me. I want the entire weight of him against me, pressed into me, merging so that there is no corner untouched, tangled together like ivy.

Large hands cup my breasts, fingers flicking against my sensitive nipples. He thrusts his hips into me, grinding the bulge in his boxers against my silk panties. I'm embarrassingly wet already, staining my underwear with my arousal.

He detaches our mouths, dipping his head down to bite through the material of his shirt, latching onto my nipple and tugging on it. I whimper, pushing into his teeth.

"I want you to make me bleed."

The words float in the air and heat my skin. I lick the taste of him off my lips.

"Make me yours." He swivels between my thighs, the head of his cock brushing my clit. The friction from our clothes heightens the pleasure. "I want to be yours."

My addictive, obsessive fucking heart sobs with joy. Warmth spreads across my chest like internal fireworks setting off. There is something to be said about belonging to someone. Completely, utterly, entirely.

I've belonged to Thatcher for years. My entire life, it feels like.

But I've never known what it's like to own another person. To look at them and know they want you to stake your claim. For the world to recognize you are a part of them.

The engraved letter *T* on my back tingles, burning for me to return the favor.

My hand fumbles for the knife next to me, holding it in a tight fist. It's a weapon that represents violence and bloodshed, but in this room, between us, it's much more than that. It's the way we make our way into each other's soul, carving out places for each other into our bloodstream.

"Are you sure?" I find myself asking as I drag the edge of the metal across his chest.

"I want a constant reminder of who my home is." He brushes the bridge of his nose against mine, holding himself up with his hands. "I want to look at your mark every day so that I never forget the parts of me that have always belonged to you, darling phantom."

Tears of happiness burn my eyes, a feeling of completion settling into my bones as I place the tip of the knife to his right pec. With as much precision as I can manage, I dig into his skin, sculpting the first letter of my name.

I've only just started when his hand curls around my wrist, forcing me to pause. I'm about to ask if he's okay when he speaks.

"The sting of this blade. I feel this when I touch you. When I'm around you, it's like fresh cuts. Painful in a way I crave," he mutters. "What is that one?"

My chest expands, and I roll my lips together. I know what it means for me. I know that emotion so well it feels like I was born to experience it. I'm afraid of what it means for him though.

"I—"

"Tell me," he urges. "What is it for you?"

"Love." I say it on an exhale. "That's what love feels like for me. It stings, it hurts, because it's real and you're afraid of losing it. But it stays with you. It scars."

He nods, biting his bottom lip as I hold my breath.

I'm expecting him to pull away, but instead, he releases my hand.

"Go on." He urges me to continue.

"Does it hurt?"

"I have something to keep my mind off the pain." He smirks darkly.

I feel his fingers sink between my thighs, nudging at my pussy through my panties, grazing my clit and applying his attention there. Simmering tendrils of heat explode through me, and I tighten my thighs around him.

I sigh, my grip on the knife slipping a bit.

"Struggling to focus, pet?" He grins, saying the words. "This is permanent, you know. Don't mess it up."

My teeth grind together as I concentrate, swirling the knife into his flesh, deep enough to leave a scar. Blood drips onto his white dress shirt I'm wearing, and the heat from it warms my skin.

He pushes my panties to the side entirely. A high-pitched whimper tumbles out of me as his digits dip into my wet entrance. His fingers slowly glide up and down my slit, thumb still flicking cruelly against my clit.

A searing heat ebbs through my body as his fingers work within me, and I can't help but grind onto his fingers without restraint. I let him fuck me with his hand, feeling him press harder against that spongy spot deep inside me.

Struggling to keep my eyes open, I heave out a breath as I finish the letter, dropping the knife onto the bed, the scrawled *S* forever engraved into his chest. It'll never leave. It's with him forever. Surges of red pour onto me as he continues working me over.

I cry at the intensity, pleasure racking through me. Just as that familiar feeling builds in the pit of my stomach, Thatcher stops, pulling his fingers out of me.

He glances down at the bleeding letter, dragging a finger through the steady stream of blood before bringing it to my mouth.

"Taste how good your brand feels," he orders, pressing against the seam of my lips. I take his finger into my mouth, swirling my tongue around and cleaning it off, letting the metallic flavor invade my senses.

When I'm finished, he dips his head into the slot of my neck and shoulder, drinking down every noise I let out, a starved man receiving his first meal in decades. His tongue licks a long stripe down my throat before his teeth nip into my skin.

"I want you," I breathe, my hands sinking into his hair, pushing my hips up to drive to my point. "Please."

"You beg so sweetly," he murmurs against my skin, taking his time to pull back from me.

I lift onto my elbows, my hair falling in front of my face. I blow a few pieces out of my eyes, staring as Thatcher kicks his boxers off before kneeling in front of me. Streaks of red fall through the grooves of his abs, white hair falling forward, muscles taut and flexing.

A fallen god, a marble statue. Devastatingly gorgeous.

Even his cock is pretty, two large veins on each side leading to the leaking tip, thick and hard. My inner walls clench, aching to feel it.

I inhale sharply as he wraps a hand around the base of his shaft, tugging from root to tip until a pearl of precome drops from the head and lands on my exposed pussy.

He guides himself to my entrance, pressing into my tight hole before pulling back. He teases me like this for what feels like hours, sinking into me just a few inches before withdrawing completely.

"Look at your needy cunt weeping for me, darling phantom."

"Thatcher, please," I beg, my stomach wound so tightly, aching to feel that familiar fullness he provides.

Taking pity on me, he sheaths his entire length within my tight channel. My back arches off the bed, a tingling sensation washing over me as he buries himself to the hilt.

"I love the way you look taking my cock, pet," he hisses through clenched teeth. "I could live inside this tight pussy."

"Then do it." I hum in the back of my throat.

"Don't fucking tempt me." He finishes his sentence with a punishing thrust. "You think I won't? That I won't keep you locked in this room for days? Feed you only my cock? Make you drink down my come?"

Thatcher brings a single hand up to my throat, greedily giving it a soft squeeze as he bends at the waist to bite on my lower lip, sucking it into his mouth.

My pussy makes wet, smacking noises as he pulls out and slams back forward. Heaving his hips, rocking into me in a way that makes my eyes roll into the back of my head.

Everything is hot and achy as he fucks me. My hips meet him for each plunge, feeling him all the way in my stomach as he pumps into me like it's the only thing he was meant to do.

I rake my nails down his back, urging him to fuck me faster.

Ecstasy shoots through me when the tip of his dick brushes my G-spot. My toes clench as I release a guttural moan loud enough to shake the windows.

"That's the spot, isn't it, pretty girl?" he grunts, his breath shaky, "Tell me how good I'm making this cunt feel."

I nod my head erratically, gasping out the words "So good, so fucking good, angel."

I cry out as he goes faster, broad and muscular thighs providing enough means to continue like this for who knows how long. He pumps up into me so hard all I can hear is our skin slapping against each other as one of his hands palms my ass, jerking me into his hips.

I can feel my orgasm approaching. The coil too tightly wound in my stomach won't survive much longer.

"I can feel your pussy begging my cock to come," Thatcher groans. "This tight, pathetic cunt crying for my hot seed. You want me to fill you up, don't you?"

I nod my head, or maybe I don't. I can't tell because I'm so lost in pleasure I can't focus on anything other than my body jostling as he pounds into me. My walls tighten around him, brows furrowed and heartbeat skyrocketing at the intimacy, the passion that crackles between us.

"Thatcher!" I scream into the humid air, my fingers digging into his traps. An overwhelming heat blasts into my body like a wildfire through dry grass. A broken shriek releases from my chest as my toes curl.

"Fuck," he moans as I constrict around him, grabbing my hips with a bruising grip, forcing my body into his as he pistons into me.

My head falls back limply as I let him use my body for his pleasure. His body drapes over mine, his teeth sinking into my throat hard enough to leave a dark bruise.

He loses rhythm, becoming quicker, needier. "Shit, I'm gonna come, baby. I—"

My fingers scramble to his hair, pulling his head up so that I can stitch our mouths together, smothering him with a kiss as my hips roll into his as he stiffens.

A loud groan rattles me as he spills into me, coating my insides with his warm release, continuing to fuck his come into me with torturously slow thrusts.

Our foreheads meet as we stare at one another with labored, choppy breaths that make his sculpted chest rise and fall sharply. I let Thatcher's biceps cage me against his chest as I try to catch my breath.

If he never says he loves me, I'll be okay with it. I don't need the words to know Thatcher cares for me. It's a trivial word compared to the lines we would cross for one another.

I don't need the word when it's real.

He is my protector, my defender. A connection that will never leave or stray, no matter how it's tested. It's a love that stays with me in the quiet nights when I'm trapped in my head.

I've never needed to make myself digestible for Thatcher. Never had to curb who I am or be less. I've never had to make myself easier to love.

He has always swallowed me whole and savored every bite.

TWENTY-SEVEN
hello, officer

Thatcher

I felt their spines stiffen when I walked in.

The silvery sound of the bell above the door announced my arrival, and the patrons of the local cafe all turned their attention to me.

At first, it was just to be a little nosey, curious about who the new customer was entering the Viva Coffee on the corner of Main Street. It wasn't until they realized who it was that their brief glances became blatant stares.

Their fear was evident.

They physically shrank away as I walked further into the restored industrial-looking cafe. Shoulders hunched to hide their faces, and my favorite, the father who clutched his wife a little closer to his side.

I haven't even been arrested, yet I've been guilty in the court of public opinion since I was nine.

Lyra's emotion 101 class may have changed how I view those close to me, but it doesn't take away how good it feels to scare the townspeople. They had exiled me, turned their back on me as a child. I want them to fear me as an adult. I want them to be afraid of crossing me.

They don't deserve my newfound growth Lyra had planted and was watering cautiously.

It was them who initially made the Hollow Boys into villains. We just decided instead of trying to change their minds, we'd play the part they designed for us. We gave them anarchy; we terrorized them; we actively rebelled. I think, if anything, we had taught the citizens of Ponderosa Springs one very important lesson.

Do not create monsters you aren't equipped to handle.

Two fingers press the sleeve of my suit upward, just enough to reveal my watch. My guest is late. Correction—she wants me to think she's late. My date this evening is here somewhere, along with the six other undercover officers I'd already spotted.

I relax into the back of the chair, lifting the small white cup to my lips and taking a pull from my expresso. The rich, bitter flavor drowns my tongue as I stare out of the wall of windows to my left, the rain battering against the glass.

Another ten or so minutes go by before I hear the click of her booted heel, something inherently feminine to remind the men in her field that this isn't a boys' world anymore.

She brushes past me, the chair scraping the floor as she pulls it from the round table before gracefully sitting down. I set my coffee down, crossing one leg over my knee and leaning back into the metal seat.

"Thatcher Pierson." She's smug, overly confident that this is about to go her way.

"Odette Marshall," I reply, keeping my face passive.

I'm a gentleman—I don't enjoy crushing a lady's hopes and dreams. Not right away, at least. I'll let her enjoy her near win for a little longer.

"You look awfully good for a man on the run." She matches my stance, the blunt cut of her blonde hair swaying as she moves.

"Charmed." I give her a tight-lipped smile. "But be careful. I'm a taken man now, and she doesn't share well."

That was the exact reason I had Silas keep Lyra entertained

while I met with the detective. She's possessive, and although I am more than capable of protecting myself, it never goes well for people who try coming for me.

Alistair had made a joke the other day that I might have to invest in a leash for the killer queen, or else I'd spend the rest of my life getting rid of bodies.

I'd only smiled because I knew I'd bury bodies forever if that's what she wanted. If that's what she needed.

"Your little girlfriend isn't going to be very happy when she sees me taking you in."

"She's confident in my return."

Odette takes a deep breath, leaning forward onto the table, her arms resting there. Witty, catlike eyes stare into mine; she looks more like a femme fatale than a detective right now. I suspect if she had it her way, I'd have an entire clip unloaded in my chest.

I'd made them look quite silly chasing me around the past few months.

"You're surrounded, Thatcher." She takes her time with each word, as if I don't understand the severity of my situation. "I met with you as a curiosity, to hear your side of it before they throw your ass on death row."

I smirk, running my finger around the rim of the coffee cup. "Would you like to hear about why I requested to meet with you?"

There are a few seconds where I think she might jump across the table and strangle me. Our personalities are very different, her and I, but both of us are a little too confident for our own good.

"If it's not about the murders, then I think we're done here."

"I have something for you." My smirk spreads into a grin. "A farewell, a parting gift."

She scoffs, shaking her head. "You really think you're walking out of here, don't you?"

"No," I respond dryly, leaning forward and interlocking my fingers together on the table in front of me. "I know I will."

"What's stopping me from arresting you right now?"

I know she came here thinking she'd get her criminal, and she will—just not the one she predicted. I have no desire to go to prison, and if she just so happened to not believe the information I'm about to give her, Rook has plan B ready to go.

"Other than my innocence?" I chide. Well, it's partial innocence, but that's just semantics. She's here for a copycat killer, and I'm here to give her one. "You're not an idiot, Odette. And for some reason, I believe that you genuinely want to help."

I reach into my left jacket pocket, retrieving Godfrey's worn journal and the file Silas had put together. I slide both of them across the table in her direction, a peace offering filled with names written in blood.

She stares at them blankly, unmoving.

"In the journal, you will find everything you need regarding the identity of your killer. Victims' names dating back several years—he only recently picked up on the mimicking hobby. The Imitator has been killing far before this."

I'm impressed by how well she hides her reaction, keeping her face passive as she pulls the file into her hands, flipping absent-mindedly through the sheets, her jaw tight.

"What are these files, then?"

"I almost forgot the best part." I tap the table with my pointer finger. "You're about to be credited with taking down a decades-old sex trafficking ring with organized crime affiliation. Prepare to be on the news, maybe even write a book. You're about to be very famous, Miss Marshall."

We stare at each other, two people forced to become enemies, only because we both fell on opposite sides. Odette lives her life in black and white, right and wrong. It's the walk all those on the right side of the law try to hold on to.

But the reality is it's never that easy.

Nothing is ever that clear-cut.

"So you're just handing these over willingly? Not going to take credit for this discovery yourself?" She lays the files back on the table, grinding her teeth to keep from saying what she wants to.

She's fighting to keep the upper hand, unaware that she never had it to begin with.

"Justice is important to you. It's why you wear that St. Michael necklace." I point at the gold chain hidden beneath her blazer. "Even though you're not religious, let alone Catholic. You'll be the hero this story needs."

Shock reads on her face clear as day, and I watch her fingers twitch to reach up for the piece of jewelry around her neck, but she refrains, biting down on the inside of her cheek before sucking her teeth loudly.

"I guess you're not interested in playing the good guy? The hero?" she snips.

I laugh, cold and distant. "Not when morally gray looks this good on me."

The suit tailored to my body is Brioni, and the shade is actually steel gray, but I can never miss an opportunity to be satirical. It's all a part of my hedonistic charm.

"Why should I trust you?" She raises an eyebrow, and I know she's expecting me to lie.

"Oh, you shouldn't." I shake my head, reaching into my slacks pocket and retrieving a thin piece of white paper. "This is my address. I'll be moving back into the estate soon. If the things in those files don't add up and you still believe I'm your killer, then you know where to find me."

I'm the last person Odette should put her faith in. But I know she is curious enough to want to look into those files in front of her. She's going to let me walk out of here whether she likes it or not.

The only reason we are doing this is for Rosemary, for our freedom. This doesn't change what I am or what I do from time to time.

At the end of the day, I may not be the Imitator, but I am a killer.

The two of us will forever fall on opposite sides of the law. This is only a ceasefire in an ongoing war between us. A brief truce for the sake of a dead friend and the survival of the girls in this town.

I let her stare at me blankly for another moment longer before rising to my feet. I feel the entire cafe tense uncomfortably, both customers and police officers waiting for her command.

I take my time to snap the button at the front of my suit, reaching into my pocket and opening my wallet. I thumb through a couple of large bills before tossing them onto the table.

"Are you seriously bribing an officer in public?"

"Don't insult me, Detective. It would've been much more than that if I was." I click my tongue. "This is for your coffee, along with

Gerrick Knight's, who is sulking in the corner, the unmarked vehicles, and the three agents behind us. Enjoy."

There is a lightness in the air as I start to leave, a weight lifted from my shoulders knowing I'm walking out of here and going home to her. The initial in my chest throbs beneath my clothes.

I'm walking out of here towards a future with Lyra. A future with a woman who owns my soul and fiercely protects whatever is left of my frigid heart. I'm not sure what our days will look like, but I know they'll be better than anything I'd ever imagined for myself.

There is no dream, no goal, no hope.

It's just her.

Her dreams are mine. Her goals are mine. She is my hope.

"Regardless of what's in this, Pierson," Odette calls out from behind me, "this isn't the last time I'll be seeing you."

I slide my dark sunglasses over my eyes, smirking as I look over my shoulder.

"Maybe, maybe not." I shrug, my tone sharp. "This is the only time I'll be playing nice though."

TWENTY-EIGHT
all's well that ends well

lyra / three months later

I hate living in this fucking house.

That's a lie.

I don't hate it. I just get…frustrated.

The house that haunts Pierson Point is immaculate. Staring from the outside could never do the inside justice. It's still hard to believe that this place is my home now. That all the tall ceilings, fancy marble, and over-the-top extravagance is where I spend my days.

We're remodeling most of it, trying to find a balance between an obsessively clean and eclectic mess. The only thing we'd been able to agree on so far was that we would make the sunroom my workspace. That's currently where all my specimen jars and equipment are, along with Alvi, who is quite content with his new living quarters.

But honestly, I'd be okay living in the cabin. Anywhere, really. I just love waking up every morning to Thatch, our bodies a sleepy, tangled mess of limbs. When he's tired, he forgets all about personal space, and I always wind up plastered to the side of him or lying on his chest.

It feels obnoxious, but I don't care that there isn't a moment we aren't together. I enjoy eating breakfast with him, running in the mornings, and grabbing lunch off campus, then coming home. This has been our new routine since he'd come back to school.

The only thing I'm not a fan of is losing shit. There is so much space, so many rooms on the estate, I can never keep track of anything for longer than three seconds. Including Thatcher.

"Where is it? Where is it, where…" I mutter. "Found it!"

I raise the shoe into the air triumphantly before slipping my foot into the rogue Doc Marten. Quickly, I exit our bedroom and jog down the steps to the foyer. We are running so late, and I do not have time to play missing person with my boyfriend.

Thatcher is usually in a number of places, depending on the time of day.

In the mornings, he's in the gym; in the evenings, he's usually in the kitchen cooking something because Gods knows I will burn the house down. Recently, he's been hovering in the backyard, micro-managing the construction workers.

We'd decided together to redesign the garden. We wanted to dig up and tear down the old memories and trauma that rotted there so that we could build something new that represented our future.

However, I'm rolling the dice and betting on him being in the basement.

I turn the corner, jogging down the hall until I reach the correct door. I'm hoping he's ready because I don't want Rook and Sage to leave without saying goodbye.

It still feels weird thinking about it, knowing everyone is about to embark on their own adventures away from Ponderosa Springs. It's sad, but in a way, that feels worth it.

We all deserve to chase the things that make us happy, regardless of where it takes us. I never imagined that I would form friendships that would hurt to say goodbye to.

I know we will still be connected, bonded in a way no one can ever take away from us, but it's going to be hard watching them leave.

My heavy footfalls thud against the steps as I make my way

down them, slowing down when I hear the round tone of the piano. The song is haunting and nostalgic. It almost carries an ethereal beauty, making an otherworldly sense of solitude settle into my bones. The flow of the tune is mellow, tickling my ears with warmth. Somehow, it makes me feel distant but not alone. Dark, melancholy notes evoke a sense of gloom and death, but not one that sorrowful. It sounds like the joy of rebirth, cresting beneath a wave that has stolen all your air and coming up on the other side for fresh air.

Thatcher's back is to me as he plays.

I watch him in his softest form bow and break against every single note, fingers caressing the keys with swift kisses, swirling the shades of white and black.

When he plays, I listen.

More often than not, it's him saying something he doesn't have the words for. I hear him in these moments so clearly, as if he's whispering in my ear. There is no question about what emotion he feels or what he is thinking. The piano requires Thatcher to be candid.

It's more than just his body playing; it's his soul.

When it tumbles to a graceful end, he takes a minute before speaking to me. I don't know how we realize the other is in the room, but we do. It's a little alarm that buzzes when he steps into my space, my body always aware of him.

"What do you think?"

I take the last few steps, walking over and taking a seat on the bench next to him. We're facing opposite directions but turn our bodies so that we can see one another.

"It's haunting," I tell him, admiring the lines and curves of his handsome face as he looks at me.

His thumb reaches up, grazing my bottom lip before moving to my cheek.

"It should." He nods. "It's yours."

My chest expands. I didn't even know he'd been working on it.

When I moved in and went snooping, naturally, I found his collection of music sheets. One specifically with my name written across the top, but mine was the only one that was incomplete.

Composing music is a trophy, is what he'd told me when I asked about it. He talked about how he composes these concertos, traditionally written for a soloist and usually accompanied by an orchestra. It's made up of three parts, and each kill gets one concerto.

I'd been the first piece of music he'd ever created but the only one he'd never finished.

Maybe that was because fate knew what we didn't.

That he was never meant to kill me that night like his father had requested him to do. He'd never be able to finish the song until he could do what he was truly meant to do.

Love me.

I brush a few pieces of his hair out of his eyes, just because I can, smiling because of how complete I feel. How free.

"I wanted it to sound like mourning because a part of you died the night we met." He presses his forehead to mine, letting me breathe him in. "Thank you for loving me with what remained."

"Thank you for letting me be your ghost. For seeing me," I tell him. "I can't wait to haunt you for the rest of our lives and the ones after that."

I wish I could go back and tell the little girl who hid in the closet that one day, she wouldn't feel so alone. That one day, the boy with icy eyes and frosted hair would stay. He would wake up every day and choose to love her despite all he'd been through.

We finally got our grim fairy tale. Our happily ever after.

The ghost and the boy who was winter.

Thatcher

"Is that it?"

Rook slams the trunk of the car down with excessive force, sweat gleaming on his forehead.

"It fucking better be," he grunts, resting his back against the car when he's done loading Sage's bags.

"We have to talk every day," Sage mutters, wrapping her arms around Briar in a tight embrace.

"Seattle is only a plane ride away from LA," Briar replies.

Lyra removes herself from my side, and my cold body misses her warmth immediately.

"Don't forget about me. Monthly Loner Society meetings on Zoom."

"Never," they respond together as they pull her into their arms, all three of them a tangle of limbs.

My sourness towards thing one and thing two, otherwise known as Briar and Sage, had dwindled a little. I'm still not a fan of anyone who poses a threat to the guys but had learned to be a little more accepting.

I had no choice when they spent weekends at my house.

I look away from them, giving Lyra a moment with her friends. I find Alistair already staring at me.

"If any of you try to hug me," I warn, glancing at each of them, "I will not be held responsible for my actions."

"No one wants to touch your prickly ass." Rook pushes off the car, shoving me with his hand. "You're a fucking cactus."

We stand at our cars, having just left The Peak for the last time as a group in, well, I'm not sure how long it will be when we are all together again at a place that holds so many memories.

I remember when we were kids coming to The Peak. Setting off illegal fireworks, the first time Rosemary showed up, the time Alistair threatened to sling Rook over the edge.

This is our spot, and it will stay that way.

Though they leave this place, the bond remains. We are an interwoven web of history—you can't pluck one string without touching another. Our lives, our futures, they are eternally connected.

"Is the shop set up yet?" Silas asks from his car, his head poking out of the driver's-side window.

"Almost. B and I fly out next week to settle in, and then I'll finish before the launch." Alistair's lips curve into a smile as he looks at me. "Should I RSVP you as my first client?"

"One was enough," I deadpan.

We all carry scars from this place, just as we carry the tattoos that promise us an eternity together in the afterlife.

"*Ponderosa Springs Tribune* came out today." Rook pulls the paper from his car, tossing it in my direction.

I catch the thin papers in my hand, shaking them so I can read the cover.

Hollow Heights Dean Arrested!

A smirk hits my lips as I read all about Stephen Sinclair's dirty laundry on page one of the local paper. It had been on the news weeks ago when he was initially arrested, but it's bittersweet seeing it in writing.

If I knew what would happen when this first started, all the turmoil, all the dredged-up skeletons and death, I wouldn't change it. I'd do everything exactly the same.

I meant what I told Odette. I don't want to be a hero.

But I do want the girl, and all of this led me straight back to her.

I'm a window shopper.

I've watched other people through a thin wall of glass my entire life. Just outside, studying their routines, reading their reactions. What makes certain people tick and others laugh.

All of them drift so freely through their emotions as if it's the easiest thing in the world. It's impossible to understand for someone like me, but studying them made it easy to blend in.

I can look at someone, analyze the way they move, how they reply, and tell you what they might be feeling. If they are happy or angry. But when I look at myself, all I ever see is a blank wall.

Maybe that's what I find so interesting about Lyra.

That she shares this dark urge with me but still *feels*.

She smiles, she cries, she laughs.

Lyra shows me every day how different my life would have been had I been born to a different father.

"Are you sure you wanna stay?" Briar's question pulls my attention back to Lyra.

I watch her nod. "This is my home. Beneath it all, I've always loved this place."

My long arm curls around her shoulder, tugging her back into my side.

"Our home," I correct, feeling her snuggle into me.

I tilt my head down, dropping a kiss to the top of her head.

Lyra and I, we don't wanna leave Ponderosa Springs. Her mother was from here, it's where her grave remains, and it's the only home Lyra has ever known. Not to mention she gave me a huge list on why the bug population in this area is perfect for her future in entomology.

I was planning on saying yes before that list, but it had been entertaining watching her explain it.

Realistically, it wouldn't be possible for me to leave. My family's estate and company need to be taken care of. I want to do right by May and Edmond. It's the very least I can do for them.

"Have you decided on where you're headed?" I ask Silas, who is watching all of us from a distance.

Even though I hate that he's the only one leaving alone, I know that's what's best for him right now. He needs time to learn how to live with his schizophrenia after having his break. Silas needs to heal, and he can't do that with someone else.

The only one who will be able to fix him is himself, and he knows that.

"No."

"So you're just going to drive until what? You fucking run out of gas? Dude, just come with me and Sage," Rook offers for at least the thirtieth time.

Silas shakes his head. "I'm going to take some time. Figure out what my future looks like without her. I've been clinging to my revenge as a way to keep Rosemary alive. But nothing I do will bring her back, and I think I have to find a way to be okay with that."

The reality that no matter how many people we bury or secrets we uncover, it will never mend the wound Rosemary left when she died is difficult. We each have to find a way to accept that.

"She just wanted you to be happy," Rook says softly. "Be happy, Silas. For Rosie, yeah?"

His face doesn't move, but his eyes, there is a smile in them.

"For Rosie."

Lyra and I linger after everyone leaves, when the tears are finished being shed by the girls and the awkward hugs from the guys are complete.

Her arms curl around my waist, and my chin drops to rest on the top of her head as we look out at the roaring ocean off the cliff of The Peak.

"Are you sure this is where you want to stay?" I ask as the sun begins to set. The sky is a burnt orange as the end of another day comes to pass.

She nods, shaking my chin in the process, and we both laugh.

"I'm sure. Just think about how cool it'll be when we're old and everyone is freaked by the couple that haunts Pierson Point."

I pull back a little, looking down at her jade-colored eyes. So expressive, full of wonder and light. All things I never appreciated before because I was afraid of what they would do to me.

"You are a strange, peculiar little thing, Lyra Abbott."

"Thank you." She stands on her tippy-toes, pressing a kiss to my lips. "Do you wanna leave?"

I shake my head. "I'm content where you are. Location is only semantics."

"What about if I said to the grave?"

My darling phantom.

How does she not realize yet that I would follow her anywhere? That she will never be alone again.

My ghost.

All of those grim fairy tales had only prepared her to love me. To accept the love I give her. She is made of nightmares and crimson kisses.

If she wanted my heart, I'd give it to her. She could keep it on a shelf in one of her jars—it was never mine to begin with. Not when it's always been hers.

"Death is trivial. He can't keep you from me. I'll follow you to the grave every time and find you in each life after."

TWENTY-NINE
all these voices

silas

I hate hospitals.

The smell makes me nauseous and reminds me that I need to take my medication.

I toss my cigarette onto the ground, shove my hands into my pockets, and walk through the automatic doors. No one pays me any mind as I walk through the halls.

It was far too easy to figure out which room she was in. I need to remind my dad that hospitals need better cybersecurity. Weaving through nurses and family members, I make my way down the hall until I reach the correct door.

Knocking quickly, I wait on the opposite side until I hear, "What?"

It's snarky and annoying. She's probably desperate to be alone and craves the comfort of silence and safety.

I push the door open, standing in front of it and listening to it click behind me. Once I'm inside, I let my eyes look at her.

Brown hair with two solid white streaks in the front.

Eyes the color of honey dripping into my morning coffee.

Her face is lacking color, thin from not eating, and I can still see the faint bruises across her cheeks.

When she realizes I'm staring, she tightens her grip on the hospital blanket, shifting uncomfortably in her gown, which is slipping off her malnourished shoulder.

"Why are you here?"

What a question.

I wish I had an answer.

I don't know why I wanted to come here before I left. I'd never spoken to Coraline Whittaker in my life. I know of her because of school, but our paths never crossed. Not a single time.

We were perfect strangers that happened to clash at a tragic time.

There was no reason for me to visit her. Not now or ever, really.

"I'm not sure," I say gruffly with a shrug, my hands finding their way back to my pockets.

She rolls her eyes. "Couldn't think of a lie?"

I lift an eyebrow. "You want me to lie?"

"Would be far more entertaining than whatever this"—she waves her hand—"is."

My lip tugs at the corner. I appreciate how she's pretending, sitting in this room and acting like nothing happened to her. Like she hadn't escaped a living hell. It's a tough shield she has up, but I know beneath it is a girl waiting to crumble.

I'll let her pretend though.

"I don't need your sympathy. You can take it and get the fuck out." She turns her head away from me. "Goodbye."

"I didn't come for that either," I reassure her. "I wanted to give you this."

I pull a piece of paper from my pocket and walk it to her. I don't miss the way she flinches at my footsteps, so I lay it near her legs where she can reach it.

Her eyes are cautious, watching me, waiting for me to do something before she grabs it quickly and peers down at the writing.

"Your phone number? Seriously?"

I clear my throat, forcing my voice to work. "If you need anything in the next few days or sometime in the future, you can call me."

"Are you hitting on me in a fucking hospital?" She scoffs, anger and pain all over her face. "I'm not your dead girlfriend, dude. Stop looking at me like I'm someone you can save."

I want the comment about Rosemary to hurt more than it does, but time has made it easier. I hate that it's easier.

"I've got no interest in saving anyone." I turn my back, placing my hand on the door, ready to leave.

"You don't even know me," she calls. "We are happenstance. I could exploit this for all you know."

"Go for it. Throw it away for all I care. Won't make a difference to me." I shrug, looking over my shoulder and catching her eyes. "But I know what it's like to fight demons you can't see."

It's the most honest sentence I've spoken in a while.

Candid and raw.

My group therapist would shed a fucking tear.

We stare at each other for a moment in silence.

I was there when they arrested Stephen. I wanted to see him be taken away, but I only ended up seeing her.

Her weak body being carried from a dungeon straight to an ambulance, where she'd searched for something, anything good, and found nothing. In those few seconds, she was just a tormented girl, and I was just a guy.

She's strong—I can see it in her eyes—refusing to show even a little weakness or fear.

"Goodbye, Coraline," I say easily.

She holds her head up a little. "Bye, Silas."

The click of the door behind me doesn't sound like an ending. It feels like the beginning of something.

Stephen saw me there, while he was being forced into the back of a cop car. He saw me watching her, and one of the very last things he said before they shut his door was clear, simple.

A warning.

"Careful. That girl is cursed."

The end

Thank you so much for reading
THE BLOOD WE CRAVE PART TWO.

*Want to find out what happens between Silas Hawthorne's and
Coraline Whittaker?*
THE OATH WE GIVE will be here October 2023!
Pre-Order: **https://amzn.to/41hyem3**

Want more of the Hollow Boys?
Sign up for my newsletter to get the extended epilogue of
THATCHER & LYRA in your inbox in my next newsletter!
https://bit.ly/3B5EBgx

Curious about what happens next for the Hollow Boys?
If you want to stay up to date on news about new releases and
sneak peaks of new books join my reader group!

https://bit.ly/3gd9dkP

If you loved reading about Thatcher and Lyra's bloody less than perfect love story, you'll love Rook and Sage's burning hot romance! Find out what happens when The Fire God of Ponderosa Springs takes on the towns very own Homecoming Queen.

"5 Vengeful stars for the first book of a very promising series. It's one I'll reread over and over again." —USA Today bestselling author, Trilina Pucci

One Click THE TRUTHS WE BURN now!
https://books2read.com/u/mVaR7J

flip the page for a expert....

THE
TRUTHS
we burn

MONTY JAY

ACT I
morning star

Most say Lucifer fell for his rebellion.
I say God's favorite of all the angels fell in love.
Captivated, enthralled, consumed with the only woman he could never have.

The only woman to exist.

Adam's first wife, Lilith.

He watched from the heavens, furious that Adam made her lesser. Refused to make her his equal, although they had been created from the same pit.

Oh, the fury that burned inside Lucifer when God punished Lilith for her rebellion against her husband, turning her into a demon.

And so, Lucifer fell.

Like lightning from the heavens, he fell.

So that he could raise the kingdom in the underworld. Carving a throne from the ashes of Hell, becoming a king.

Creating a home for Lilith. A place where he could make her more than an equal.

A place where he would make her his queen.

ONE
genesis

rook / the past

Masochism.

Pleasure in being abused or dominated. A taste for suffering.

I always liked that definition—a taste for suffering. It's almost poetic, and I didn't know the Merriam-Webster dictionary could be anything but conventional.

While being dominated isn't something I necessarily enjoy in the bedroom or in life, I can always get down with a little scratch-and-bite action. For me, at least, it's less about domination and more about the hurting.

Some call it sadomasochism. That's what I like.

You see, I really love pain.

God, it's like the cure-all. The magic bullet. The ultimate escape.

The way bruises hover on my body and ache for days after. Sometimes I like to press them when they are still purple, just so I can remember where they came from, ya know?

I love the way pain explodes inside my skin, reminding me of all the things I deserve punishment for. The constant reminder that even on Earth, we must all pay for our sins.

Hell would be a walk in the park.

I practically ruled it.

"It's all your fault, Rook." His voice stings like coals against the soles of my feet. "The *Lord* examines the righteous, but the wicked, those who love violence, he hates with a passion!"

"Then shouldn't he hate you as much as he hates me?" I spit back.

A son is supposed to be his father's proudest achievement. I am his reckoning.

The straightlaced, self-righteous lawyer had disappeared the fucking second he passed the threshold of this house. The tie had loosened, his hair disheveled from pacing, and I can smell his whiskey-coated breath as I walk away from the kitchen, headed to the front door.

"Don't you dare walk away from me, you bastard!"

Sometimes it's not even the physical pain I need. I enjoy verbal abuse; it bites into me just as deep, just as brutal, making my toes curl, my body light up with chill bumps. It's the only time I feel normal.

And nothing has been normal since I was seven.

Before I was excommunicated from my own father.

My scalp burns as he curls his fingers into the back of my scalp, gripping my thick hair and jerking me back into his space. Damn, man, I should cut this mop.

The earlier Bible verse rubs my skin raw, blistering my bones. Violence done without the name of God is something hideous, but as long as you're quoting scripture before beating your son, it's alright.

It's holy, the work of prophets.

If we were going by Dante's rules, I'd fall just above my father, spending eternity in the river of boiling blood in the seventh circle of Hell, while he walks for eons in the pits of hell, dancing in the sixth ditch of Malebolge.

Was any of it true?

Did sins rank worse in the underworld? Different punishments given based on your crimes against humanity?

"Pulling fucking hair? What are we doing now—we in a bitch fight?" My words are simply fuel to the already raging fire inside of him.

I could fight him back when he tosses me to the ground, do more than catch myself as my palms dig into the wooden floor, keeping me from banging my head on the hard surface, but I don't.

His wingtip shoe punches into my ribs, making me grunt at the abruptness of the discomfort. I roll to my back, breathing out with a grin and staring up at the ceiling, wondering if God is laughing the way I am right now, happy that the devil is being punished on earth.

My laugh comes out cold and breathless.

It's amazing what you find funny when you've seen what I have. When you've been through what I have. Comedies featuring Seth Rogan and Will Ferrell just don't do it for me anymore.

"You're getting old," I choke out. "I can barely feel these now. You should hit the gym."

"Ah!" he yells loudly, charging down on top of me, both knees on either side of my chest, his fist connecting solidly with my face. I taste the blood from my split lip, the metallic sting warming my tongue. "I should just kill you! You should have died—it should have been you!"

Throbbing pain shoots through my skull as he grabs the front of my shirt, picking up my upper half from the ground only to toss me straight back down. Damn, that's going to give me a headache.

Over and over again, he lifts me up just to sling me back down. I'm swimming in my head, stars dancing in the corners of my eyes. Another concussion added to the growing list of injuries received from the man who created me.

"Then do it! Kill me!" I shout in my haze, feeling every ounce of this. Drowning in it. Allowing it to submerge me completely.

I hear his heavy breathing when he stops shaking me, and I stare up at the man who once taught me how to throw a baseball, who would toss me up on his shoulders so I could see over crowds, a man who used to look at me with fatherly love.

Now all I see inside of his eyes is the bloodshot misery I put there. The anguish I gifted him. I'd killed the part of him that believed in happiness, in good, in everything light.

This is my land of atonement.

This is what makes the pain feel so fucking good.

Knowing I deserve it.

"I hate you." He seethes. Spit flies from his tongue and smacks me on the face. "You're nothing but the devil. You will pay for this, all your wickedness."

There it is.

My darling nickname. His favorite for me.

The devil.

El diablo.

Lucifer.

I had been an angel once, when I was a kid, before I was cast out of the good graces and left to burn.

Church used to be somewhere I didn't mind going. When my mother was alive, and we were all happy. Now I'd catch fire walking through the door.

We stay there, staring each other down with enough contempt and fury to power New York City during a goddamn apocalypse. Deep breathing and damning history that will never be washed cleaned from our memories.

I have taken the man who thinks logically and analytically, turned him into a brash, impulsive beast. I made him into an older version of myself, both of us caught in our own version of purgatory.

I've ruined my father.

And every day he makes me pay for that. With his hands, his words, his religion.

A blaring horn seems to snap him back to a bit of his sanity as I swallow, trying to shove the dryness down my throat. "Welcome to the club."

I push his hands off me as he climbs off my body, leaving me lying there without a hand to help me up. Not like I thought he would assist me, but it was worth noting.

Even at seventeen, I stand taller than him as I rise to my feet. A couple of inches allows me to stare down at him, my hair falling in front of my eyes some. "At least have the balls to finish the fucking job next time."

His shoulders heave as he takes breaths, coming back to reality.

He stalks to the kitchen to grab the whiskey glass on the table, raising it to his lips and pouring it down his throat.

The irony of it all is that he grabs his Bible off the counter next to it.

"You think God is going to help you while you're drowning your liver? Gluttony is pretty high up on his lists of what not to do."

I might be a bastard, but at least I'm not a hypocrite.

Ignoring my statement completely, he states, "Don't you question my faith, son. And I don't want you hanging out with them anymore. Burning down that willow tree was the last straw, Rook. You have no idea the strings that needed to be pulled to clear you of that."

I chuckle, grabbing my hoodie from the back of the couch. I pull it over my head, tugging it down my body. "Final straw. First straw. Doesn't matter, man." Turning to face him as I walk backwards, I spread my arms wide. "You can't keep me from them. It'll never happen. Just like I can't keep you from polishing off that entire bottle tonight. Remember, I'm the devil. The devil does as he pleases."

I don't bother denying the tree. He knows I did it. Hell, everyone knows I did it. But without any proof, with no witnesses, there isn't shit they can do, and that is the beauty of it all.

Walking around knowing everyone sees me as a chaotic arsonist, from the police to teachers—they all know what I am.

The Antichrist is what they call me. Pooled from the loins of Satan. Hell on planet Earth, or in this case, hell for Ponderosa Springs.

I love it.

How they clutch their rosary when I walk by. Whisper three Hail Marys because just glancing at me is a sin.

I love that they know all the things I've done and can do nothing to stop me. Not now, not ever.

There is no stopping me.

Stopping us.

And you know what? Fuck that tree.

He looks at me, dead eyes full of disgust. "You make me sick." He grabs the neck of his whiskey bottle and walks away to the den, not speaking another word to me before I leave.

I tug the door open, slamming it behind me with a thud, not

307

missing a beat as I walk down the driveway towards Alistair's car. The tinted windows shield his hateful ass from me, but I already know there is a permanent scowl awaiting me behind the glass, even if he's in a good mood.

Slipping into the passenger seat, I lean back into the headrest with a deep breath. There is a pause of silence, and I can feel Alistair staring at the side of my face.

"Is there something I can help you with, Caldwell?" I ask, still looking forward.

"Yeah, you have blood on your fucking chin. Clean that shit up." He reaches into the glove box, tossing white napkins into my lap.

I take them easily, wiping at my chin. The red stains them almost immediately. Tomorrow, the cut will be nothing but a dull ache, and in a few days, I'll probably peel the scab back just to feel it hurt all over again.

Unless he hits me again and splits it back open.

Either way.

"I spar with you almost every other day. You can hit him fucking back."

Rubbing harder to make sure it's all off, I respond, "I can handle it."

He shakes his head, pulling out of the driveway and heading towards the Peak to meet up with the other guys. The last few days of summer are fading to black, senior year of high school slowly approaching, and I'm not looking forward to seeing so many faces.

I spend ninety percent of my time surrounded by the same four people, and I'd like to keep it that way.

I reach into my black jeans for my pack of Marlboro Reds and pull one stick from the pack.

"It's not about you handling it. I'm aware you can take a punch. It's the fucking principle, Rook. How are you just going to sit back while your dad beats the shit out of you?"

Balling up the napkin, tightening my fist around the material, and tossing it onto his floorboard, I lean back and shut my eyes. Out of habit, I flick the Zippo through my fingers, rolling it around a few times before striking the flint and putting the flame to the tip.

"How about you let me worry about my father, alright? I'm fine.

One more year and we'll be off at college, far, far away." I inhale the smoke deep into the bottom of my lungs. "I've been dealing with this since I was a kid. I can do one more year. So just drop it, bro."

An aggravated grunt fills the car before I watch him press his foot farther onto the accelerator, and I barely blink when we hit eighty-five and climbing. If we die in a crash, we die in a crash.

Everyone ends up in the same place at some point, six feet under. Doesn't matter how we get there.

Ya see, we all feel the same way. Well, all of us except for Silas's lovestruck ass.

Thatcher, Alistair, and I want out of this town so damn bad we would claw our way through barbed wire to get there. Even if it means dying. We *will* get out of this place. Each of us has different reasons, but it all comes down to the history that's attached to us. The memories we can never escape here because this town is a coffin.

It suffocates you with your past, never letting you move on. Never letting you forget.

"I hate when you say 'bro.' It's fucking annoying."

I laugh, pulling my hood onto my head. "Yeah, well, I hate when you're a grouchy asshole, but that's not changing anytime soon."

"Whatever, smartass."

Music drowns out our voices as we tear down the road. Alistair has mad control issues, so until we reach our destination, I'm stuck listening to metal, which is fine every once in a while. But my ears start getting numb after the seventh guitar solo. For two people who are so close, our musical tastes couldn't be more different.

My eyes find the pines that blur together outside of the window. We fall farther and farther away from the town limits. Just before we enter the next shitty small town, he hooks a right, taking us down a dirt path hidden between towers of trees.

I spot Thatcher's and Silas's vehicles as the sun falls beyond the horizon, already parked. We pull in next to them and get out, walking the rest of the way to the edge of the cliff.

The Peak is a small piece of land on the coast, overlooking the deep blue waves of Black Sands Cove, a small beach where locals spend most of their summer months. Our spot is secluded, overlooking those below us. It's where we come to hang out most of the time because we don't exactly enjoy being home.

It's always better to just be away from our parents. Alone, with each other.

"RVD! Thank heavens, Thatcher is seconds away from torching his eyebrows off."

Her voice is smooth, softer than any of ours, and it can only belong to Rosemary Donahue.

The rich girl with enough balls to be seen with us and the only person who calls me by my initials. The only person I know willing to risk her reputation for the guy she loves. A sister to all of us. She infiltrated our group before we even had time to realize there was an intruder amongst us. I look over to her in Silas's lap, both of them sitting in a chair beside a circular stack of wood.

Her auburn hair catches the wind, hitting him in the face, but I know he doesn't mind it.

"The lack of confidence in me is a bruise to my ego, Rosie," Thatcher responds, holding a can of lighter fluid.

"Bullshit," Silas scoffs. "There is no bruising that massive ego."

Thatch is good at a lot of things—talking his way out of a mass murder, winning the hearts of millions, stabbing things—but starting fires is a little too messy for the clean freak.

"Take a seat, Thatch. We don't need you ruining your hair."

I receive a middle finger as I take the container from him, letting him walk past me to his seat. Placing my dart between my lips, I squirt the liquid in a circle around the wood, swirling it into the center, making sure each piece has fuel on it.

Excitement pools inside my stomach, knowing what's coming in a matter of seconds.

Fire is a key element in my existence. Every strike of a match, every flick of a flame is a compulsion. There is no stopping it. I'm always thinking about it, dreaming, contemplating it.

The way some people are driven to kill others, obsessed with cleaning or locking their door eight times before bed, that twitchy itch in your hands—that's what happens to me without it.

Fire is my flesh. My bones. It's my home.

It's my way of balancing myself out.

310

Getting the shit kicked out of me for punishment can be demeaning, but controlling one of the most unpredictable elements in nature, that's an unruly amount of power.

Every single time it burns, I feel content. A warmth spreads across my chest, down my arms, all the way to my toes. It brings me back to a time of remembrance when my life wasn't a rotting dumpster fire.

And I'll spend the rest of my life chasing that high.

My pyromania is the drug and the cure.

I flick the cigarette into the center of the wood, watching the cherry connect with the lighter fluid. There it is, the spark that starts it all. A buzzing fills my head as it catches, combusting together until the flames reach higher and higher.

Every piece of wood is soaked with dark orange, the heat making my skin sweat as the flames reach right above my chest.

I could fucking come just staring at it. Thinking about the destruction it would bring to the town, the people inside of it, the capability of damage it holds. And in that moment, I feel like the only person who could control it.

I take my seat between Alistair and Thatcher, tilting my head back and shutting my eyes for a moment, listening to everyone else talk.

"Are you four going to be at the homecoming fundraiser before school starts this year?" Rosemary asks naively.

"Possibly," Alistair answers. "Probably not in the way you'd like us to, but it is a possibility."

I grin, knowing what we have planned for that stupid fucking fundraiser.

"Nothing too illegal, okay? I don't feel like bailing my boyfriend out of jail."

"As if we'd ever get caught," Thatcher adds.

"Maybe you can join us this go around, Rose," I add, joking obviously because of her overbearing boyfriend who happens to be my best friend. "Might be fun."

I can practically hear his grip tighten around her waist and his teeth grind from across the crackling fire.

"Over my dead fucking body. She stays out of the shit we do

when night falls in Ponderosa Springs," Silas says.

"When night falls? Is this where we scoot in closer and tell ghost stories?"

"Fuck off, Rook. You know what I mean. She doesn't need to get involved with that shit."

"I can handle myself, you know, and like Rook said, it might be fun, babe," Rose argues, and I just know Silas is going to ream my fucking ass later for even bringing it up, so I might as well keep it going.

"See? Let the girl live, Si."

"Remind me why I'm friends with you again?"

Laughter resounds into the night from four of the closest people to me. Laughter is such a strange sound for me, something so normal and human. You'd never think we would be the kind of people capable of the things we've done, the things we would do.

We are bad people who do very bad things. Very well.

I sigh, tossing my hands behind my head. "Because you need me," I say. "Who are we without each other?"

The question soaks into their skin. While all of us have our own secrets, ones that we'll take to our grave, there is a mutual understanding that connects us. One that others would never comprehend.

A darkness, a hunger that lives inside each of us.

Separately, we are just kids born with tragedy leaking from our split veins.

Together, we are utter chaos.

AFTERWORD

I spent an entire year with Lyra and Thatcher. I'd be lying if I said I loved every second, but I find myself missing them more often than I thought. Usually when I finish a book, I shed the old characters and try to morph myself into the new. But these two, I think they will always be with me. Lingering. They are a once in a lifetime couple.

Okay, here is my little village, everyone stand up and give the following people a round of applause because I wouldn't have finished the duet without them.

Fletcher, Always. Always. Always.

Tril, Ramz, Kat. I love you three. You make me a better author, better person, and friend. Thank you for helping me push through. Cheers to us and years of friendship.

To my lovely Alpha's Kandace and Shaunna. Your feedback is so vital to me and these stories. Thank you for putting up with my random voice messages.

All the formatters, editors, and designers you are all Rockstars. I'm forever thankful.

Oh, and you didn't think I'd forget about you, did you? The reader. The risk taker. The dreamer. Did you know you're my favorite person on the planet? Thank you for choosing me to go on adventures with. Each and every one of you, mean so very much to me. My words have no home without you. Thank you for not leaving me homeless, that's so cool of you.

All the love in my dark, horror loving heart.
—MJ

BOOKS BY MONTY JAY

THE HOLLOW BOYS
The Lies we Steal
The Truths we Burn
The Blood we Crave Duet

THE FURY SERIES
Love & Hockey
Ice Hearts
Shattered Ice
Blind Pass

STANDALONE
Courage for Fools

STAY CONNECTED

Author of edgy romance about broken heroes and the lovers who help them find their HEA's. Monty Jay likes to describe herself as a punk rock kid, with the soul of a Wild Child who has a Red Bull addiction. When she isn't writing she can be found reading anything Stephen King, getting a tattoo, or spending time with family.

Join my Newsletter
https://dashboard.mailerlite.com/
forms/131111/64162720563332108/share

Follow me on Instagram
https://www.instagram.com/author.montyj/

Add me on Facebook
https://www.facebook.com/author.montyj

Made in United States
Orlando, FL
11 October 2024

52546226R00183